Welcome to my worlds . . .

In response to fan demand, this is a collection of short stories I wrote for Berkley many years ago. Originally published in three separate anthologies, they are now brought together in one volume and are a sampling of some of my universes.

"Fire and Ice" comes from my League series. Completely rewritten with new scenes, and more pages, it's the story of Adron, the son of Nykyrian and Kiara from *Born of Night*. He is, without a doubt, one of my most tortured heroes. Originally written as a novel, I cut it down to a novella just so I could see it in print since at that time no one would publish a full-standing futuristic novel. I'm thrilled to see it included in this collection.

Next is the fantasy piece "Knightly Dreams." The idea was born on a road trip and looks at my personal belief of where characters come from and what happens to them if writers abandon them. It's quirky and odd, and completely unrelated to anything I've ever written, but I love it just the same and I hope you will, too.

Lastly is "Dragonswan," which was the first of my Were-Hunter stories to see print. A companion series to my Dark-Hunter world, it explores my clan of shape-shifting dragons and features Sebastian, who's been mentioned in several of the Dark-Hunter books. I adore my dragons and hope to write a book about Damos one day soon.

If you'd like more information about the worlds and to see character profiles, please visit my website, sherrilyn kenyon.com. In the meantime, I hope you have a great read and that you'll come back to my worlds many more times.

Hugs,
Sherrilyn

IN OTHER WORLDS

SHERRILYN KENYON

BERKLEY BOOKS, NEW YORK

THE BERKLEY PUBLISHING GROUP
Published by the Penguin Group
Penguin Group (USA) Inc.
375 Hudson Street, New York, New York 10014, USA
Penguin Group (Canada), 90 Eglinton Avenue East, Suite 700, Toronto, Ontario M4P 2Y3, Canada
(a division of Pearson Penguin Canada Inc.)
Penguin Books Ltd., 80 Strand, London WC2R 0RL, England
Penguin Group Ireland, 25 St. Stephen's Green, Dublin 2, Ireland (a division of Penguin Books Ltd.)
Penguin Group (Australia), 250 Camberwell Road, Camberwell, Victoria 3124, Australia
(a division of Pearson Australia Group Pty. Ltd.)
Penguin Books India Pvt. Ltd., 11 Community Centre, Panchsheel Park, New Delhi—110 017, India
Penguin Group (NZ), 67 Apollo Drive, Rosedale, North Shore 0632, New Zealand
(a division of Pearson New Zealand Ltd.)
Penguin Books (South Africa) (Pty.) Ltd., 24 Sturdee Avenue, Rosebank, Johannesburg 2196,
South Africa

Penguin Books Ltd., Registered Offices: 80 Strand, London WC2R 0RL, England

This is a work of fiction. Names, characters, places, and incidents either are the product of the author's imagination or are used fictitiously, and any resemblance to actual persons, living or dead, business establishments, events, or locales is entirely coincidental. The publisher does not have any control over and does not assume any responsibility for author or third-party websites or their content.

IN OTHER WORLDS

A Berkley Book / published by arrangement with the author

PRINTING HISTORY
Berkley mass-market edition / July 2010

Copyright © 2010 by Sherrilyn Kenyon.
"Fire and Ice" copyright © 2004, 2010 by Sherrilyn Kenyon, a previous version was published in *Man of My Dreams*.
"Knightly Dreams" copyright © 2005 by Sherrilyn Kenyon, previously published in *What Dreams May Come*.
"Dragonswan" copyright © 2002 by Sherrilyn Kenyon, previously published in *Tapestry*.
Cover design by George Long.
Cover illustration by Don Sipley.
Interior text design by Laura K. Corless.

ISBN: 978-0-425-23320-7

BERKLEY®
Berkley Books are published by The Berkley Publishing Group,
a division of Penguin Group (USA) Inc.,
375 Hudson Street, New York, New York 10014.
BERKLEY® is a registered trademark of Penguin Group (USA) Inc.
The "B" design is a trademark of Penguin Group (USA) Inc.

PRINTED IN THE UNITED STATES OF AMERICA

10 9 8 7 6 5 4 3 2 1

FIRE AND ICE

ONE

"So you're a badass assassin, huh? You don't look like much to me."

Adron Quiakides paused his drink halfway to his lips. His blood rushed through his veins like lava as he narrowed his gaze on the beefy human in front of him.

His elite military training allowed him to size the bastard up in a nanosecond. Dressed in black because he thought it made him look tough, the man wore an abundance of weapons in plain sight, which said he didn't know how to use any of them properly. The obnoxious idiot was hoping the sheer number alone would deter anyone from messing with him.

As if . . .

His clothes were two sizes too small to show off the muscles that were out of proportion with the rest of him, no doubt from steroid abuse. He stood with his hip cocked, blustering and preening for a group of like-minded cling-ons who were laughing at his braggadocio.

Bully. Trash. Free assassin too incompetent in his trade to pay his own bills.

In short, he wasn't worth the cost of a blaster charge to eliminate him from the master gene pool. Lucky day for him because in the past, Adron wouldn't have hesitated to perform that public service.

Adron knocked back his drink with one gulp, then poured himself another. "You have three seconds to evaporate or I'm going to spray your brain matter all over your crew behind you."

The man laughed, then sneered at Adron's black silver-tipped cane resting against the table. "You're a pathetic cripple. What can you do besides get drunk and glower? I'm surprised they even let something like you in here with the rest of us." He turned to his friends. "Help me, guys. Help me. You have to protect me from the drunken waste. I'm so scared. Please don't hurt me," he mocked. "Look, I'm cry-ing like the little bitch I raped last night."

Adron's fury fled as that old familiar cold seized him. Without hesitation, he kicked the table over, knocking the man back. Even though his body screamed out in agony at his movements, he rose, yanked one of the blasters from the bastard's belt, and aimed it between his eyes.

One shot. One kill.

That was the assassin's creed, and true to his promise he dispatched one more piece of vermin out of this plane of existence.

Too bad he hadn't done it one day sooner before the trash had found his last victim.

Screams erupted as several patrons ducked for cover or ran for the door. Others merely looked on in curiosity at the blood splatter. Typical *Crona* behavior.

Adron chucked the blaster at the man's body, then calmly retook his seat and adjusted his coat around him.

Edsel, the owner, who was a man in his late twenties, came forward with a heavy sigh as he looked over the body. He picked up the cane from the floor and handed it to Adron. "I would ask what happened, but I've got a pretty good idea." He returned the table to its previous position. "How anyone with even a single brain cell can mess with you is beyond me. Not like you don't telegraph to the world that you're only one step this side of crazy—looking for someone to kill and alleviate your boredom." He glanced back at the body. "Then again, he has no brains at all . . . now. Impressive shot, by the way."

Adron held out his card but didn't speak. He didn't like wasting breath, and Edsel knew the card meant he'd cover all damages and buy drinks for anyone disgruntled over the bloodshed. Not to mention the small fact that it seriously hurt to speak. So he'd learned to keep his comments to the bare minimum when dealing with people.

Edsel took the card and kept bitching. "Thanks." He held the card up between his thumb and forefinger. "This is the only reason why I still let you in here—'cause you always make good on the messes you make, unlike the other drunken bums. Though why every few times you're in here some asshole has to challenge you, I'll never understand. Stupid dregs. If they can't tell you're lethal, they're too dumb to live. Hell, I consider this a public service. You probably do, too." Edsel stepped back as a waitress brought another bottle of Tondarion Fire and set it down in front of Adron.

Edsel motioned to the patrons who were staring at them. "Go on, everyone. Just a little misunderstanding. The fireworks are over. You're all safe now." Then added under his breath, "As long as you don't screw with a pissed-off assassin. Morons."

He motioned for his security to come over. "Guys, get this cleaned up. I don't want to see it, and I know no one else does either." Then louder, he spoke to the crowd again. "Free drinks for anyone who has brain matter on their body or clothes. Sorry for the frayed nerves and inconvenience. What can I say? This is an exciting place."

Edsel shook his head as he turned to Adron. "I'd ask if you have a permit for that killing, but I don't want to be laying next to him on the floor. Don't worry. Any authorities come in, I'll tell them you ran for the door after the shooting."

Adron scoffed as he knocked back another drink. He ran from nothing, which was exactly why he was here tonight. *Damn fucking bastards.*

Edsel and the others faded into the crowd.

Adron narrowed his gaze on the dead man's friends who'd been laughing earlier. Their faces were pale as they tried to come to terms with what had happened and the speed with which he'd eradicated their sick buddy from their putrid lives. They might have wanted to avenge the dead man, but their common sense prevailed, and one by one they walked over to the bar to claim their free drinks.

The waitress cast one last terrified glance at him, then

scurried off to what she perceived as a safe distance. Once upon another life, he could have tracked her to the farthest corners of infinity and killed her.

But those days were gone.

Adron poured himself another drink and savored this one a little slower than its predecessors. His pleasures in life were minimal, and consuming buckets full of the yellow-orange liquid gave him the solace his battered soul craved.

Because tonight, more than ever before, his memories hurt.

He glanced at his chronometer and winced. This very hour marked the eighth anniversary of the night he'd made the "noble" decision he would spend the rest of his life paying for.

Fuck all of you.

But in the end, the only one who'd been really screwed was him.

Adron gripped the bottle tight in his right hand, unable to believe it'd been so long since he'd last walked without a pronounced limp. Moved without pain. Spoken without his throat aching from the effort of it.

Eight years since he'd experienced any comfort or peace whatsoever.

He'd lain in bed for hours trying to sleep. Trying to forget, and finally he'd realized the only way to silence his demons was to drown them out. And nothing worked better than Tondarion Fire, which he'd been out of at his place.

Forgetting the glass and the manners his mother had drilled into him, he tipped the large bottle to his lips and let the fire pour down his throat.

"Hey, baby," an attractive redhead said as she sauntered over to him and propped a thin hip against his table. "You want some company?"

He tried to wave her away, but she didn't take the hint. Angry over her stupidity, he cleared his throat and braced himself for the pain of speaking. "I have company." His deep raspy voice grated on his ears. "Me, myself, and I."

She raked a hungry look over his body, then leaned across the table to show him her ample breasts. "Well, there's enough of me to make all three of you happy."

There had been a time, once, when he wouldn't have hesitated to take her up on that offer.

But then life was nothing if not ever-changing, and usually it altered on the hairpin of a second.

She licked her lips. "C'mon, handsome, buy me a drink."

Adron glared at her. She wasn't the first woman to proposition him tonight. And in truth it mystified him that any woman would bother, given the vicious scars on his face. But then, the women in the Golden Crona weren't all that discriminating, especially not when they sensed money.

"Sorry. None of us are interested."

She sighed dramatically. "Well, if any of you change your minds, you let me know." With one last wistful look at him, she headed back into the human and alien crowd that drifted through the packed bar.

Adron shifted uncomfortably in his seat as a bone-deep pain shot through his left leg. Clenching his teeth, he growled low in his throat.

One would think the amount of painkillers he lived on, when combined with the alcohol, would squelch any amount of ache or kill him. But it barely numbed his physical hell.

And it did nothing for the burning agony in his heart.

"Damn it all," he snarled under his breath. He threw his head back and finished off his drink.

He grabbed a passing blue-fleshed waitress and held the bottle up with two fingers to let her know he wanted more.

A lot more.

As he waited for her to return, he saw another woman headed his way. The fierce glare he narrowed on her sent her fleeing in the opposite direction.

He was through playing around. Tonight he intended to get fully flagged, and he pitied the next fool stupid enough to approach him.

Unless they came bearing more alcohol.

∘   ∘   ∘

Livia typpa Vista had lived the whole of her life in protective custody. More hostage than princess, she'd long grown weary of everyone's dictates for her behavior, and at age twenty-six, she'd had enough.

She was not a child.

And she was not going to marry Clypper Thoran in two weeks. Not even if he were the last male in the universe.

"You will do as you are told and you will not question me. Ever."

She winced at her father's imperious command. High Eminence he might be, but she, not her older brother, had inherited his stubbornness. No matter the cost, she refused to marry a Territorial Governor sixteen years her father's senior. The very thought made her flesh crawl.

Since Clypper had demanded a virgin for his bride, she knew a way to thwart them both.

After tonight, she would be a virgin no more.

Tomorrow, her father would kill her for it. But better to die than to be married to a cruel, goat-faced ancient who groped her with cold hands every time he got near her. *That will not be my future.* The one thing she had control over was her body, and as of tonight, she was taking charge of it.

As the cold rain poured over her, Livia stared at the sign above her head. The Golden Crona. Her maid, Krista, had told her about the club. Inside it held all manner of heroes and villains, and though she would rather give her virginity to a hero, she honestly didn't care. So long as he was passably attractive and gentle, he would be good enough for the night.

Gathering her courage, she opened the door and stopped dead in her tracks.

Never had she seen anything like it. A sea of aliens and humans danced and bobbed through the smoky bar that smelled of sweat from many species and of cheap alcohol. The obnoxious music was so loud, it made her ears throb.

A big, orange reptilian male frowned at her as she hesitated in the doorway.

"In or out," he snarled. "Make a choice quick. I ain't got all night and it's cold outside—so close the damned door."

She took a deep breath to fortify her courage. That, and she mentally conjured an image of Clypper's fat jowls and beady, lust-filled eyes. Shuddering, she stepped inside and let the door pulse closed behind her.

The reptile man blocked her from entering. "Twenty-five credits."

What was he talking about? "Excuse me?"

"Twenty-five credits. You pay or I toss you out on your ass."

Livia arched a brow at him. It was on the tip of her tongue to put him in his place, but then she remembered he had no idea who she was.

And she must keep it that way.

If anyone learned she was a Vistan princess, she'd be sent back to the hotel where they were staying and her father would beat her just for having left without proper escorts and chaperones. For that matter, he'd beat her for being in public dressed like she was.

Not to mention the fact that her time was short. She had to find a man before someone missed her and started a search.

Pulling out the money she'd stolen from her brother, she paid the fee.

The alien put an iridescent mark on her hand before he allowed her access to the bar.

Her heart pounding in fear, dread, and a dash of excitement, she surveyed the large room full of people. "It's time to find him." She walked through the crowd and flinched as several unwashed humans eyed her with interest. They definitely weren't any better than Clypper.

Most appeared worse.

Livia quickly amended her list of qualifications to include a man who bathed.

A tall, dark human male smiled at her, displaying a set of black teeth. Okay, she would also add one who knew how to use a toothbrush.

As she crossed the room, she saw a brunet at the bar who looked like a hopeful prospect. She headed for him. But as soon as she drew near enough to see his face clearly, she froze.

It was her father's personal runner.

If she knew how to curse, she would definitely curse at her luck.

Just don't let him see me.

Falling back into the crowd, Livia kept an eye on him while trying to scan the beings around her for her target. Surely, there was someone here who could . . .

A commotion at the entrance caught her attention.

Livia turned to look.

No! She panicked at the sight of her father's royal guard swarming into the bar. Immediately, the gray-clad soldiers began questioning patrons as they spread out to cover as much of the bar as they could.

Fear tore through her. For them to be here in force and that grim meant Krista had volunteered her location, and no doubt her intent as well. She groaned at the very thought.

Father's going to kill me.

How could Krista betray her? Her maid had been so helpful in the planning and execution of her escape.

But then for some unknown reason, Krista lived in fear of Livia's father, and one scowl from him would have easily caused her maid to tell everything.

Right down to the grittiest of details.

She cringed at the thought of her father's reaction. But at least Krista, unlike her, would be spared his wrath. Krista was protected by their laws. Only a male of her own family could punish her, and since Krista had no living male relative . . .

Livia was not so fortunate, and there was no telling what her father would do to her for this.

Chastity was one of the highest virtues any woman could possess on her world. In fact, men and women were allowed to mix only during meals, at chaste royal functions, and when married couples performed conjugal duties. For a woman to seek out a man not related to her was strictly forbidden.

And punished severely.

Publicly.

She shook the fear away. She'd known the consequences before she set out. Either way, she was going to pay for her indiscretion, and if she had to pay, then she was going to make sure she completed the deed.

Clenching her teeth, she scanned the room for a hiding place. At the back of the club were a line of booths. She headed for them.

Unfortunately, all of them were occupied.

Drat!

"Hey, babe." A rough-looking man stopped her as she tried to move past him. "You want some company?"

She considered it until he reached out and roughly grabbed her arm. He pulled her toward him, his hand biting fiercely into the flesh of her upper arm. "C'mon." He gave her a slick smile as he roughly ran his hand though her wet hair. "What say you and me head to the back?"

She jerked away from him before he hurt her any more. "No, thank you." Turning, she saw the guards heading her way as they skimmed the crowd.

Her heart hammering, she ran to the last booth and sat on the empty bench before the guard saw her.

"What the hell are you doing?"

She shifted her gaze from the guard to the man who sat

across from her. Livia's breath caught in her throat as her gaze focused on his face.

Oh . . .

My . . .

He was more than passable.

In fact, she'd never in her life seen a man so incredibly handsome. His features were sharp and aristocratically boned. His dark-blond eyebrows arched finely over the most piercingly blue eyes she'd ever seen.

Dressed all in black, he had long white-blond hair tied back into a neat queue. Clean-shaven and washed, he was gorgeous. An air of refinement and power clung to him.

But his eyes were cold while he watched her. Guarded. They warned her that he was lethal in nature. And by the set of his jaw, she could tell he didn't want company.

He tugged at the black gloves over his hands as he eyed her with malice.

She should get up and leave, especially since he had a fierce scar that ran across his cheekbone to his hairline and then down along his jaw. It looked like someone had intentionally carved it there, which made her wonder just what kind of man he was.

What had he done to deserve such a wound?

Biting her lip in indecision, she glanced back to the guard who was steadily headed this way.

What should she do?

Adron arched a brow at the woman, who had yet to leave him. He was drunk, but not so drunk that he didn't realize the wet little mouse sitting across from him didn't belong in this dive. He could smell the innocence on her.

And it turned his stomach.

Her dark-brown hair was loose, spilling over her thin shoulders in waves.

She had large, angelic eyes. Brown eyes that had no past haunting her. They were completely guileless and honest.

A shiver ran over him. Who in this day and age had eyes like that? And what right did she have looking at him with them?

"I'm hiding from someone," she confided. "Do you mind?"

"Hell, yes, I mind." He gestured to the door with his bottle. "Leave."

Livia frowned at the stranger. His angry tone set her back, and if it weren't for the fact that one of the guards was scanning the booths, she would have left.

Think of something. Because if she didn't, she was sunk.

The guard stopped two booths up and held out a small digital palm frame she knew had to contain her royal portrait to the aliens sitting in it. "Have you seen this woman?"

Her plan in ruins, she knew only one way to thwart her father. She got up from her seat and sat next to the stranger.

He scowled at her.

Before he could say anything, Livia leaned forward and kissed him.

Adron sat in stunned silence as she placed her tightly closed lips over his. It was the most chaste kiss a woman not related to him had ever given him.

By the way she held his head in her hands, he could tell she thought this was the way a kiss should be given. But worse than the innocence he tasted—he hadn't kissed a woman in over eight years, and the feel of those plump, full lips on his was more than his drunk mind could handle.

And her smell . . .

Gods, how he'd missed the sweet, intoxicating smell of a woman. The warmth of a warm body pressed up against him. The feeling of a gentle hand on his flesh . . .

Closing his eyes, he let go of the bottle and cupped her face in his hands as he took control of the situation.

Livia trembled as he opened her lips and slid his tongue into her mouth. She'd seen people kiss like this in plays and movies, but no one had ever dared such insolence with her before. She tasted the sweet, fragrant alcohol on his tongue, smelled the warm, clean scent of him as he ran his hands over her back and held her so gently that it made her shiver. Her body burned from his gentle kiss.

He's definitely the one. This was the man she would give her virginity to. A man with tormented blue eyes and a tender touch. A man who made her breathless and weak, and at the same time hot and strangely powerful.

In his arms, she truly felt as if she had control of her life. Her body.

And she liked it.

Adron had never tasted anything better than her mouth. He felt her inexperience as she hesitantly met his tongue with hers. His body roared to life with a long-forgotten heat that demanded more than just her lips. The fact that she could arouse him through his pain . . .

That in and of itself was a miracle.

No, it was heaven, and he'd lived in hell for so long that he'd forgotten the taste and feel of it.

"Excuse me," a man said as he stopped in front of them. "Have you seen this—"

Adron broke away from the kiss only long enough to pass a lethal glower at the newcomer. "Go away or die."

Fear flickered deep in the man's eyes. It was a look Adron was used to.

Without another word, the man left them.

Adron returned to her lips.

Livia moaned as he deepened his kiss. The guards and her fear forgotten, she sighed in pleasure. Foreign emotions tore through her as he buried his lips against her neck and sent white-hot chills through her. His arms tightened around her waist as her breasts swelled.

What was this deep-seated hunger she felt?

This unbearable ache?

He made her light-headed and breathless. And she wanted him desperately. "Would you make love to me?"

Adron pulled back in surprise. Had he been sober, he would have sent her away, but there was something about her that called out to him in a way he'd long forgotten. It'd been an eternity since he'd last slept with a woman. Years of bitter, aching loneliness and pain.

And here she was offering herself to him.

Don't even think about it.

But for once he didn't listen to that inner voice. Instead, he found himself getting up from the booth and leading her through the crowd.

Livia didn't know where they were going, but she made sure none of the guards saw her as they left the bar. In the back of her mind, she was terrified. She didn't know anything about this man.

Not even his name.

Never in her life had she done anything so compulsively foolish. And yet she instinctively knew he wouldn't hurt her. There was pain in his icy blue eyes, not cruelty.

Even so, had she not been so desperate, she would never have done this. Not even for him.

He kept a possessive arm draped over her shoulder as he walked by leaning heavily on a silver-tipped cane. She wanted to ask him what'd happened to his face and leg, but didn't dare lest it cause him to reconsider, something that would spell the end for her.

He led her outside the club, to a transport.

After they got in, it took them to a high-end apartment building that wasn't all that far from her hotel. At least that would make it easier for her to get home once this was over with.

Livia relaxed a tiny bit as they entered the grand lobby. Thank goodness she wouldn't be taken in a dark, filthy back room somewhere. Krista had well prepped her on what to expect. Right down to an estimation of how long a man would take before he let her go.

Taking a deep breath for courage, Livia figured she would be back in her hotel room by midnight. There would be questioning, and eventually her father would learn the truth.

God have mercy on her then.

But she'd made her decision, and once her mind was set on something, that was it. She would not be swayed.

Without a word to each other, they took a lift to the top floor.

Once it opened, he led her into an opulent apartment that

was almost the size of her palace wing, which was huge. And as soon as he closed the door, he pulled her into his arms.

This time his kiss was fierce. Demanding. And it stole her breath as he pressed her back against the wall. Her head swam at the powerful feel of his hands roaming over her.

What are you doing? You can't go through with this. You don't even know him.

Shut up, conscience. She had no time or patience for it. This had to be done. It was her life, and she was going to claim it. No one would tell her what to do with her body again. And she wouldn't allow her first time to be with an old man who made her skin crawl.

With that thought in mind, she started unbuttoning his shirt.

Adron sucked his breath in sharply at the feel of her hand against his bare chest. Her touch seared him. He could only vaguely recall someone other than doctors, nurses, or therapists touching his flesh in more years than he wanted to account for.

To her credit, she didn't cringe or comment about the multitude of scars that bisected his body. She didn't even seem to notice them.

That was why he hadn't been with a woman since that long-ago night. He hadn't wanted to explain the scars. To recount where they'd come from and relive the horror and agony of it. To have to face his lover in the early morning light where the scars stood out against his skin like nauseating beacons. He was thoroughly repulsive, and he knew it. He didn't need to see his own disgust mirrored in the eyes of someone who regretted touching him.

Perhaps that was why he'd chosen a stranger tonight. He owed her no explanation. Owed her nothing at all.

He never wanted to see pity or repugnance on another woman's face when she looked at him. If he lived forever, he'd never forget the sight of his ex-wife when she saw him in the hospital right after he'd been wounded. *My God, they turned you into a freak. You're revolting!*

But there was nothing in Livia's dark brown eyes except curiosity and hunger. She didn't seem to judge him in any way, and that he needed more than anything.

Livia bit her lip as she ran her hand over the taut muscles of his stomach and torso. She'd never seen a man's bare chest before, at least nowhere other than in movies. Fascinated by it, she ran her hands over the smooth, tawny skin that was stretched tight over hard muscles. Like velvet over steel. The contrast amazed her, and she had a strange urge to place her mouth on his skin to taste it. Her cheeks warmed over that thought.

How extremely inappropriate . . .

"You feel so wonderful," she breathed.

Adron pulled back to look down at her. There was a peculiar note of awe in her voice, a gentle hesitancy in her touch. And in that instant, a feeling of cold dread consumed him.

He was drunk, but he wasn't *that* drunk. "You're a virgin."

Her face turned bright red.

"Shit!" he snarled as he stepped away from her. His hard cock ached and his entire body burned. Leave it to him to find the only virgin he was sure had ever set foot inside the Golden Crona.

Gripping his cane, he limped his way to the bar and

poured another drink. But the watered-down alcohol did nothing for him except piss him off more.

Suddenly, she was behind him, leaning up against his back as her slender arms wrapped around his waist.

He shook all over from the sensation, from the feel of her small breasts against his spine as she laid her head on his back. And in that moment, he was lost to her.

Damn it to hell.

She stood up on her tiptoes to whisper in his ear. Her breath scorched him and sent chills skimming over his entire body. "I want you to make love to me."

"Are you insane?" He turned to look at her.

She shook her head. "I want to give my virginity away. I don't want it taken from me."

"Taken by whom?"

She dropped her gaze. "Fine. If you don't want me, I'll go find someone who does."

A strange wave of jealousy stung him as he thought of someone else inside her.

What do you care?

And yet for some unknown, stupid reason, he did. He didn't want someone else taking what she'd offered him. The thought of another man . . .

It called out the assassin in him and made him want to kill anyone who even looked at her.

He caught her hand as she moved away from him. "What's your name?"

"Livia."

"Livia," he repeated. It suited her and those guileless doe eyes that stung him soul deep. "Why would you give yourself away so cheaply to something like me?"

Livia paused as she saw the self-loathing in his icy eyes. He hated himself. It was so obvious, and she wondered why. "Because you seem nice."

He laughed bitterly at her answer. "I'm not nice. There's nothing *nice* about me."

That wasn't true. He had yet to be mean to her. He was hurting, she knew that. And it made him snappish.

But it didn't make him cruel.

"I need to go," she said quietly, regretting that he wouldn't be the one after all. "There's not much time before I have to return, and I have to take care of this by the morning."

"Why?"

She bit her lip as she felt her face flush again. In the morning, she'd be inspected by Clypper's doctors. If she didn't find a man tonight, she was doomed and bound for the altar.

"I just do." She let her gaze wander over his lush body. He had broad shoulders and a lean, firmly muscled frame. His white hair contrasted sharply to the black he wore.

He was gorgeous.

But he didn't want her.

So be it . . .

Adron saw the steely determination in her eyes. She was going to find herself another man to sleep with. He knew it.

He should let her, and yet . . .

Why not me? Don't I deserve something after all I've been through?

One tiny, fucking moment of happiness?

Ever since he'd lost his agility, he'd avoided women. He'd been afraid of embarrassing himself with his stiff clumsiness and pain. But Livia would have no one to compare him to. She wouldn't know if he completely sucked in bed.

Adron gripped his cane. He remembered a time when he could have scooped her up in his arms and run with her to his room. A time when he could have made love to her flawlessly for hours and left her begging him to stay.

But those days were lost to him forever, and he was trapped inside this broken body.

One night . . .

Was that really too much to ask?

"My bedroom is this way." He grabbed a bottle of light alcohol and headed down the hallway.

Livia hesitated as she realized he was inviting her to join him after all.

Excited and terrified, she followed him down the elegant marble hallway and into a room at the end of it. The master bedroom was every bit as large as her own at home. A king-sized bed was set against the far wall, looking out over the city below them where the lights twinkled like fallen stars.

He set his bottle down on the nightstand, then moved to a chair by the bed. His features stern, he sat down slowly. Pain made his jaw rigid as he bent his leg and moved to take off his boots.

She wanted to know what had happened to him but didn't dare ask for fear of making him angry again.

So she went to him and took his foot in her hand.

He looked up at her, his eyes startled as she pulled the boot free.

"You know, I've never done anything like this before," she whispered.

"Seeing that you're a virgin, I would think not."

Licking her suddenly dry lips, she removed his other boot.

Adron could feel her nervousness, her uncertainty, and he wanted to soothe her. "I won't hurt you, Livia. I promise."

She smiled a smile that wrenched his gut. How he wished he'd met her before that fateful night. Then he could have been the lover she deserved. He would have been able to take her all night. Slowly. Teasingly.

He had no idea what he'd be like now. But he would try to pleasure her. Do his damnedest to make sure her first time was at least a decent memory.

His groin tight, he pushed himself up and moved slowly to the bed. He sat on the edge and leaned his cane against the wall where he could get to it in the morning.

Before he knew what she intended, she sat in his lap and kissed him.

Adron inhaled the sweetness of her breath as he ran his hands over her back. He'd never expected a virgin to be so bold. And she was a quick learner. She deepened her kiss and teased his tongue with hers.

Oh, yeah, this could be fun.

He unbuttoned her shirt to expose her lacy bra. She moaned as he ran his hand over her satin-covered breasts and squeezed them gently in his hands. Gah, how he'd missed the way a woman felt in his arms. He was all but drooling at the thought of tasting her breasts.

Livia shook all over at the foreign throb between her legs. And when he released the catch behind her back and her bra fell open, she shivered. No man had ever seen her naked before, and it took all her courage not to run away.

24

He stared at her bare breasts as he ran his hands over the taut peaks. He traced slow, simmering circles around her, sending chills all over her body. "You are so beautiful," he breathed. Then he dipped his head down and took her breast into his mouth.

Livia sucked her breath in sharply as his tongue swirled around her flesh, teasing, licking. Never had she felt anything like it. With every lick, her stomach fluttered. She leaned forward, cradling his head in her hands. Her body was on fire. He trailed his hands over her bare back, down her hips, and when he cupped her between her legs, she groaned.

He looked up at her, his eyes dazed and hungry as he breathed raggedly. Then he rolled her over, onto the mattress, and shut the curtains, He turned the lights off with a control he had on the nightstand.

She heard him remove the rest of his clothes in the darkness, but she couldn't see anything at all.

Adron ached to see her naked, but he didn't want any light whatsoever for her to see his damaged body. She might change her mind if she realized what an ugly monster he was. His cock hot and heavy for her, he unfastened the stiff, prickly brace on his left leg and let it fall to the floor. Next, he removed the one on his hand and arm.

Then, slowly, carefully, he pulled her clothes from her.

He ran his hand over her smooth, hot skin, delighting in her murmurs of pleasure. He'd never taken a virgin before, and the knowledge that he was her first lover added even more excitement to the moment.

No man had ever touched her.

No one but him.

Even with his wings broken and clipped, he soared at that knowledge.

Livia moaned as he covered her with his long, hot body. She'd never felt anything like all that lean, hard strength spread out evenly against her bare flesh. He kissed her fiercely as he separated her thighs with his knee. Then he pressed his thigh against the center of her body, the hairs on his leg teasing her intimately.

She ran her hand over his back, feeling the rugged terrain of scars, muscle, and skin.

"My name is Adron," he whispered a second before he traced the outline of her ear with his tongue.

"Adron," she repeated, testing the syllables. It was a strong name that suited him.

He stroked her with his thigh, his tongue, and his hands. Arching her back, Livia welcomed his touch. It was so wickedly erotic to feel him all over and yet see nothing of him. It was like a vivid and yet surreal dream.

Reaching up, she freed his hair and let it fall around his face, then buried her hands in the silken strands of it. He leaned down and placed his lips in the crook of her arm where he suckled her flesh.

Adron swallowed as he pulled back, wanting desperately to see her face. Instead, he lifted his hand to trace the contours of it. He could feel the tiny cleft in her chin, imagine the small oval face overwhelmed by large brown eyes that tugged at a heart he'd thought was dead.

She was breathtaking. And for tonight, she was his.

All his.

Closing his eyes, he moved himself down her body, then

cursed as a wave of fierce pain lanced up his leg and across his back.

She tensed beneath him. "What's wrong?"

Adron couldn't answer. The pain in his leg was so intense that it instantly quelled his desire. He rolled over onto his back and struggled to breathe.

"Adron?"

The concern in her voice ate at him. Gah, he was a pathetic waste of humanity.

"My leg," he said between clenched teeth. "I need the painkillers on my nightstand."

"Which leg?"

"Damn it, get my medicine."

"Which leg!" she insisted.

He groaned out loud, hating himself for the fact he couldn't keep it in. But the pain was just too much. "The left one."

She took his knee into her hands.

He cursed as even more pain tore through him. "Stop!" he snarled.

"Just relax . . ." She massaged the joint.

A strange warmth came from her hands, seeping deep into his skin. He frowned as the ache began to diminish.

Suddenly, it was gone entirely.

For a full minute he lay there, tense, waiting for it to return.

It didn't.

In fact, nothing hurt. Not his chest, not his arm, not his knee. Nothing.

"What did you do?"

She placed her hand against his chest. "It's only temporary. But for a few hours, it won't bother you at all."

Adron couldn't believe it. He'd learned to live in a state of constant, unrelenting pain. Physical agony so severe that he couldn't sleep for more than a couple of hours at a time.

Until now.

The absence of it was unbelievable. His heart swelled with joy. He was free. Even if it was only temporary, he still had a moment to remember what he'd been like before his body had been cruelly, vengefully taken from him.

And it was all because of her.

He pulled her into his arms and kissed her precious lips.

Livia felt his heart pounding under her hand, and she heard the laughter in his voice.

"Thank you."

She smiled. Until he moved down her body with his kisses. She moaned as fierce pleasure tore through her. His hands and mouth felt incredible against her bare skin.

This was so much more than she'd expected. Krista had told her that a man who didn't know her would be quick with the deed, then let her leave.

But Adron was taking his time. He seemed to actually savor her body.

It was as if he were really making love to her. And she wondered, if he was this tender with a stranger, how much more so would he be if they actually knew each other? If he actually cared for her?

But tonight was all they'd ever know. When it was over she'd leave, and this moment would be nothing more than a treasured memory she'd carry with her the rest of her life, which would probably be really short once her father found out what she'd done.

That was tomorrow.

Tonight, there was just the two of them.

And she would revel in it.

Adron drank in the smell and taste of her skin as he nibbled the bare flesh of her hip. Her taste was addictive, and her smell . . .

He could breathe in the sweet floral scent forever.

Her soft hands caressed his hair and neck in a way that made him burn. He'd never thought to have another night like this.

A night with no demons. No memories.

She engulfed him, and he gladly surrendered himself to her. She was his angel of mercy, delivering him from his sins and darkness. Delivering him from his loneliness and solitude. He would treasure this peaceful moment for the rest of his life. It would warm him and keep him company when his body returned to being hateful.

His heart tender for her, he spread her legs and placed his body between them.

Livia bit her lip, expecting him to enter her.

He didn't.

Instead, he kissed a small path down her thigh while he buried his hand at the center of her body.

She groaned from the pleasure of his touch. It was sweet, pure bliss. And he took his time circling her with his fingers, delving, stroking, caressing.

"That's it," he breathed against her leg as she rubbed herself against his hand. "Don't be embarrassed."

She should be, and yet she wasn't.

At least not until he took her into his mouth.

Blind ecstasy ripped her asunder. "Adron? Are you supposed to do that?"

He gave her one long, deep lick. "Does it feel good?"

"Oh, yes."

"Then I'm supposed to be doing it." Without another word, he returned his mouth to her.

Livia writhed in his arms as his tongue tormented her. And when he slid his finger inside her, she thought she would perish from the pleasure. Krista had told her to expect pain, but there was nothing painful in his touch. Nothing but heaven. She threw her head back as he swirled his finger inside her, around and around, matching the rhythm of his tongue. Assaulted by fierce, fiery sensations, Livia felt her body quiver and jerk as if it had a mind of its own.

Her ecstasy mounted until she could stand no more, and then just as she was ready to beg him to stop, her body ripped apart.

She screamed out as her release came hard and fast. Still he toyed with her. His finger and tongue pleasured her until the sensitive flesh couldn't bear his touch any longer.

"Please," she cried. "Please, have mercy on me."

Adron laughed at her tone and was amazed at the foreign sound. He couldn't remember the last time he'd laughed.

He pulled back, but kept his finger inside her for a moment longer. He could feel her maidenhead still intact. His body burned, demanding he take her. But he couldn't do that. He hadn't done any real damage to her yet.

Once he broke that barrier, there would be no going back. No second chances.

It would be like when he decided to . . .

30

He flinched at the memory. His life had been completely ruined by one impulsive act. He wouldn't let her ruin hers the same way.

She was kind and gentle. A pure heart in a world of corrupt ones.

He wouldn't spoil that. He couldn't.

Closing his eyes, he was mystified by what he felt for her. At the fact that he was able to pull himself back and rein in his treacherous body.

It had been years since he'd done anything noble. Years since he'd *wanted* to do anything noble. And for the first time in almost a decade, he felt like the man he'd once been.

And it felt good.

He reached down for the blanket and covered her with it.

Livia paused as he spooned up to her back and held her close. She reveled in the feel of his arms around her, but he didn't seem to be making any move to . . .

"Adron?"

"Yes?"

"We're not through, are we?"

He rubbed his cheek against her shoulder. "I gave you your pleasure, Livia. What more do you want?"

She turned to look at him, but in the darkness all she could see was the vaguest of outlines of his face. "But you didn't . . . You know."

"I know."

"Why?"

"Don't you think you should wait until you find someone you care about?"

"I care about you."

31

Adron snorted. "You don't even know me."

She turned in his arms and reached up to place her hand against his scarred cheek. "You're right, I don't know you. And yet I've already shared my body with you. I want you to finish."

He pulled away from her. "Livia—"

"Adron. If you don't, I'll be forced into marriage with a man I despise. I don't want him to touch me the way you have. Please help me. If I'm not a virgin, he'll refuse the marriage. I can't marry him. I can't."

Her words tore through him. An image of Alia flashed through his mind. He'd been forced for political reasons to marry her. And she'd shown him a whole new meaning to the word *hell*. It was something he'd wish on no one.

Livia skimmed her hand over his chest, down across his stomach. His gut contracted fiercely at her touch as her nails brushed at the hairs between his legs until she held him in her hand. His cock tightened and swelled even more. In that instant, he knew he was lost.

And when she kissed him, his entire world came undone.

Livia was unprepared for his reaction. He growled low in his throat and rolled her over, pinning her against the mattress. He was wild and untamed as he kissed her lips, then buried his face against her neck where he licked and teased her flesh, burning her all over. He reached down between them, stroking her until she lost all reason, all sanity. His gaze locked with hers, he spread her legs wider. She felt the tip of his cock against her core.

In a sweet gesture, he took her hand in his and held it above her head. He kissed her lightly on the lips and slid himself deep inside her. As he filled her, she bit her bottom lip to keep from crying out at the unexpected pain that intruded on her pleasure. He was so large that her body ached at the foreign feel of him.

But at least it was done.

She was a virgin no more.

Adron held himself perfectly still, waiting for her body to adjust to his. The last thing he wanted was to hurt her, but by the fierce grip she had on his hand, he knew what she was hiding.

He also knew better than anyone that a person couldn't feel pleasure and pain at the same time.

And he refused to hurt her tonight.

Reluctantly, he let go of her hand and raised himself up on his arms to look down at her. He was used to the darkness. So much so that he saw her eyes tightly shut.

"Don't be afraid," he whispered, skimming his hand down her body until he touched her between her legs again.

Livia sighed as his hand stroked her nub. The pain receded behind a wave of building delight.

"That's it," he said before he slowly started to rock his hips against hers.

Livia arched her back as his hot touch washed away the pain. He felt so good inside her, and every stroke seemed to reach deeper as she clung to his broad, muscular shoulders. She'd never imagined it could feel so wonderful.

Adron watched her face as she surrendered herself to him. He ground his teeth at the incredible feel of her. She was so wet and hot beneath and around him. He'd forgotten the pleasure to be had in a woman's arms.

Had forgotten the incredible feel of someone just holding him in the darkness.

He lowered himself and took her into his arms, where he cradled her head in his hands as he thrust against her. Her breath fell against his bare shoulder, burning him.

She turned her head to kiss his neck as she ran her hands over his back.

He growled, scalded by the bliss of it. *Gah, let me die right here and right now.* Before the pain returned. Before he remembered what a worthless piece of shit he was.

Desperate for her, he didn't want this moment to end.

Livia wrapped her legs around his lean waist. He held her so tenderly that it touched her deep inside her heart. Krista had told her he would use her without any feelings for her whatsoever.

But it didn't feel like that.

Not the way he held on to her like she was unspeakably precious.

He returned to her lips, and she moaned at the taste of his tongue. He stroked her faster. Deeper. Harder. She held him close as her pleasure started building again. Oh goodness, what was it about him that made her feel like this?

And this time when her release came, he joined her. He growled low in his throat as he delivered one last, deep stroke and shuddered in her arms.

Adron collapsed on top of her. Completely spent, he lay there, holding her as he waited to drift back down from heaven and into his body. So much for meaningless sex. There had been absolutely nothing meaningless about what they'd just shared. And what terrified him most was the fact that he didn't want her to leave.

He didn't want to return to the vacant emptiness of his

life. He'd been alone for so long. Had lived without anyone other than servants and family.

But she'd changed that, and he didn't want to go back.

"That was amazing." Her breath teased his ear. "Can we do it again?"

He laughed, and was shocked to feel his body already stirring. "Yes, we can." In fact, he wasn't going to stop until she again begged him for mercy.

TWO

Adron came awake slowly to the most incredible feeling he'd ever known.

Livia by his side.

She lay nestled in his arms, facing away from him. He wasn't sure what time they'd finally fallen asleep. All he knew was that he'd never experienced such peace. Such warmth.

And there was no pain. Neither physical nor mental.

Reveling in the moment, he buried his face in her hair and inhaled the fresh, sweet scent of her as he pressed his skin to hers.

His body stirred immediately.

How?

After the night they'd shared, he should be sated for days to come, and yet here he was craving her in a way that was almost inhuman. He didn't understand it.

He pulled away to kiss her shoulder, then froze as he saw her skin in the faint morning light. Frowning, he ran his hand over her bare shoulder and the vicious scars that marred her back. She'd been beaten. Severely by the looks of it.

Was she a runaway slave?

She sighed contentedly and snuggled against him. Adron forgot the scars as her buttocks collided with his erection. He tightened his arms around her while he nudged her legs apart with his thigh. God help him, but he wanted more of her.

Livia came awake to the sensation of Adron behind her, filling her again. "Oh my goodness," she breathed as he thrust himself deep and hard into her body. Biting her lip, she groaned in pleasure. "Don't you ever get tired?"

"Not of you, I don't."

She smiled at that. No one had ever made her feel so treasured. And she had to admit, a woman could get used to waking up like this.

Closing her eyes to savor his long, luscious strokes, she surrendered herself to him.

She came an instant before he did.

Livia rolled over to see a gentle smile on his face as he stared at her in wonder.

"Thank you, Livia. For everything."

She returned his smile. "Thank you." She placed her lips against his.

Adron's senses swirled as he cupped her head in his hand. He was definitely going to keep her in his bed for the rest of the day.

"Adron, you're not going to believe what—" His father's

voice broke off the instant his bedroom door swung open. Gaping at them lying entwined on the bed, his father froze.

Then, all hell broke loose.

Livia dove beneath the covers at the same time a fetid curse rang out.

Adron looked from her cowering in his bed to the six men surrounding his father. Two of them wore royal Vistan robes, marking them as an emperor and his heir. The other four wore the dark-gray uniform of imperial bodyguards.

"I told you it was true!" the elder Vistan snarled at Adron's father. His dark-brown eyes were filled with hatred as he tilted his head to look up at Adron's father. At six foot six, and a former League assassin himself, his father wasn't the kind of man you addressed in anything except the most reverent of tones.

Not unless you wanted to die, anyway.

And he saw the warning glint in his father's eyes that denoted a wrath the Vistan emperor would do well to fear.

"The informant was correct when he said your son left with her."

Adron arched a brow at the contemptuous sneer on the man's face. And it was then he realized the Vistan emperor had hair the same color and hue as the woman cowering in his bed. And as he scanned the younger Vistan heir, he saw further confirmation of who Livia really was.

Shit.

He'd slept with a Vistan princess.

"You whore!" Her brother threw the covers back and grabbed Livia by the wrist.

Adron removed her brother's hand from her and shoved

him back. "She didn't do anything wrong." Oblivious to his nudity, he left the bed and put himself between Livia and her family. "You touch her and I'll tear your heart out."

Rage descended on her brother's face, but Adron saw the fear in the man's eyes as he took in Adron's height, build, and vicious scars.

Her father, however, wasn't so easily intimidated. "Take her," he said to his guards.

Livia hung her head as she wrapped the sheet around herself. The guards lifted her from the bed and took her to stand before her father.

Adron ached at the frightened look on her face. And the sight of his bloodstained sheets kicked him hard in the gut. There was no doubt what the two of them had done.

Or how innocent she'd been before he'd touched her.

Her father raked her with a scathing glare. "Modesty isn't becoming of a whore who spreads her legs for a man she meets in a filthy bar."

Before Adron realized what he was doing, her father yanked the sheet from her body. Tears filled her eyes as she tried desperately to cover herself with her hands.

"Take her outside and beat her."

Rage flooded him. "Damn you to hell." He grabbed the first guard and shoved him away from Livia.

He pulled her behind him to protect and cover her. Then he retrieved the sheet from the floor and wrapped it around both of them. Livia stood so close to his back that he could feel her trembling.

And it made him even angrier. How dare they ruin this and embarrass her so. What kind of people were they?

If her father wanted a fight, Adron was ready to give him

one. No one would hurt her for what she'd given to him. Not unless they wanted a taste of him first.

Her father narrowed his gaze threateningly, and Adron saw the look in his own father's eyes that warned of death if her father attacked him. "Boy, this is no concern of yours. You've done enough damage." Her father took a step forward.

So did Adron's father. And Adron knew that look preceded death and dismemberment.

He had to do something.

And in that instant, he knew exactly what.

Adron refused to release her to her father. "Whatever concerns my wife, concerns me."

Livia froze as soon as the words left Adron's lips. Last night, she'd had no idea that he was the Andarion heir. But Emperor Nykyrian Quiakides she knew. They'd been introduced a few days ago when she and her family had arrived for a meeting and the preliminary nuptial preparations.

Indeed, it was business with Adron's father that had her getting married on Kirovar to begin with.

Now that the two men were together, she saw the similarities between father and son. Nykyrian had the same white-blond hair, the same firm, sculpted jaw. They also shared an identical height and build.

And a lethal air that was truly frightening.

Her father shifted his cold stare from Adron to her. "Is this true? Are you his wife?"

Livia swallowed. If she said yes, Andarion law would recognize them as married.

"Adron," his father said sternly. "Do you understand what you're doing?"

Adron turned to face her. He tilted her chin up with

gentle fingers until she looked into those icy blue eyes that were laced with pain and torment. "It's entirely up to you. You're welcome to stay here with me if you want to."

Aghast at his offer, she stared at him. She'd never known a man so honorable. He could have left her to her father's wrath, and yet here he was offering her sanctuary. There weren't many men who would be so thoughtful, and it brought tears to her eyes that he would be so kind.

"Are you sure about this?"

"No." A hint of a smile played at the edges of his lips. "But then, I've never been sure about much of anything in my life."

She glanced past him to her father's angry face, and her brother's. If she went home, they would have her beaten until she passed out. But if she stayed . . .

She had no idea what that would be like.

The known or the unknown.

"Take her," her father ordered.

Adron turned and put himself between them.

"Quiakides, tell your son to step aside. He is interfering with royal Vistan business."

For the first time, Livia noticed the deep, angry scars bisecting Adron's body. His back was completely covered by them. It looked as if someone had once carved him into pieces.

Her gaze fell to the skull-and-dagger tattoo on his left shoulder that marked him as a League assassin. She trembled. She knew absolutely nothing about him.

Nothing except for the kindness of his touch. Nothing except for the way he'd made her feel when he kissed her. The way he made her feel wanted. Safe.

And in that instant, she made up her mind. "What happens to me is the business of my husband."

Her father's face turned to stone. "Then your ties to our house are severed." He glanced at her brother. "Come, Prinam."

Her brother's features softened a degree before he caught himself. Without a word, he followed her father from the room as the guards fell in behind them.

Nykyrian stepped forward with an amused light in his green eyes. "Some things must run in our blood."

Adron frowned. "How do you mean?"

"Ask your mother one day about how we married." He smiled at Livia. "In the meantime, welcome to our family, Highness."

Adron's frown deepened as he regarded his father suspiciously. "You're being awfully understanding about all this. Should I be afraid?"

Nykyrian laughed. "Probably. I hope this means you'll rejoin the world again. We've missed you."

A tic started in Adron's jaw.

Livia wasn't sure what the undercurrent was between father and son, but there was something just below the surface that she didn't understand. Some history that they had yet to work through.

Still, his father's face was kind and not the least bit judgmental as he looked back at her. He honestly seemed glad to have her with his son. "You know, you'll have to bring your wife to the palace to meet the rest of your wayward siblings."

"And Mom?"

His father inclined his head.

Something strange flickered across Adron's features. Something Livia couldn't define, but it looked as if Adron wanted to avoid his mother. "When?"

"Tonight."

Adron curled his lip as if he'd rather be gutted. "Will Jayce be there?"

"He is your brother."

Hatred flared in Adron's eyes. "He's your son. He ceased to be my brother the day he refused to uphold the League's Code."

Nykyrian sighed, then looked at Livia with sympathy in his eyes. "I hope you know what you've gotten yourself into."

The bad thing was, she didn't.

"You two have a good day. I have an international incident I have to go prevent over this." Nykyrian went to the door and paused. "God help me," he said under his breath before he left. "Let the bribes begin."

Now that they were alone, the reality of what she'd done came crashing down on her.

She was married.

To a complete stranger.

"Well, isn't this interesting." Adron turned to face her. "I don't know about you, but when I went to the Golden Crona last night, I never intended to find a spouse."

She laughed nervously. "Since I was there to avoid one, I can honestly say that never crossed my mind either."

He cupped her face in his hands and smiled a warm, dimpled smile at her. And when he kissed her, she shivered at the tenderness of his lips.

"You taste so good." He nibbled the corner of her mouth. "I could kiss you forever."

Desire stabbed her at his words. "You're not so bad yourself in a lethal, I'll-kill-you-if-you-look-at-me-wrong kind of way."

He laughed, then scooped her up in his arms.

Livia gasped at the unexpected feel of his strong arms surrounding her. But as he reached the bed, he staggered.

Agony contorted his face as he let go of her and fell to his knees.

"Adron?" She knelt beside him. She could tell by his face that he hurt too much to speak. "Here, lie on the floor."

Livia helped him lie down, then took his knee in her hand. She did her best to summon her powers, but they refused to come.

No!

Adron held his hand to his head as if something vile were being plunged into his brain. He writhed in misery, and she ached that she couldn't help him.

Her heart hammering, she rushed to the nightstand.

"The injector," he snarled from the floor. "There's a bottle for it in the drawer."

Livia found them and took them to him.

He placed the bottle in the injector, then held it against his stomach and pulled the trigger. Sweat drenched his body as he shook all over. She could only imagine how bad he'd have to be hurting.

Not knowing what else to do for him, she covered him with the blanket and then held his head in her lap. She brushed her hands through his damp hair, trying to give him whatever comfort she could.

Adron tried not to fight the pain. It hurt less when he did,

44

and yet it ripped through him with such a torturous fury that it left him weak. Drained.

Damn it! The brief reprieve had only made it hurt all the more as it returned.

He stared up at Livia as she brushed her hand through his hair and held him close. He'd never before allowed anyone near him when he was like this. Not when he had a choice about it, anyway. But there was something about her that soothed his tattered spirit.

Better still, he didn't see contempt or pity on her face. A peaceful calm stared at him from her brown eyes, as if that were what she wanted to leave with him.

After a few minutes, his pain ebbed enough that he could move again.

He sat up slowly, carefully, but it felt as if every muscle in his body had been shredded. He started to push himself to his feet.

She moved to help him.

"Don't," he said with more rancor than he meant. "I can stand on my own."

She took his angry tone in stride. "Can I get you anything?"

"A bottle of alcohol." He slowly made his way back to the bed so that he could lie down.

"Adron, it's morning. Shouldn't you eat something?"

He glared the glare that had never failed to send his enemies running for cover. "Get me something to drink."

She dressed, then returned a few minutes later with a glass of milk.

He could have beaten her for that shit. It was something

his mother or sister would have done to piss him off. "Damn it, Livia! I'm not a child."

"Then stop acting like one."

Before he could respond, the door chime sounded.

She bit her lip. "Should I answer it?"

"I don't give a damn what you do just so long as you leave me alone."

Livia sighed at his hostile tone as he shifted slightly in the bed, then grimaced.

Leaving him, she went to the door and opened it to find a tall, attractive brunette barely dressed. The short red halter top was scooped low, and the tight black leather skirt would have given Livia's parents the vapors.

The woman removed her sunglasses so that Livia could see the red irises and white pupils that marked the woman as a full-blooded Andarion. "You must be Livia." She grinned cheerfully, flashing her fangs. "I'm Zarina." She said her name like Livia should recognize it.

She cocked a brow at the odd stranger.

Laughing, Zarina explained herself. "I'm Adron's baby sister. Dad just told me about the marriage, and I had to come meet you and make sure Dad hadn't snapped a wheel and started hallucinating or something."

Unsure what to make of Adron's unconventional sister, Livia let her in.

"You're really, really cute." She stepped inside and dropped her bag on Adron's couch. "But I wouldn't have pegged you for his type."

Was she trying to be offensive? "Excuse me?"

"Adron always had a thing for expensive ho's with the

intelligence of backwash. You look like you actually have both a brain and a soul."

Livia scowled. "Should I be offended?"

Zarina laughed. "Please don't be. I pride myself on being socially inept. But the only people I ever intentionally offend are my bevy of brothers. And speaking of, where's Big Bad Angry One? Dad said he was actually up and walking around without his cane. That I have to see."

Before Livia could answer, a loud crash sounded in the bedroom. She ran back to Adron with Zarina one step behind her.

As soon as they entered the room, she saw him leaning with one hand braced against the nightstand. She gasped at the sight of blood covering him, the bed, and the floor. And every time he coughed, more blood came up.

"Oh, God." Zarina pulled her link from her pocket.

Terrified, Livia went to her husband.

He opened his mouth to speak but only coughed up more blood. His entire body shaking, he fell back against the bed, where he writhed in agony.

When she tried to touch him, he pushed her away.

Zarina joined her at the bed. "An MT unit is on its way."

Livia locked gazes with Adron. She saw the torment and the shame in his eyes. He was embarrassed. But for her life, she couldn't imagine why.

Then it dawned on her. He, a proud League assassin, was naked and helpless in front of his baby sister. If everything else wasn't bad enough . . .

He had that indignity to suffer.

She glanced to Zarina. "Can you give us a minute alone?"

Zarina hesitated before she nodded. "I'll go call our parents and let them know." She left the room and shut the door.

Adron scowled at her. "What are you doing?"

"I'm cleaning you up."

She saw the anger and relief in his eyes before he stopped fighting her. She figured the anger was for himself because he needed help cleaning up, and the relief for the fact that he wouldn't be transported naked.

Something that was confirmed by the weak, bashful "Thank you" he whispered to her once she had him dressed.

She'd just handed him another clean towel to keep the blood off his clothes when the MTs arrived. Zarina joined her as she moved into a corner to give them room to work.

They inserted a tube down Adron's throat and gave him another injection while they started an IV. He just lay there, and his calm acceptance of their actions told her he was well used to things like this.

Dear Lord, what had happened to him?

And what had caused this episode? Could it be because of what they'd done? Could having sex kill him?

The thought horrified her.

As the air gurney passed her, Adron gave her a tired, sheepish look, then turned away.

Zarina draped her arm around Livia's shoulders. "C'mon. I'll give you a ride to the hospital."

Livia followed her to a transport and got inside first. "What happened to him to cause all those scars?"

Zarina winced as if the memory were too painful to even contemplate. "Eight years ago, Adron was the League assassin who was assigned to terminate Kyr Omaindon."

Livia knew the name well. Kyr's bloodthirsty cruelty was the stuff of nightmares. He'd blazed a two-year trail of rape and slaughter through the Brimen sector.

Zarina raked a graceful hand through her hair. "When Adron entered Kyr's home to execute him, Kyr grabbed one of his servants and locked himself inside his study. The woman was pregnant, and Adron blamed himself for letting her get taken."

Livia remembered that famous standoff. There had been days of media coverage. It had ended when one of the League assassins had allowed his hands to be cuffed behind his back and then traded for the pregnant woman.

Now she knew the name and face of that assassin.

Worse, she knew his gentle touch.

Tears gathered in her eyes as she tried to imagine the courage it'd taken for Adron to be bound, helpless, and given over to a monster in order to save a stranger he'd never even met.

Zarina drove through the crowded sectors that blurred past outside. "Kyr decided to make an example out of Adron. He wanted to ensure that the League thought twice about sending another assassin after him. So he tortured Adron for over a week. They hunted for him everywhere, but found nothing. No traces of either of them."

A tear slid down Zarina's cheek. Angrily, she swiped it away. "It was the longest twelve days of my life. My entire family searched everywhere we could think of—used every resource we had. Finally my brother Jayce found him barely alive inside a Dumpster. There was so little left of Adron that Jayce barely recognized him as a human being, never mind his own brother."

Livia blinked away her tears as she imagined what it must have been like for Jayce to find his brother in such a condition—not knowing if he'd live or not. Never mind the pain the rest of them had felt, especially Adron himself.

"If Jayce saved him, why does Adron hate him so?"

"Because, according to League Code, when an assassin finds another assassin who has been permanently maimed or disfigured, he's supposed to terminate him. The idea is to die with honor and dignity."

Livia ached for her husband and his family. "Jayce couldn't do it."

"No, he couldn't. The two of them were too close. Plus, Jayce would never have been able to face the rest of us if he'd killed him or let him die. Not when all we wanted was to have him home safe and sound." Zarina sighed wistfully. "I wish you could have seen Adron back before he was butchered. He was something else." She gave a sad smile. "He was always rushing around at warp speed, joking, laughing. Now there are days when he can't even leave his bed for the pain. And I can't even remember the last time I saw him smile, never mind laugh. I don't think he's capable of it anymore."

Livia remembered catching a glimpse of that playful Adron last night when he'd made love to her. And he had a beautiful laugh—if only she'd known then how rare a thing it was. "What happened to Kyr?"

Zarina's face tightened. "My father and uncles tore him to pieces. Literally. His was a death I'd only wish on him and no one else. There's probably some poor engineering person who's still finding chunks of him in the sewer where they dumped him."

Livia had never condoned violence of any sort, but after seeing Adron and the constant pain he lived in, she understood their actions. Even as a pacifist, she would have done serious damage to anyone who hurt her child like that.

Now, she just wanted to make it better for him.

If only she knew how . . .

But one thing was certain, she wasn't going to leave him like this. Alone. Tormented. Isolated. She owed him too much for that. He'd given her a new life free of over-the-top restrictions and stern punishments.

Her throat tightened as she realized that for the first time in her entire life she was outside in the world without being covered from head to foot, with no guards scowling at her and no old chaperones warning her not to speak or touch anything.

She was free because Adron had stood up for her for no other reason than he was a decent human being. Such a man deserved happiness and love.

Somehow she would make him laugh again. Even if it killed her.

THREE

Adron shoved the oxygen mask off his face.

His doctor gave him a peeved glare. "Would you stop that? You need it."

"I can't breathe with it on."

"You can barely breathe, period." Theo put the oxygen mask back in place.

Adron narrowed his eyes at the man, but as usual, Theo didn't care. Over the last eight years, their battle of wills had become legendary with the hospital staff.

Theo brushed a hand though his graying black hair while he scowled at Adron. "I can't believe you'd even try to have sex in your condition. What were you thinking?"

That his wife had the best ass he'd ever seen . . .

Adron jerked the mask off. "I'm not a friggin' eunuch."

"No, you're not. But that's about the only part of you that didn't get cut off and that still works the way God intended it to." Theo put the mask back in place. "You need to remember you're a man whose internal organs are barely fused together. Their functionality is minimal at best, and any strain on them can kill you. How many times do I have to tell you that you can't put any pressure on your abdomen?"

"Well, if I have to die, I'd rather go out with a good bang."

Theo curled his lip. "You're not funny."

His throat tight, Adron closed his eyes. An image of Livia drifted through his mind, and he cursed it.

Theo checked his IV. "If you'd wear your chest brace like you're—"

"It's hot and it chafes. I can't even move in it."

Sighing, Theo set his electronic chart aside. "Like it or not, Adron, one misplaced fall and you could break something and kill yourself. Your body is as fragile as a roshuna flower."

Yeah, there was something an assassin really wanted to be compared to. He, the baddest of the bad—the man who'd once made the worst scum in the universe piss in fear—was now a goddamn delicate flower.

I wish I were dead.

Adron removed the mask again. "I don't care. I'm not going to wear that monstrosity. It makes me look like a freak." Which he was, but by the gods, he had no intention of letting everyone know just how damaged he really was.

He did have *some* pride left.

Theo rolled his eyes. "One day, that stubbornness is going to get you killed."

Yeah, but obviously not soon enough.

More roughly than before, Theo replaced the mask. "By

the way, there's a reason why I don't give you medicine to completely numb your pain. You need to feel it to know the limitations of your damaged body. Tell your wife it was a nice thought, but in the future you better not let her help you. Not unless you want to become my permanent guest here at Hotel Hell. Now keep that damn mask in place or I'll have your hands restrained."

In one last act of defiance, Adron made an obscene gesture.

Letting out a sigh of supreme disgust, the good doctor walked away.

Theo stopped at the door and turned back to face him. "And the next time you want to have sex, you better find some way to do it without putting any strain on your chest or abdomen. I'm not kidding, Adron. You do this to yourself one more time and I will geld you for it."

∘ ∘ ∘

"**Hey,** big brother."

Adron opened his eyes to see Zarina leaning into the room. He tried to muster a smile for her but couldn't. The pain was just too much right now. Not to mention she wouldn't be able to see it anyway for the mask covering his face.

Still, he was glad to see her. No matter how bad he felt, Zarina and her offbeat sense of humor could always make him feel better.

"Theo the Bad said it was okay to see you. How do you feel?" Zarina took a hesitant step inside his room, and it was then he saw Livia behind her and all thoughts scattered.

His wife had her long brown hair braided down her back. The blue conservative pantsuit caused her pale skin to glow, and those large doe eyes held so much tenderness in them that it made him ache to be whole.

To be able to love her like she deserved . . .

Adron clenched his teeth as a wave of desire tore through him. He couldn't stand to see her, knowing she belonged to him, and yet he could never again have her.

It was the cruelest blow of all.

I'm not even a man.

He turned his head away from them so he wouldn't be reminded of what an abomination he'd become. Wouldn't remember the man who could have made love to her all night long without tiring.

Now . . .

He looked down at his bare, scarred arm that disgusted him. The twisted flesh. The puckered skin . . . How could Livia not be repulsed by him? Even he hated himself. "Get out and leave me alone."

"Adron?"

The sound of Livia's gentle voice washed over him like a gentle caress, and it tore through him like glycerin on glass. *Gods, it wasn't fair!*

She came forward, and when he felt her touch on his scarred arm . . .

Forget the pain of his injuries. They were nothing compared to the mental damage that touch wrought. "Get away from me!" He pushed Livia back and glared at his sister as his monitors blared. "Take her to a lawyer and get us divorced. Now! I mean it, Rina. Don't you dare ignore me."

Theo came running in with two nurses behind him. "Out," he snapped at the women. "I told you not to upset him."

Livia felt her tears swell at the sight of the doctor forcing Adron to lie down and the sound of Adron cursing them all.

Her throat tight, she looked up at Zarina. "What did I do?"

"It's not you, sweetie." Zarina hugged her to her side as they left the room and headed down the hallway. "Adron is just blaming you for what Alia did."

"Alia?"

"His first wife."

Livia stumbled at the news. "He was married before?" *Please don't let him still be married.* That was one question she hadn't even thought to ask.

She nodded. "Yes. And she was one serious bitch. To this day, I'd love to rip her cold heart out and feed it to her. Since she was the Wurish heiress, her father had negotiated a marriage between them when they were both in their teens. Alia had agreed only because she wanted a trophy husband, and as the youngest commissioned officer in League history and the next in line to inherit my father's empire, Adron was a choice candidate for her.

"But they never really got along. She was too selfish and bitchy. I think half the missions he took were to escape having to be around her. He spent so much time away from home that he was all but a stranger to us. Then three weeks after Adron had been found—while he was still fighting for his life—my mother, father, and I were in his hospital room, trying to give him reasons to live through the pain. All of a sudden, Alia showed up with divorce papers. She handed them to him and told him she was too young to be nursemaid to some cut-up cripple."

Horror for him filled Livia as she gave Zarina an incredulous stare. "How could she do such a thing?"

"I have no idea, but if I live an eternity, I will never forget the look on Adron's face. I saw something inside him die that day. But honestly, between you and me, I think it's the best thing that could have happened to him. He didn't need her in his life, and it was good riddance to self-indulgent trash. I just wish the bitch had had better timing."

Zarina stopped and leveled a hard look on her. "And speaking of timing . . . are we going to a lawyer's office?"

Livia bit her lip in indecision. Adron had been through so much that she wondered if he was still mentally sound. His physical scars she knew; it was the ones she couldn't see that scared her.

She searched Zarina's eyes for the truth. "Tell me, is he psychotic or abusive?"

"No. But he is angry and extremely bitter. He was never the type of person to depend on anyone for anything. It humiliates him every time he has to ask for something, and right now he needs help to do even the simplest of things."

She could understand that. She'd never liked being dependent either. And if what she'd seen was his worst, she could definitely withstand it. "Then take me home."

Zarina smiled. "I knew I liked you for a reason."

o   o   o

Over the next few days, Livia spent as much time as she could learning about Adron while she waited for him to come home.

Zarina and Adron's twin brothers, Taryn and Tiernan, were tremendous sources of information. And that afternoon, they'd provided her with a box full of files and pictures.

Sitting alone in his media room, she pulled out a handful of old discs to watch.

The first one was of Adron with a tall, dark-haired man. Adron appeared to be around the age of twenty, with the dark-haired man a little younger. Adron's long blond hair was loose, spilling over his shoulders as the two of them played a complicated electronic board game.

Goodness, but she barely recognized her handsome husband. His face intact, his eyes glowed like blue fire while he drummed his fingers impatiently on the table.

"C'mon, Devyn, move already. You're like watching ice freeze. You keep this pace up and my grandkids will be able to finish the game for you."

"Shut the fuck up, Adron, I'm thinking."

"Yeah, I can see the smoke coming out of your ears. What? You strip a gear or something trying to think? Want me to call Vik over to take your turn for you?"

Devyn made an obscene gesture at him.

Before Devyn could do or say anything else, water poured down over the two of them, drenching them completely and short-circuiting the board.

Adron held his hands out as his expression darkened in anger. "What the hell?"

The men looked up to see a young Zarina with a hose, leaning over the wall while she laughed at them.

Adron's gaze narrowed dangerously. "Oh, Reen . . . You're going to die. Painfully."

Dropping the hose, Zarina shrieked and ran, but Adron caught up to her the moment she came around the fence.

"Get her, Adron!" Livia recognized the voice as Tiernan's or Taryn's. One of the twins must have been the one filming them. "Make her pay!"

Adron slung Zarina over his shoulder as he sprinted across the yard with her.

Zarina pounded on his wet back as she tried to squirm out of his hold. "I'm going to tell Dad on you if you don't let me go! Put me down, you overgrown bully."

He stopped in front of an inground pool. "You got it." He flipped her over his shoulder, straight into the water.

Zarina came up sputtering and coughing. "Oh, that's it! Devyn! Help your baby cousin! I need my avenger."

Devyn came running. His dark hair was cut short and his eyes glowed with mischief. He grabbed Adron by the waist, and the two of them fell into the pool.

Adron broke the water's surface, laughing.

Devyn grabbed him from behind and dunked him while Zarina pounded on his head.

"No!" Adron's mother, Kiara, shouted as she ran to the pool. Her eyes were wide with fright, and her beautiful face was stern. She looked like she was about to cry. "No playing like that. You know better. One of you could get hurt."

Adron shoved Devyn back before he swiped his hair out of his eyes. "Mom, it's okay."

Kiara shook her head, causing her long mahogany braid to spill over her shoulder. "No, it's not. I couldn't live if I lost one of you, and you both know what Shahara would do if she saw you and Devyn fighting in the deep end of the pool. Now get out of there, all of you, and stop playing around."

Subdued, the three of them climbed out of the pool.

Subdued, that was, until Devyn sneaked up behind Adron and pulled his shorts down.

Livia gaped at the sight of Adron completely naked.

So, her husband had never worn underwear . . . She smiled at the knowledge.

Cursing, Adron jerked his pants up and ran after his Devyn.

"Adron!" Kiara shouted, but the laughter in her voice took the sternness out of her tone. "Don't you hurt him."

"I'm not going to hurt him, Mom. I'm going to *kill* him."

"Aunt Kiara, help!" Devyn came running back around and put Kiara between them. Not that she was much of a wall, since she didn't even reach their shoulders.

"Adron," she said sharply. "You touch one hair on his head and his mother will skin you alive. You know it. And there's nothing I can do to stop her."

Adron paused as he glared at Devyn. "It's all right. You have to sleep sometime."

"Yeah, but I have a mecha bodyguard who doesn't." Devyn gave a taunting laugh before he stuck his tongue out.

Adron flashed an obscene gesture. "You suck, you little bastard."

Kiara glared. "Adron, I raised you better than that."

Devyn continued to torture him.

Livia laughed at their loving play, and as she watched more files, she realized that Zarina had been right. Adron had been a kind, fun-loving soul who took very little seriously.

Somehow, she was going to find that man and return him to the world.

∘ ∘ ∘

It was a full month and three more surgeries before Theo finally allowed Adron to leave the hospital. All he wanted to do was go home and be left alone. He didn't want to see any more pity on his mother's tear-streaked face. See the guilt in his father's eyes over the fact that there was nothing he could do.

He just wanted solitary peace away from everyone. A nice alcohol-induced fog . . .

His brother Tiernan moved to help him from the transport. Adron leveled a scowl that made him shrink back.

"Jeez, you ought to bottle that look. I know armies that would pay a fortune to have something that toxic in their arsenal."

Grinding his teeth, Adron got out even though the strain of it made him sweat. "Why are you still here?"

"Dad wanted me to make sure you got home safely."

"I'm home. Now leave."

Tiernan scoffed. "Why would I want to do that? I mean, heaven forbid I should be around someone who actually likes me. It's so much more fun to be here with you insulting my manhood and questioning my parentage every five seconds."

Ignoring him, Adron made his way into his apartment building, to the lifts, and did his best not to remember who had been with him the last time he'd crossed this lobby.

Livia.

Her name and face still haunted him. And in spite of himself, he wondered where she was. How she was doing.

"I don't care."

Tiernan stepped into the lift beside him. "What was that?"

"Nothing."

Adron didn't speak until he was back in his apartment. He limped to the bar and searched for something to drink. But nothing was there. Not even the watered down crap. Obviously his family had paid another visit to clean his place out while he'd been gone. "Damn it, which one of you did this?"

"I did it."

He froze at the sound of Livia's voice behind him. That dulcet tone tore through him like jagged glass.

Bracing himself, he turned to face her. But all the bracing in the world couldn't prepare him for the sight of her standing there, dressed in white and looking like a precious angel. Her dark hair was pulled up, with wisps of it falling around her face and shoulders. Daylight shone through the strands, making them glow.

But that was nothing compared to those large eyes that seared him. To her Cupid's-bow lips that compelled him with a memory of how sweet they'd tasted. Every part of his body surged to life as his cock hardened. And all he wanted was to feel her hands and mouth on his naked skin.

I'm not kidding, Adron. You do this to yourself one more time and I will geld you for it. Too bad Theo hadn't made good on that threat. Because all he wanted was a taste of his wife, and it was the one thing he couldn't have.

Livid over that fact, he snarled at her. "What are you doing here?"

"I live here."

"The hell you do." He turned on his brother. "I want her out of here. Now."

Tiernan held his hands up in surrender. "According to your own words, she's your wife. There's nothing I can do."

"Tiernan," he said in warning.

"Adron," he shot back.

Livia moved forward, and by all appearances, she didn't look a bit shaken by his anger. "Thank you for bringing him home, Tiernan. I think I can handle it from here."

Tiernan arched a doubtful brow. "I don't know if I feel right leaving you at his mercy. He can let blood with that tongue."

"I'm used to people insulting me." She directed a meaningful stare at Adron. "As well as being unwanted. I promise you, there's nothing Adron can say to make me cry."

And in that moment, Adron felt low. He'd never wanted to hurt her.

Turning away, he headed for the bedroom.

Livia said good-bye to Tiernan, who let himself out of the apartment, and then she followed after Adron. In spite of her brave words, she was terrified. Even though he was her husband, he was a stranger to her in many ways.

But then, she was used to living in fear, too. At least Adron wouldn't beat her.

She hoped.

As she entered the bedroom, she found him lying on the bed, fully clothed, with his arm draped over his eyes. His long, lean body was a feast that made her heart speed up.

Strange how lethal and powerful he was while relaxing. But even more frightening was how much she'd missed him. His presence filled the room and added . . .

She couldn't define it. Even though they'd been together for only one night, she felt connected to him. And she'd missed him more than she'd ever missed anyone.

Now that he was here, she wanted to make him happy again. "Are you hungry?"

"No."

"Well then—"

"I want to be alone."

She sighed sadly at his sharp tone. How could she reach the Adron she'd seen in his files? The Adron who'd been so tender and kind to her?

Was it even possible?

Don't give up on him . . . That was what his mother had said to her yesterday when Kiara had called to tell her that Adron was coming home. *I know he's hard to be around, but he's a good man, and in spite of what he says, you mean something to him. He wouldn't have married you unless you did. So please, for his sake, help him find a reason to live. I want to see my baby smile again. Just once.*

How could she deny his mother so simple a request? Only today, that request didn't seem as easy as it had yesterday.

Today it seemed impossible.

But she'd promised to try, and so she would. "It seems to me you've spent far too much time alone. Perhaps a little time with—"

"Damn it, why are you still here?" He glared at her with

such loathing that it stung her. "Why didn't you do what I told you to?"

She took a deep breath and counted for patience as she reminded herself that he was in a lot of pain. *He doesn't mean it.*

What if he does?

No. She refused to believe that he would hate her after he'd protected her. So she answered with the simple truth. "Because I have nowhere else to go. My father has completely disowned me over our marriage. If I go home, he'll have me arrested and publicly beaten."

Adron winced as he realized the extent of the damage he'd done to her. How could he have been so stupid and selfish? And for what? One night of sex that had almost killed him?

What kind of life could he give her? He couldn't do anything. He was worthless and weak.

Pathetic.

And she deserved something better than him. A life that didn't include wiping his crippled ass.

"If it's a question of money—"

Her expression said that he'd insulted her to the core of her soul. "I don't want your money."

"Then what do you want?"

Her guileless stare pierced him. "You."

He shook his head slowly. "You must be deranged."

"Why? Because I want to be with you?"

"Yes. In case you haven't noticed, I'm not exactly pleasant to be around. Hell, *I* don't even want to be around me most days."

She moved to sit on the bed beside him. So close that he ached to pull her into his arms, but he refused to. He wouldn't do that to either of them.

It wouldn't be fair or right.

She brushed a strand of hair back from his face, her fingertips burning his skin as she touched him. "You know, while we were making love, I felt a connection with you. Did you feel it, too?"

"No," he lied.

She *tsk*ed at him with a light in her eyes that made him feel like a heel for not telling her how he really felt about her. "I don't believe you. You were too tender. You held me too close. I might be innocent, but I'm not stupid. I know men don't treat women that way."

He gave her a droll stare. "And how do you know that?"

"Zarina told me so."

He grimaced at her. "Oh, jeez. You discussed sex with my baby sister?"

"Yes. She was very informative."

His gut twisted at the thought of Zarina having any kind of carnal knowledge. "I can imagine."

"I also talked to your mother and she said—"

He cringed in pain, and for once, it wasn't from his injuries. "Ah, gah, Livia. That's even worse! Why would you talk to my mother about sex with me?"

"I didn't have anyone else to ask."

He let out puffs of aggravated breaths over what she'd done. How could she? Did she have no shame whatsoever? "You could have looked it up online like everyone else does."

"I tried, but all I got was porn vids and while it was . . . well, it was kind of gross and not very informative. Just a lot of huffing and puffing and body parts. So I thought your mother and sister might have some insights to share. After all, your mother had five kids and—"

"Stop! I don't even want to think about my mother having sex with my father. I know for a fact that she was artificially inseminated and he never touched her. Grandpa Zamir told me so and I believe him."

"That's not what she says."

He groaned out loud in utter misery. Yes, he was being childish, but this was not a topic he wanted to talk about, and it definitely wasn't something he wanted to think about. "Am I not in enough pain that you'd torture me with this shit on top of it? What did I ever do to you to make you want to kill me?"

"Why are you being such a baby over this? I'm the one who was kept cloistered."

"Because my mother and sister are sacred beings, unsullied by the hands of a man, and if you tell me differently, especially where Zarina is concerned, I swear to God, I'm donning my assassin's uniform and gutting whatever bastard touched her."

Livia pressed her lips together to keep from laughing at him when it was obvious he was deadly serious. Even so, she liked teasing him like this. And deep down, she suspected he might not be as ticked off as he was acting.

Deciding to give him a bit of a reprieve, she changed the subject. "So, are we just going to sit in here all day?"

All the humor fled from his face. "No. You're going to leave."

"I'll leave when you do."

Adron growled at her. "Do you have any idea how much pain I'm in? It hurts to breathe. Most of all it hurts to talk, so if you don't mind, I'd like to just lie here in silence."

She sighed at the anger and bitterness in his voice that seemed to be a permanent part of his life. What he'd done for that woman and her child had been beyond decent and heroic, and she didn't want him to lose sight of the sacrifice he'd made.

For someone else's happiness.

He was a hero and she only wanted to see him smile.

Just once.

"Fine." She slid from the bed and pulled a small photo frame out of his nightstand. "I wanted to show this to you. It came by messenger while you were in the hospital."

Adron frowned as she handed him the blank frame and turned it on. Static flickered until the image of a fragile brunette woman and a small blond girl appeared.

The two of them were smiling at him and waving.

Livia watched his stoic face as her heart filled with warmth over what he'd given them. It was enough to bring tears to her eyes.

"Hi, Commander." The woman picked up the little girl and kissed her cheek. "On the anniversary of what you did, I just wanted to say thank you. This is my daughter, Dalycia. I don't know if you remember me or not, but I'm the woman you saved from that psycho, and this is the daughter I had six weeks later. Say hi, Dalycia."

"Hi, Commander." The little girl waved and smiled with that innocence that came only with childhood. "Thank you for saving my mommy and me." She unfolded a hand-drawn picture of a man, a woman, and a little girl holding hands in a patch of flowers with a rainbow overhead. "I drew this for you to say thank you. See"—she pointed to the man—"it's you saving us, and we're all happy 'cause we're alive and the bad man isn't."

Livia watched the agony play across his face as the woman and child continued to talk to him.

All of a sudden, he snarled in outrage and threw the frame against the wall, shattering it into a thousand pieces.

"Adron!" she snapped, losing patience with him.

He turned on her then with a vicious snarl before he let fly a curse so foul she blushed. "What? Did you think showing me that shit would make all of this okay? Did you think I'd look at them, then cry and say how grateful I am they live while I'm trapped like this?"

He gestured to the scars that bisected his body and twisted his leg. "What about the children *I* wanted to have, Livia? I can't even have sex without spending a month in the hospital, or dying from it." He cursed again. "All I want is five fucking seconds where I'm not trying to breathe through absolute agony. Five seconds where I can move and not ache to the marrow of my bones."

The bitter torment in his eyes scorched her. "I'm only thirty-five years old, and all I have to look forward to is a future where I'll slowly, painfully disintegrate into an invalid who can't even wipe his own ass. Do you really think I'm okay with being dependent on you or anyone else? I was an assassin, and now I have less mobility than a withered-up hundred-year-old man. I'm nothing but a worthless piece of shit who should have died that night. And them telling me how grateful they are doesn't make this okay with me. It never will."

His words brought tears to her eyes. She'd stupidly thought it would make him feel better to know how much his sacrifice had meant to the ones he'd saved.

But she was wrong. Nothing would ever make him feel better.

"I'm sorry," she whispered. "I was just trying to help. But you won't let anyone help you, will you? You'd rather just wallow in self-pity. Fine. I understand. I won't bother you anymore." Her heart breaking for him, she turned with as much dignity as she could manage and left him to it.

She didn't stop walking until she reached the sitting room. Wishing for an answer that wouldn't come, she curled up into a ball on the couch and bit her lip to hold back the tears. She wouldn't cry.

But inside, she bled for him. Ached for what he'd once been. Even now she could see him laughing and playing games with his sister and brothers.

How she wished she'd known him then.

Suddenly, she felt a hand on her head. Looking up, she found Adron standing beside the couch. His brow was damp with sweat, and she saw the whiteness of his lips as he struggled with his pain while he leaned heavily on his cane.

"I'm sorry," he said, his voice tense. "I know you were just trying to help. But I passed the point of help a long time ago." He shifted his weight and winced. "Look, I know about your people and customs, and I know you were raised inside a cage. The last thing you need is to be saddled with

70

a man who can barely walk. Why don't you just go and get your own place and live? I'll be happy to put you on all my accounts. You'll never want for anything."

It was a generous offer he made. But she couldn't accept it. "I can't do that."

"Why not?"

"Because I love you."

FOUR

Adron couldn't have been more stunned if Livia had reached up and slapped him. "You don't even know me."

"Yes, I do. You try to hide what you are, but I see it. It shines through your bitterness with a brightness not even you can extinguish."

He scowled at her. "And what am I?"

"You're kind and decent. You have a good heart."

He snorted at her infantile naïveté. "I have no heart at all. What I have is a mechanical substitute that pumps blood though a broken body, and half the time it malfunctions."

She rose from the couch.

Adron flinched as she touched him. God, how he wanted to kiss her.

No, he wanted to slide himself deep inside her until he was lost. Until he forgot everything except the peace he'd found there that one night they'd spent together. Was that too much to ask?

She took him by the hand and led him into his media room. "Zarina said that it's painful at times for you to sit, so I thought I'd make a few modifications for you."

He stared at the new sofa. It was twice the size of his old one and looked more like a small bed. She'd piled pillows up all over it. Girlie pillows that looked out of place with his dark, masculine tones.

Biting back a nasty comment over that, Adron sat down and leaned against the pillows, amazed at just how good it did feel.

Until Livia sat down next to him. His body reacted instantly to her nearness. "You're killing me."

"I don't want to kill you." She leaned forward and captured his lips with hers.

Closing his eyes, he savored the taste of her. Over the last month he'd done little except dream of her kiss. Dream of touching her again.

She ran her hands over his body, making him burn even more.

And when she touched his cock through his pants, he cursed. "Livia, stop. I can't make love to you."

She smiled patiently at him. "That's okay. I'm making love to you."

He frowned as she started unbuttoning his shirt.

Adron opened his mouth to protest, but then she dipped her head to his neck. He sucked his breath in as her tongue gently laved his skin. And as she nibbled and licked his flesh, she unbuttoned his pants, slid her hand down, and took his swollen cock into her hand.

His head light, he couldn't speak while she caressed him. Couldn't move. All he could do was feel her making love to him . . .

He trembled as she blazed a scorching trail down his chest with her mouth. Slowly, carefully. Her touch blistered him and went so much deeper than his skin.

It touched his soul.

His eyes shuttered, he watched her while she licked and nibbled the flesh of his stomach, and when she took him into her mouth, he thought he'd die from the pleasure of it.

Her dark hair fanned out across his lap as he buried his hand in her soft curls and watched her teasing him.

Adron ground his teeth as her tongue and mouth massaged him from base to tip. She was relentless in her tasting. Never had he felt anything like it. Her actions were so selfless, so kind.

Why would she care?

Why would she do this for him?

I love you.

Her heartfelt words tore through him. No woman had ever said that to him before.

Only her.

And for his life, he couldn't understand what about him she could possibly find lovable. Or even tolerable, never mind desirable.

The woman was insane.

But she touched him on a level that defied explanation. A level he'd never known before. Throwing his head back against the pillows, he growled as he released himself into her mouth.

Still, she didn't pull away. Not until he was completely weak and spent.

His breathing ragged, he stared at her in awe. "I can't believe you did that for me."

"I told you, Adron, I love you. I would do anything to make you happy."

"Then kiss me."

She did.

Livia moaned as he ran his hand under her shirt and gently squeezed her breast. Bracing her arms on each side of him, she carefully straddled him while making sure not to put any pressure on his chest or abdomen. Theo's warnings had been explicit, and she would never do anything to hurt him.

Adron cupped her head with one hand while he reached around behind her with the other one and released her bra.

"I love the way you feel in my arms," he whispered against her lips. "I love the way you look when your cheeks are flushed and your eyes bright."

He skimmed his hand down over her breasts, to her stomach, and then down to where she ached for him. "And I love the way you look when you come for me." He gave her a tender smile. "You make me feel like a man again, Livia. You make me whole."

Shamelessly, she rubbed herself against him. And when she came, she cried out from it.

Adron smiled at her then, and held her close.

They spent the rest of the day lying naked in each other's arms, caressing and stroking, and just talking about absolutely nothing important.

It was the best day of Adron's life, and he kept her up until the wee hours of the morning for fear of it ending.

∘ ∘ ∘

That day was followed by three more days of bliss.

Adron was constantly amazed by the woman fate had miraculously thrown into his life. She was funny, intelligent, and so incredibly giving that it cut him up inside. It pained him to think of her spending the rest of her vivacious life strapped to him as he slowly decayed.

"Hi."

He looked up from the book he was reading to see her standing in the doorway. Her hair was still damp from her bath, and her eyes glowed mischievously.

"Hi," he said hesitantly. There was no telling what that look might mean. If he'd learned anything about her, it was to expect the unexpected.

She walked slowly toward the bed. "Would you like to go out for a bit today?"

Yes, he would. More than she'd ever know. But he was in too much pain. Even holding the electronic reader in his hand, which weighed only a few ounces, was hard for him. "I can't."

"C'mon, Adron. You told me your therapist said you needed more exercise."

"Yeah, but not today. My leg's too stiff. Why don't you call Zarina?"

"Because I'd rather be with you."

The woman was the biggest fool he'd ever known.

She sat down beside him on the bed. "Here." She placed her hands on his knee.

Adron tensed as warmth from her hands seeped into his leg. After a few seconds, all pain was gone and his knee felt like it had before Kyr had torn him apart. "How do you do that?"

"My mother taught me. She comes from a long line of great healers." She gently massaged his knee and leg, which made another part of him swell and ache. "I wish I could get you to her. She'd be able to heal you in an instant."

"Really?"

She looked askance at him. "You don't believe me?"

"Let's just say I have a hefty dose of skepticism. I have three friends who are Trisani, and not even they were able to repair me."

"Really?"

He nodded. "Yeah. Not even Nero, who's the most powerful Tris I've ever heard of. He was sick for days after trying to repair me. And after that, I quit believing in anything."

She rolled her eyes at him. "Feeling better now?"

"Yes."

"Then join me. I'd love to have the pleasure of your company this afternoon."

How could he say no to that? Besides, he hated being home all the time. It was why he'd installed the heavy blinds over his windows—he didn't want to see the beauty of what he couldn't enjoy. Looking outside on gorgeous days was nothing but torture that reminded him of all the times he'd jogged and played without any thought of a time when he wouldn't be able to do that anymore.

He left the bed but didn't go far before she stopped him. "You still have to use your cane. I don't want you back in the hospital."

He growled as she handed it him. "I hate this thing."

"I know." She wrapped her arms around his and took him outside for the first time since he'd returned from the hospital.

He blinked against the bright sunshine that was harsh against eyes that weren't used to being in it. "So, where are we going?"

She hailed a transport. "I want to go to the park."

"Why?"

She leaned forward impishly. "Because, and I know this is a new concept for you, we might actually have fun. Can you imagine? You might even smile and the world could come to an end over it."

He touched her cheek and watched the way her eyes sparkled with life. "I've never allowed anyone to talk to me the way you do."

"That's what Zarina said last night. She also said she was amazed I was still breathing."

He laughed at her as the transport pulled up. It was true. As an assassin, he'd had a notoriously short fuse on his temper. But for some reason he tolerated her gentle teasing.

She slid into the transport first, and he took a little longer to get inside. While he adjusted the cane, she typed the address into the monitor. Her smile warmed him as the car took off and she held his hand.

Gods, her hand was so tiny compared to his. So frail. Yet she stood strong against him when no one else would. His temper didn't frighten her.

Nothing did. And that amazed him most.

Once they reached the park, he allowed Livia to lead

him toward the large pond where children and adults were fishing, swimming, and skipping waves. He hadn't been here in at least a decade. But back in the day, he, Jayce, and Devyn had spent many an hour scoping out women and playing toss here.

Livia paused next to a rental station. "Want to try a paddleboat?"

He scoffed at the mere idea. "I'm too old for a paddleboat."

"You're thirty-five, Adron. Not an ancient by any stretch of the imagination."

"I'm too old for a paddleboat," he reiterated with more venom than he intended. "And even if I weren't, I couldn't pedal it anyway." Which was why he was so angry. He didn't want another reminder of how crippled he was.

"I'll do it."

He curled his lip. "I'm not helpless."

She glared at him as the color rushed to her cheeks. "I know that. It's okay to let others help you from time to time, Adron. Why are you so afraid of it?"

He clenched his teeth and looked away.

She took his chin in her hand and turned his head back so that he met her questing gaze. "Answer me."

Rage clouded his vision as agony coiled inside him, and he saw his future with a clarity that sickened him. "You want to know what I'm afraid of? I'm afraid every morning when I wake up that this will be the day when I can no longer move for myself. I know it's coming. It's just a matter of time until I have no choice, except to have someone else clothe me, feed me. Change my diaper. And I can't stand it."

"Then why don't you kill yourself? Why are you still here?"

Before he could stop himself, the truth poured out. "Because every time I think of doing that, I can hear my family praying over me while I was in the hospital. I hear my mother weeping, my father begging me not to die on them." He swallowed. "I could never intentionally hurt them that way. It would devastate them both, and while I'm a pathetic asshole, I'm not that selfish."

The love in her eyes scorched him. "You are the strongest man I've ever known."

"Weakest fool, you mean."

She shook her head and gave him a tender smile. "Come, husband. We're going to have fun even if it kills you." She stopped at the kiosk and rented a paddleboat, then led him to it.

Reluctantly, he got inside and let her take them out to the center of the pond where he could feel the sun warming his pale skin. *Gah, I must look ghastly.* He'd lived inside so long that his skin had none of the tan it used to.

She looked up at the sky and smiled. "It's a beautiful day, isn't it?"

Adron leaned back and stared at the sky to see what about it made her so happy. The light blue was covered in soft, white clouds, and the warmth of the sun felt good on his skin. She was right, it was exquisite. "It's okay."

She huffed at him. "You're such a pessimist."

In spite of himself, Adron ran a hand down her bare arm that was exposed by her sleeveless tunic. He touched the faint scar on her shoulder and frowned. Most of her back and hips were covered with whip scars, and every time he saw them, he wanted the throat of whoever had hurt her. "Who beat you?"

A hint of sadness flashed on her face, but she quickly recovered as she dangled one hand in the water. "My father."

"Why?"

She leaned forward and whispered as if imparting a great secret to him. "Brace yourself. I know you're going to have a hard time believing this, but I tend not to do what other people want me to."

Smiling at her dire tone, he laced his fingers through her hair. "I think I like that about you."

"So not what you said to me yesterday."

"Yesterday I was stupid, and I'll probably be stupid again later today and tomorrow . . . and probably many more times after that."

"Then it's a good thing I ignore you."

He laughed at himself—something he hadn't been able to do in a really long time. Which was another reason for him to be grateful to her.

Livia watched the way Adron leaned back on his elbows as he stared at her. His white shirt was pulled taut over the muscles of his stomach and chest. His broad shoulders were thrown back, his biceps flexed with the promise of leashed strength and power while the wind teased his white-blond queue.

Goodness, he was gorgeous even with the scar on his cheek. How devastating could one man be?

And it wasn't just his looks. There was a regal air that clung to him. One that was at odds with the soldier he'd once been. She had a hard time reconciling those two parts of his past. "Tell me something . . ." She paused her pedaling. "Why was a royal heir in the League?"

He scratched his chin before he answered. "I wasn't the heir at the time I enlisted."

The knowledge surprised her. "No?"

"No. My older sister was the heir." The pained expression on his face was profound and went deeper than the one he wore when his body hurt him.

"You have an older sister?"

He nodded. "My father's daughter from a relationship he had long before he met my mother."

"What happened to her?"

"She and my father fought over Thia's choice of fiancé. In a fit of anger, she stormed out of the palace and vanished. All of us have been trying to find her for years, but we've had no word of her. We don't know if she married him, died, or whatever."

"I'm so sorry, Adron."

He didn't speak as he glanced away, but his grief reached out to her and made her sorry that she'd asked.

Now it all made sense to her. That was the real reason he hadn't killed himself even though he didn't really want to live. His family had already lost one child, and he'd seen their grief firsthand.

Had felt it himself.

"You must miss her."

"All the time. She used to arm-wrestle me to the ground and kick my butt every time I went into her room."

She smiled at the teasing in his voice.

A tic started in his jaw. "She was the best confidant I had

growing up. I could tell her anything and know it would never reach the ears of my parents."

She reached out and took his hand into hers. "Tell me something, Adron. Something you've never shared with anyone else. Not even Thia."

He stroked her fingers with his thumb and waited so long to respond that at first she thought he was refusing. Finally, he gave her a sheepish grin. "I'm the one who glued Zarina to the toilet seat when she was seven."

Livia burst out laughing. "I was serious."

"I am, too. I'd meant to get Jayce, but she made a mad dash for the room and ran into it before he did. Poor Taryn ended up taking the blame for it."

"And you never confessed?"

His expression was one of absolute horror. "If you'd ever seen my father truly angry, you'd know the answer to that. I was only thirteen, and Zarina was just a tiny kid who wouldn't go to the bathroom for months after that without someone testing the seat for her.

"My father was a giant to me back then. Not to mention the fact that you never knew when his assassin's training was going to kick in and override all paternal instincts—not that it ever did, but there was always that fear back in the day that he could mentally snap and break one of us in half. Given his wrath over it, there was no way in hell I was going to confess."

"So what happened to Taryn?"

"He was restricted from playing ball for the whole summer season."

Livia frowned. "That doesn't seem so bad a punishment. Why were you afraid to own up to it?"

"Because I knew my father would punish me twice as severely since I not only did it, but I let someone else pay for it. My father's a firm believer in justice." He squeezed her hand. "It was a cowardly thing, I know, and I spent the whole summer staying home with Taryn trying to make it up to him."

"Did he know you were the one who did it?"

He shook his head. "No. Like I said, only Thia and Devyn ever kept my confidences, and even then I didn't trust them with that one. It's always been my guilty secret."

And now it was hers, too.

It made her warm inside that he'd trusted her with it.

His grip tightened on her hand. "What about you? Who were you running from at the Golden Crona?"

Her face flamed as he brought back a memory she'd done her best to bury. "It was horrible. My father was going to marry me to Clypper Thoran."

He gaped incredulously. "The Giradonal Governor?"

"Yes."

Adron frowned as he stared at her. "Good Lord, he's what? A hundred and fifty?"

"Eighty-two."

He shuddered. "Your father was going to marry you to an eighty-two-year-old man?"

She nodded, grateful that he shared the same repugnance she'd had over the event. "He wanted a trade agreement with them, and Clypper wanted a virginal wife."

He let out a long, audible breath. "No wonder you didn't mind getting stuck with me. One way or another, you were bound to end up as some man's nursemaid."

She lost her temper at him then. "You know, I'm tired of

84

your self-pity. Instead of thinking of all the things you no longer have, you should concentrate on what you do have."

"And what is that?"

"A family who loves you. *All* of them. And though your body is damaged, at least your mind isn't."

"Yeah, well, being trapped in an invalid body happens to be my worst nightmare."

Livia glared at him. "I would rather be crippled than mindless. My worst fear is ending up as a vegetable, trapped in a whole, sound body. So from where I'm sitting, you have nothing to complain about."

His frown deepened. "Why would you fear something like that?"

"I saw my grandmother die that way. It was terrible. She lay comatose in a hospital bed, hooked to monitors and machines for almost a year before they finally let her die. Even though she'd told everyone that she didn't want to live with that indignity, that she wanted to be free to die. No one listened."

"Why did they do that?"

"Because they couldn't let her go." Her look intensified. "If your mind was gone, Adron, you couldn't be here with me now. You wouldn't be able to see the sky above us, hear the children laughing or anything else. You'd be trapped in cold, awful darkness with nothing."

Adron flinched as his mind conjured a perfect picture of the horror she described. "Okay." It was too gruesome even for him to contemplate. "You make a good a point." She'd obviously given this a lot of thought. "You're right, I am a self-pitying bastard. But I'll endeavor to be a little less so."

"Promise?"

"As long as you're with me, yes."

"Good, because I have no intention of leaving you."

Adron scowled at her choice of words. Not that he doubted her, it was just that fate had a way of slapping down all the best intentions, and a weird premonition went through his mind.

It was one of her dying, and that was the only thing that could still frighten him.

FIVE

Weeks went by as Adron tried to keep his word to her. Some days it was easier than others. And today it was particularly difficult.

"Come on, Adron," his therapist said as she increased the weight on his leg. "You can lift it."

Grinding his teeth against the pain, he hated the patronizing tone Sheena always used whenever he worked out. Like a mother coaxing a small child to eat his vegetables.

"That's it. You're doing fine. Good boy."

"Go to hell," he snarled.

"Adron!" Livia snapped at him as she came forward to stand beside him. "You behave."

Adron curled his lip. This was the first time he'd allowed her to come with him to his therapy in the hospital. And if she kept that tone up, it'd be the last.

Sheena smiled at Livia good-naturedly. "It's all right. He says that to me a lot. I've learned to ignore it."

Livia reached out and took his hand in hers. Adron's heart pounded at the softness of her touch.

Gods, he'd gotten so used to her. Had become dependent on having her with him . . . and that terrified him more than anything else.

What would he do if he ever lost her?

Livia narrowed her eyes at him. "You play nice."

"Yes, ma'am." Holding her hand over his heart, he nodded. And then he lifted his leg even though it felt like it was shredding every muscle he had.

Sheena's smile widened. "See, I knew you could do it."

He ignored her.

Sheena moved to the next machine. "Okay, let's try some pulls now."

Adron let go of Livia and sat up slowly. But no sooner was he upright than he felt the familiar burning in his chest. Two seconds later, his nose started bleeding and he coughed up blood.

"Damn it," he snarled as Sheena grabbed a towel and handed it to him. He lay back down while Sheena called for Theo.

Without a single word, Livia brushed his hair back from his damp forehead. The tenderness of her touch and look scorched him. And it made him yearn even more for a way to love her as she deserved to be loved.

"Are you okay?"

He held the towel to his nose and mouth. "I just damaged another internal organ. Who knows which one. Since they're all pretty much soup, it could be . . ." His voice trailed off as Theo came in with a gurney and three orderlies.

Theo shook his head. "You know, Adron, if you want to spend the night with me, there are easier ways of going about it. You could just ask."

He wasn't amused by Theo's playfulness as the orderlies picked him up and placed him on the gurney. "I want to go home."

"Maybe tomorrow." Theo put an oxygen mask on his face.

Adron pulled it off.

Livia put it back on.

Adron met her gaze and made no more attempts to remove it.

"I'll call your parents." Holding his hand, she walked beside him as the orderlies pushed him through the all-too-familiar hallways.

When they reached the scanning room, Adron reluctantly let go of her.

Livia's heart was heavy as she watched the doors close behind him. How she wished she had her mother's healing powers. Her mother could make him whole again.

So could you.

True, but if she did, she'd lose him forever. It was something she couldn't do no matter what because in the end, she was too selfish to heal him if it meant losing him.

He's in constant pain . . .

And that broke her heart, but not as much as it would break if he lived a whole life without her.

o   o   o

Adron lay in bed, listening to the monitors whirring and beeping. It was absolute misery to be stuck in this cold, sterile place.

Alone.

There was nothing he hated more than hospitals. Even worse, Livia had left him a little over an hour ago to run some errand she swore couldn't wait.

Disgusted, he watched his vitals flash on the screen. He'd watch the monitor, but there was nothing on. Gah, time moved so slowly when there was nothing to do. His father was in a meeting. His mother off with his sister.

No one knew where his brothers were, and here he stayed.

Stop feeling sorry for yourself.

That was easier said than done when there was nothing else to do. And for the last eight years, this had made up the majority of his life.

"Damn, what did you do to him?"

Adron scowled as he heard one of the twins' voices. He looked to the door to see both Taryn and Tiernan coming in with Livia. All of them had their arms full with bags and boxes.

"I didn't do anything." She set her bags down on the floor, then popped Taryn, whose hair was longer, playfully on the back of the head. "And you promised me you'd behave."

Tiernan laughed as he set his box on the chair next to the bed. "Like that'll happen."

Adron's frown deepened. "What are you people doing?"

His brothers pointed to Livia. "She did it," they said in unison.

"Did what?"

She responded by opening up the box in Tiernan's hands. "You two get this set up while I work on the other box."

Adron huffed as they ignored him, until he realized what they were doing. They were turning his hospital room into something that resembled a hotel.

Tiernan hung dark curtains while Taryn set up a reading light next to the bed. Livia handed him his reader.

Unable to speak past the lump in his throat over her thoughtfulness, he pulled her toward him so that he could kiss her.

"Ah, gah, people, please. We're in here with you. Do you mind? Could you not be so affectionate until we leave?"

"Yeah," Taryn agreed. "I have a shipment to make tonight and can't afford to be blind from my older brother groping his wife." He shuddered. "It reminds me of walking in on Jayce when he was a teenager, getting out of the shower. I'm still having violent flashbacks."

Tiernan snorted. "Please. That I could take. Try walking in on Thia on the can. I swear I tried to get Nero to erase my memories of that."

Taryn arched a brow. "Why didn't he?"

"He tried. Instead of erasing that, he undid three weeks of chemistry class. I damn near flunked over it."

Tiernan laughed evilly as he stepped down from the chair. "Knowing Nero, he probably did it on purpose."

Livia's eyes were bright. "Are they always this entertaining when they're together?"

"Depends."

"On?"

"Whether or not they're plotting against you. Taryn's

like a head injury. It's only funny when it happens to someone else. And Tiernan . . . I think there's now a hurricane on Chrinon VI named after him."

She burst out laughing.

The twins sobered.

Taryn gave her an incredulous stare. "Thank you, Liv."

"For what?"

Tiernan answered for him. "For making Adron human again. It's been a long time."

"Screw you, Tier." But Adron had to give her credit, too. It'd been too long since he'd teased with his family or with anyone else like this.

"Yeah, bro, since when was Adron ever human? More like a festering subspecies of some kind. You know. Like a pimple on the ass of a warthog."

Adron tossed a pillow at Taryn, who caught it and laughed. "You better be glad I'm strapped down."

Taryn threw the pillow back at him.

It rebounded off his head. Adron hissed and threw himself back as if in pain.

The three of them ran to his side.

Taryn reached him first. "Do I need to call a nurse?"

Adron laughed at them as they surrounded him with terror in their eyes. "You are all so gullible."

Tiernan let out a sound of extreme disgust. "You bastard. I thought you were hurt."

Taryn picked the pillow up and beat Adron with it. "I hate you."

Adron snatched the pillow out of his hands. "You suck, too." As he tried to put it back behind him, Livia took it from his hands and placed it where he wanted.

"You're all terrible. I feel sorry for your poor mother having to referee all of you. It's a wonder she has any sanity left."

Taryn grinned. "Personally, I'm not sure she does."

Suddenly exhausted from the activity, Adron leaned back and watched as they put his room together. When it was done, his brothers left and Livia pulled the chair closer to his bed.

"You need anything else?"

"Yeah. You not to leave."

"I'm right here, sweetie, and there's no place else I'd rather be."

And right there she stayed for the entire week he was sentenced to his hellhole. Even though it was selfish of him, he loved it, and her presence there made time fly in a way it never had before.

Once it was over and they were back in his apartment, he took her to bed and didn't emerge except to attend to basic needs like food and drink.

° ° °

Livia came awake slowly. She blinked her eyes open to find herself lying in bed, wrapped in her husband's arms.

Adron was still asleep, but even so, he had a tight grip on her as if he were afraid she'd vanish.

Smiling, she picked his hand up and placed a kiss over his scarred knuckles.

Then she heard someone in the outer room. At first, she assumed it was the cleaning lady who came twice a week, until she heard one of the twins call Adron's name.

"Hey, bud." He threw open the door. "I need . . ." Tiernan

took one look at them lying naked in the bed and turned around to give them his back.

"Sorry, Livia. I assumed by three o'clock in the afternoon the two of you would be up and about."

Adron rubbed his stubbled cheek against her shoulder as he came awake. "I need to learn to lock my bedroom door."

She laughed.

Tiernan made a sound of agitation. "I'm going to go out there and wait until you two are dressed."

Adron brushed his hand over her hair, and she felt his erection against her hip. "Why don't you keep walking until you get to the other side of the front door?"

"Ha-ha." Tiernan paused in the doorway and turned back toward them. "By the way, your wife has a great body."

Heat exploded across her face as Tiernan shut the door.

Adron gave her a stern frown. "Say the word, and I'll kill him for you."

She smiled. "It's okay. If you did that, Taryn would miss him."

"Hardly. He'd probably fall down in gratitude. You know, when they were babies, Tiernan used to shove Taryn down and grab his bottle away, then drink it."

"No, he didn't. Tiernan's too sweet to do something so mean."

He scoffed. "Don't let Tiernan's polite, mild-mannered demeanor fool you. He's every bit as lethal as Taryn, and he hits twice as hard. Take it from someone with firsthand experience. The only difference is, unlike Taryn and his pirate garb, Tiernan will be in a suit when he cuts your throat. No one expects an ambassador to go bad, but believe me,

Tiernan's not a pacifist. I'd put him up against any assassin the League ever trained . . . including me in my prime."

She still had a hard time believing that. There was an aura about Taryn that said he could be vicious if provoked. But Tiernan . . . he was like an adorable baby brother who never lost patience with anyone. Not even Zarina.

With a low groan, Adron rolled over slowly and reached for his injector and medicine on the nightstand.

Livia cringed as he gave himself a shot in the stomach. How she wished he didn't have to do that every few hours. But it was either that or his body locked up with so much pain that he couldn't move at all.

Unfortunately, he would have to do it for the rest of his life.

His features strained by the effort, he left the bed and dressed. Every few minutes, he'd have to pause and wait for the pain to subside before he could resume dressing. She wanted to offer to help, but he wouldn't appreciate it.

By the time he finished, his brow was damp with sweat from the strain. He gave her a sheepish look before he grabbed his cane and left the room.

While he went to speak to his brother, she headed into the bathroom for a shower.

She took her time, letting the hot water cascade over her skin, until she felt someone watching her bathe. Turning around, she saw Adron leaning against the wall, staring straight at her.

She dropped the cloth in her hand. "You startled me."

"Sorry, I didn't mean to. I was just wishing I could join you."

It amazed her how comfortable she'd become around

him when she was naked. Her nudity had long since ceased to bother her. As did his. In fact, she'd learned every dip and curve of his tawny flesh. Every scar.

She glanced over to the tub a few feet away where he took his baths. "Want me to join you?"

He smiled. "Yes, I do."

Livia turned the shower off and ran them a tub full of water. Adron got in first, then pulled her in on top of him.

"Careful," she warned as a wave of panic went through her. "I don't want to hurt you."

"You could never hurt me." He claimed her lips with his.

Livia moaned. Oh, but she would never get tired of his kisses. His touch.

Adron pulled back to stare at her in awe. Her lips were swollen from his kiss and her cheeks red from his whiskers. He ran his hand over her ravaged skin, hating that he'd chafed it.

"I'm sorry about that." He reached for his razor in the cubbyhole in the wall above his head.

She sat beside him, watching him shave with a frown on her face. "Wouldn't that be easier with a mirror?"

"Probably."

"Then why don't you use one?"

He paused and looked away from her as his gut knotted. "I don't like looking in mirrors, and I damn sure don't want to do it first thing every morning." It was bad enough to catch sight of his mangled face accidentally. The last thing he wanted to do was look at it on purpose.

She took the razor from his hand, and to his shock, she shaved the mutilated side of his face. "You are incredibly handsome."

Adron stared at her doubtfully. "When I was younger, I was really vain about it. Zarina used to tease me that I looked at my reflection so much that one day the bogeyman was going to come and steal my face." He dropped his gaze to the floor. "I guess she was right. He did."

Livia rinsed the soap from his face. "I think you're gorgeous."

"I think you're insane."

She shook her head as she started shaving his other cheek. "You know, there is a bright side to all you suffered."

"And that is?"

She hesitated as if gathering her thoughts. "Tell me truthfully, Adron. If Kyr hadn't scarred you, would you have taken me home that night at the Golden Crona? Would you have even looked twice at me?"

Adron opened his mouth to deny it, but he couldn't. She was right. She was beautiful to him now, a vital part of his life. But she wasn't the kind of woman he'd chased after when he was single. Like Zarina had said, he'd been a vain asshole. Though Livia was pretty and sweet, she wasn't one of the tall, sleek knockouts he'd been with. The kind of women who knew how to tease and torment a guy with their looks and body.

The truth was, as pretty as she was, he would never have looked twice at her before Kyr had crippled him.

That thought cut him all the way to his soul. How could he have been so stupid as to not look any deeper than the surface?

And she deserved someone much better than him.

"I wish I could be whole for you . . . I wish I could hold

97

you and dance with you, take you in my arms and make love to you the way I want to."

"And I'm just grateful I have you at all. It's not your body or face that I love, Adron. It's your heart, your soul, and your mind."

He trembled at her words, then pulled her to him and kissed her. She moved carefully into his lap.

Adron nibbled her lips as he felt her sliding her hand over his shoulders, down his arms.

She lifted her hips, then impaled herself on him. They moaned simultaneously.

Bracing her hands on the edge of the tub, she rode him slow and easy, making him blind from the pleasure of her body surrounding his. And for the first time, he was grateful to Kyr. Grateful that the bastard had opened his eyes . . .

Grateful he'd found Livia.

God help him if anything should happen to her. She was the one thing he could never lose. The one thing that could truly destroy him.

His throat tight, he watched her as she climaxed in his arms. The pleasure on her face tore through him. And as he felt her body tighten around him, he surrendered himself to his own release.

Livia started to collapse against his chest, then barely caught herself before she hurt him. She smiled at him, but she saw the turmoil in his eyes, felt him go rigid over her action. It always hurt him when he realized the frailness of his body.

She would give anything to remove that look from him forever.

Would you give your life?

That was the question that haunted her every day. And what scared her most was that the answer was starting to become yes. She'd much rather he have his happiness than she hers.

"I love you," she whispered.

As usual, he said nothing as he shifted away from her.

Livia sighed. She hadn't meant to hurt his feelings. But it was too late. He was closed off from her again.

SIX

By the time they dressed, it was nearly dinnertime.

"You want to go out to eat?"

Adron's question startled her. It was so unlike him to volunteer to leave. Normally she had to pull him out while he threatened and protested every step of the way.

She wanted to go eat, but he'd been doing really well with his pain today. He'd taken only half his normal dosage of medication. The last thing she wanted was to tax his strength and make him hurt again. And going out always made him tense. He didn't like the way people stared at his face or his cane.

But it was nice of him to offer.

"No, it's okay."

He looked at her skeptically and used her words against her. "C'mon, you can't spend your life locked in this apartment. The fresh air will be good for you."

"Are you sure you feel up to it?"

"Truthfully? I hate being stuck here all the time. I was never a homebody before."

"Yeah, but I know how much you loathe being in public."

He shrugged. "I've learned to like going out with you. People don't bother me as much as they used to. And I don't really see them when I'm with you anyway. I'd much rather look at you than anyone else."

How could she say no to that?

"Okay." She got up and put on her shoes while Adron got her coat and held it for her.

They didn't go far, just a few sectors over to a quaint restaurant she'd discovered with Zarina and his mother a few weeks ago.

Adron sat beside her with his arm draped over the back of her chair as they waited for their food. For some reason he liked to twist a lock of her hair around his forefinger. She wasn't even sure if he realized how much he did it . . . if he even knew he did it at all. But anytime she was near him, he played with her hair.

And it always warmed her.

"I don't believe it."

Adron went rigid at the unfamiliar deep voice.

Livia turned her head to see a man who looked so incredibly similar to her husband that she knew he must be the elusive brother, Jayce—the only member of Adron's family she had yet to meet.

Jayce's green eyes were warm with friendship as he paused beside her chair. His long blond hair was braided down his back, and he wore a black League assassin's street uniform. Something so dark, it seemed to absorb light. Dark-red daggers were engraved down the sleeves, and each was topped by a crown that marked him as the most lethal of his kind. A command assassin of the first order.

But for his playful eyes, he would have been terrifying to meet. They, however, softened his features and made him appear almost human.

Smiling, he extended a gloved hand to her. "You must be Livia. It's great to finally meet you. My parents think the world of you."

Before she could move or speak, Adron knocked his arm away. "You're not welcome here. Why don't you slink off into the hole you crawled out of?"

Jayce curled his lip. "Oh, that's real original and ma-ture. Why don't you call me Mr. Stinky Pants while you're at it?"

"Fuck you."

A tic worked in Jayce's jaw. To his credit, he kept his cool and took a deep breath before he spoke again. "Look, can't we just put the past behind us and be brothers again?"

Adron's response was so crude that it sent heat over her face.

Jayce went flush with his rage. "Fine, wallow in your self-pity, you disgusting asshole."

He turned to leave.

"That's right," Adron snarled, "turn your back on me, you coward. That's what you were always best at."

Jayce whirled about and grabbed Adron out of his chair.

Livia gasped as she rose to her feet to stop them. "You need to let him go."

Jayce ignored her. "Don't you ever call me a coward. You, of all men, know those are fighting words."

But Adron didn't back down, and the hatred in his eyes was searing. "Why not? It's true, isn't it? You dare wear a League uniform, yet you betrayed your oath to them and you betrayed your oath to me. You are nothing but a self-righteous coward."

After that, everything happened in a blur.

Jayce bellowed, then swung.

Adron ducked and caught Jayce a staggering blow against his jaw.

Trained and honed as an assassin, Jayce acted on auto-pilot as he returned the blow with one of his own. A fist straight into Adron's heart. It was so fierce it would have been debilitating on a healthy man.

On Adron . . .

Livia heard the horrendous sound of bones breaking. The force of the blow knocked Adron back into the table.

Before he hit the floor, Livia knew he was seriously injured.

"Oh, God, Adron," Jayce gasped as he knelt beside him. "I'm so sorry. I didn't mean to. It was completely re-flexive. Oh, God, I'm sorry."

Adron couldn't answer.

Livia watched, horrified by the paleness of Adron's face as his breath rattled loosely in his chest. She'd never seen panic in Adron's eyes, but she saw it now, and that scared her most of all.

Jayce called for an MT unit, but it was too late. Adron's breathing was growing shallower by the heartbeat. He started coughing up blood.

Livia cupped his face in her hands.

Adron touched her arm and tried to memorize her features before he died. He should never have provoked Jayce. His brother had always had a hair trigger on his temper.

Just like Adron.

But now it was too late. Jayce had finally done the one thing he was supposed to have done when he found Adron lying in the Dumpster.

He'd killed him.

Adron reached up and placed a hand to Livia's soft, creamy cheek. His angel of mercy. At a time when he'd wanted to die, she alone had given him a reason to live.

He didn't want to leave her. Couldn't stand the thought of not having her with him.

But it wasn't meant to be.

Her face faded from his sight, and then everything went black.

"No!" Livia screamed as his hand fell from her face and he went limp in her arms. "Don't you dare leave me!"

But it was too late. His skin was already discoloring.

Jayce laid him on the floor and prepared to resuscitate him.

"Damn it!" The agonized cry tore through her as Jayce realized he couldn't give him CPR. Adron's body couldn't sustain it.

In that instant, Livia did the only thing she knew to do. She reached down deep inside her and summoned all the power she possessed. She didn't care what it cost her. She couldn't live without Adron. And if it meant her own life, so be it.

Almost instantly, her hands were hot. Hotter than they'd ever been before. She placed them against Adron's chest and willed her life force into him.

Jayce shielded his eyes as an unbelievably bright orange halo surrounded Adron's body.

∘ ∘ ∘

Adron came awake with a jolt. At first, he thought he was dead. There was no pain anywhere in him.

His body felt strange. Different.

It felt whole.

Then he became aware of Jayce touching his face and of a strange weight on his chest.

"Adron?" Jayce gasped in disbelief.

Looking down, Adron realized the weight on his chest was Livia.

His heart pounding, he sat straight up with an agility he hadn't possessed in eight years.

And in that instant, he knew what she'd done. She'd healed him again.

As he pulled her into his arms, he saw his blood-covered hand and scowled at it in disbelief. The scars were completely gone from it.

Not even the scars on his knuckles remained. What had she done?

"Livia?" He held her against him.

She didn't answer. It was like she was . . .

Dead.

Adron tilted her head and saw the ghostly paleness of her face.

"Livia?" He tried again, shaking her gently.

She didn't respond.

Jayce tried to help, but Adron pushed him back. He didn't want anyone touching her. "Livia? Please talk to me. Please."

The MTs came in, and he reluctantly released her to their care.

More terrified than he'd ever been before, he followed them out of the restaurant and to the lift that would take them to the hospital.

∘ ∘ ∘

For the first time in years, Adron sat in the antiseptic waiting room while Theo tended Livia. He finally understood some of what his parents had felt while they waited for word of his multiple operations.

The fear and uncertainty tore him apart. And he and Livia had known each other only a short time.

How much worse must this have been for his parents?

"Adron?"

He looked up as his mother and father joined him. His mother's eyes brimmed with tears as she took his face in her hands and touched his undamaged cheek. "What happened to your scar?"

Jayce, who'd followed him to the hospital and had stayed with him, answered. "Livia cured him. I don't know how she did it, but one minute he was practically dead, and the next he was perfectly fine."

His father frowned. "What did the doctor say about you?"

Adron pulled back from his mother's touch. "He wants to do tests on me later." But Adron didn't give a damn about himself.

Livia was all that mattered.

His mother nodded. "Did you call her parents?"

Adron's chest tightened at the memory. "I tried. Her father told me she was no longer his concern and he didn't care what happened to her."

Disgust contorted his mother's beautiful face. "How could he?"

Adron shrugged. He didn't really want to talk at the moment. Then again, Livia was the only person he liked talking to, period.

Please don't die . . .

The pain of the thought of being alone again was all he could focus on. Everything else was insignificant.

His father smiled as he passed a glance from Adron to Jayce. "It's good to see the two of you in the same room without bloodshed."

Adron exchanged a wary, shamed look with Jayce. This was all his fault. If he'd just left Jayce alone, none of this would have happened.

I'm such an asshole.

Jayce turned away.

His parents went to get something to drink.

Once they were alone, Jayce approached him. "I'm really sorry about all this."

Adron glared at him. He was tired of Jayce's excuses. "If you'd killed me when you were supposed to, none of this would have happened."

Jayce curled his lip as his eyes blared a cold, harsh rage. "Tell me honestly, could you have killed me if you'd found me lying half-dead and helpless?"

"Rather than see you suffer, yes."

Jayce's entire face went blank. "Then you're a better assassin than I am. Because I would never have been able to live with myself had I killed my own brother."

"Adron?"

He turned as Theo joined them.

Theo hesitated in front of him. "This is weird, isn't it? I'm not used to having discussions with you while you're dressed and upright."

"You're not amusing."

Theo looked apologetic. "Sorry, nervous humor." He cleared his throat and a feeling of dread washed over Adron.

Theo was avoiding something bad.

"Well?" he prompted.

"She's firmly in a coma. Whatever she did, it caused a great deal of neurological damage to her. Honestly, I've never seen anything like it. It's as if she burned up part of her brain."

Like her grandmother . . .

Adron choked on a sob as he thought of her lying helpless in the dark. Alone.

It was her worst fear.

Why had she done it?

For him . . .

Oh gods, he couldn't breathe for the agony in his heart. He wanted to scream out at the injustice. Wanted to rail against everyone and everything.

He wanted to hate Jayce for this, too.

But in the end, he knew the only one really to blame was himself, and that stung most of all.

He leveled a fierce stare on Theo. "Will she come out of it?"

"Honestly . . . I doubt it. There's too much damage. She's only alive right now because of the machines." Theo gave him a hard, cold stare. "My professional opinion is that we should turn everything off and let nature take its course."

Adron fell back against the wall as his heart shattered into a thousand pieces. He felt the tears in his eyes, felt the bitter, swelling misery that overwhelmed him.

He couldn't let her go.

Not after everything she'd done for him. Everything she'd come to mean to him.

But then, he couldn't let her live when he knew she wouldn't want to. It was too cruel.

And all he felt was a desolate agony so deep, so profound, that it made a mockery of the one he'd learned to live with over the years.

He grabbed Theo by the shirt. "Don't you dare let her die. You hear me?"

Theo looked aghast. "All we have is the shell of her body, Adron. Her mind is already gone."

"Only half of it, right?"

"Well . . . yes."

"Then there's a chance." And half a chance was better than none. "You keep her heart beating until I get back."

"I'll do my best."

And so would he.

Releasing Theo, Adron ran from the hospital with a

SHERRILYN KENYON

strength and agility he hadn't known in years. Livia had one chance for survival, and no matter what, he was going to give it to her.

Even if it killed him.

∘ ∘ ∘

"What are you doing here?" Livia's father demanded as Adron forced his way into the throne room where the older man was overseeing his advisers.

Oblivious to the roomful of men who gaped at him, Adron approached his father-in-law. "I have to see Livia's mother. Now."

"It is forbidden."

That wasn't good enough. "The hell it is. Livia's dying, and her mother is the only one who can save her."

Her father's face stoic, he seemed completely immune to the news. "If she dies, so be it. That is the will of God. She has disgraced us with her disobedience. I told you and her that she was forever severed from this house, and so she is. Her affairs are your problem, not ours."

"I need to see her mother." Adron started for the side door.

"Guards!" her father called. "Remove him immediately."

Adron knocked the guards back until they called for re-inforcements. Seriously outnumbered, he fought as best he could, but eventually they seized him and dragged him back in front of her father.

"You can't let her die." Adron struggled against their hold.

The smugness on her father's face disgusted him. "Had you wanted her to live, you should never have shamed her."

110

"Damn you!"

"Remove him from this planet."

Against his will, Adron was pulled back from the throne, but as he fought against the guards, he saw a teenaged servant girl watching him from the shadows with concern and pity on her face.

Adron met her frightened gaze and hoped that she could get a message through. "Tell her mother Livia needs her. Please . . ."

"Krista!" Livia's father snapped. "Get out of here. Now!"

The girl scampered off, and the guards threw him out of the palace.

Adron struck the closed door with his fist as more guards came to escort him back to his ship. He bellowed in rage. "So help me, if she dies, I'll see all of you in your graves!"

But no one heard him.

Defeated, he turned and headed back to spend as much time with Livia as he could before death stole her completely away from him.

o   o   o

Adron paused in the doorway of the hospital room as he listened to the familiar monitors beep and hiss. Only this time, they weren't connected to him.

He knew from his own experience that she could hear them. Knew what it felt like to lie there unable to communicate. Alone. Afraid.

He wanted to scream at the unfairness of it all.

His throat tight, he crossed the room and sat on the bed beside her.

"Hey, sweet," he whispered, taking her cold hand into his. He cupped her face with his other hand and leaned over her to brush his lips against her cool cheek.

"Please open your eyes, Livia," he whispered as tears blinded him. "Open your eyes and see what you did. I'm actually sitting here without grimacing. There's no pain at all. But you know that, don't you?"

Adron traced the outline of her jaw. And then he did something he hadn't done in a long, long time.

He prayed.

He prayed, and he yearned to feel her sweet arms wrapped around him. To hear the precious sound of her voice saying his name. Just one more time.

Why wouldn't she open her eyes and look at him?

Hours went by as he stayed with her, talking more than he'd ever talked before.

Sitting by her side, he held her hand to his heart and willed her to wake up. "I don't know why you stayed with me. God knows, I wasn't worth it. But I don't want you to leave me alone anymore. I need you, Livia. I can't live without you in my life. I can't . . . I'm not that strong. Please open your eyes and look at me. Please."

"She can hear you, you know?"

Adron tensed at the voice behind him that intruded on his last few precious hours with his wife. Assuming it was a nurse, he didn't bother to look. "I know."

"Are you going to unplug her?"

He choked at the thought. And for the first time, he understood exactly how Jayce had felt when he'd pulled Adron from the Dumpster.

God, he'd been such a fool to hate his brother for loving him.

His throat tight, he was blinded by tears. "I can't let her go. Not while there's a chance."

"It's what she wants."

"I know." He knew it in a way no one else ever could. He'd been there.

The nurse came forward and placed a gentle hand on his shoulder. "She wants me to tell you that she is with you. And that you were well worth it. She loves you more than her life."

Frowning, he looked up to see a small woman wearing a cloak that completely shielded her identity from him. "Who are you?"

She lowered the cowl. Her features were angelic, and he knew her in an instant. She was Livia's mother.

And he saw the silvery-green eyes of a race that was more myth than reality. "You're Trisani?"

She nodded.

Adron gaped with the knowledge. The Trisani were legendary for their psychic abilities. So legendary that they had been hunted almost to extinction. Those who survived were very careful to stay hidden away from large populations where they might become enslaved or killed by those who wanted or feared their powers.

She stepped to Livia's side and removed the IV from her daughter's arm. Then slowly, piece by piece, she took the monitors off.

"It's time to wake up, little flower," she whispered. She placed a gentle hand on Livia's brow.

Stunned, Adron watched as Livia's eyes fluttered open. "Mama?" she breathed.

Her mother smiled, then kissed her on the forehead. She passed a hand over Livia's body.

Adron felt weak with relief as joy spread through him. Livia was alive.

Her mother took his hand and Livia's and held them joined in hers. Adron's heart pounded at the warmth of a touch he'd thought was lost to him forever.

Livia looked from him to her mother. "You had Krista send me to the Golden Crona, didn't you?"

Her mother nodded. "You two were destined for each other." She looked at Adron. "And to answer your unspoken question, Commander, yes, it's permanent. Livia healed you completely, but . . ." She turned a sharp glare at her daughter. "You are not to call on your powers anymore. Your human half isn't strong enough for them."

"I know, but I couldn't let him die."

"Understood. But don't *ever* do it again." She raised her cowl. "Now I have to return before I'm missed." She paused in the doorway and turned back. "By the way, it's a boy."

Adron frowned. "What's a boy?"

"The baby she carries. Congratulations, Commander. In seven months, you'll be a father."

EPILOGUE

One year later

Livia paused in the doorway as she watched Adron giving their infant son his three A.M. feeding. Propped against pillows, Adron sat on the bed, wearing nothing except a sheet draped modestly over his lap as he held the bottle and stared adoringly at baby Jayce . . . named for the uncle who'd been key in bringing them together.

Adron laid his cheek against the top of the baby's bald head and held him close. "I've got you, little bit," he whispered. "Yes, I do."

Jayce kicked and cooed.

She laughed.

Adron looked as if she'd startled him. "I didn't know you were back."

"I can tell." She moved to sit next to them. Then she leaned against Adron's raised leg to stare at the beautiful baby that lay on his unscarred chest.

Jayce smiled at her as he wrapped his tiny hand around her finger.

Adron brushed a loving hand through Livia's soft, mussed hair. Thanks to her, he'd come a long way from the bitter alcoholic she'd found tossing down drinks in the back of the Golden Crona.

She'd found a broken, bleeding man and made him whole again. Not just in body, but in his heart. She'd reunited him with his family and with his soul.

Over the last year, he'd watched her grow ripe with his baby and had held her hand as she struggled to bring Jayce into the world.

Life turned on the hairpin of a second. He'd always known that, but on one rainy, cold night in the back room of a filthy dive, his life had taken a sharp turn into heaven.

Redemption is never where you expect to find it. And he, a bitter cynic, had found it in the arms of a guileless innocent.

Livia furrowed her brow as she caught the intensity of his stare. "What are you thinking about?"

He traced the outline of her lips with his fingertip. "I'm thinking how glad I am that I traded myself for that woman. How glad I am that my brother couldn't kill me. But most of all, I'm thinking just how damn grateful I am that you saw something in me worth saving."

He leaned forward and kissed her gently on the lips. "Thank you for my son, Livia, and for my life. I love you. I always will."

KNIGHTLY
DREAMS

ONE

"**Well,**" Taryn Edwards said into her cell phone as she stood beside the road, watching the steady Dallas traffic pass by her broken-down car, "I would throw myself under the nearest bus, but considering my luck today, I'm sure it would break down less than a millimeter from me and just ruin my clothes. . . . Probably break my watch, too."

"You wear a Timex."

She snorted. "Trust me, today not even my Timex could take a licking and keep on ticking. Give me a Tonka truck and I'll squash it with my ink pen."

Janine's laughter echoed through the static. "Taryn, is it really *that* bad?"

Holding her cell phone in a tight grip, Taryn looked at her stalled-out Firebird, which was the prettiest, most expensive lawn ornament she'd ever purchased.

Of all the rotten luck, especially since all she wanted to

do was get home and drown her woes in gallons of Ben & Jerry's Phish Food. "Considering the fact that I'm stuck out in this wretched heat wearing high heels with a black car that currently wouldn't go downhill with a hurricane pushing it, I'd say yes."

Janine laughed again. "Do you need me to come pick you up?"

"No. I appreciate the thought, but I have to wait on the tow truck, which seems to be the only thing moving slower than my DOA Firebird."

"Jeez," Janine said. "You are in a pissy mood."

That's because I just caught my boyfriend in his office with his secretary showing her a position I'm sure would qualify them for the Kama Sutra Hall of Fame. . . .

Pain sliced through Taryn's heart as she remembered the sight of them going at it on his desk. Unable to breathe for a moment, she wanted desperately to tell Janine the whole story, but the last thing she needed was to cry on the side of the road. Her dignity was all she had left, and she had no intention of giving Rob that last piece of her.

"Taryn, why don't we . . ."

All of a sudden the phone, much like her car, went dead. "Janine?"

Nothing.

Taryn tried to redial the number, but the static was so severe, she couldn't hear anything.

"Great," she mumbled, turning the phone off and glancing at the shopping center across the street. It would be a bit of a hike through screaming traffic, but at least it had a grocery store where she could grab something cold to drink and a few shops she could browse in to pass the time until the tow truck could get here.

And with any luck, a car or truck might plow into her and put her out of her misery.

Dodging traffic, she made her way over to the shopping center. Damn, she actually arrived without bodily injury. It really wasn't her day.

Disgusted by that, she headed for the grocery store, but as she drew near the entrance for it, she happened to see the small bookstore next door.

Taryn paused and frowned at the cozy-looking place. When had they opened that? She couldn't recall ever seeing it here before.

She stared up at the hand-painted sign: DAYDREAMS AND RAINBOWS.

How odd.

Well, thank God for small favors. A good book would cure her woes tonight almost as much as Ben & Jerry.

Heading inside the cheery store lined with bookshelves, she saw an elderly woman straightening the books on the wall to her right. There was something about the old woman that appeared youthful, almost sprite-like as she came off her ladder to greet Taryn. The woman moved with surprising agility. Her platinum gray hair was pulled back into a tight bun, and she wore a pair of faded blue jeans and a pink summer sweater.

The store smelled like musty old books, and there was a small café in a corner on the far left where a pot of coffee percolated.

"Welcome," the woman said, her brown eyes bright

with friendship. "I'll bet you're looking for something to read."

For the first time that afternoon, Taryn smiled. "You must be psychic."

The woman laughed as she closed the distance between them. "Not really. You are in a bookstore, after all." She winked as she came to rest in front of Taryn. "So, what's your pleasure? Thrillers, science fiction . . ." The older woman tapped her chin as she studied Taryn. "No. *Romance*. You look like you need a good romance to read."

Taryn wrinkled her nose at the very thought. She'd given up reading romance novels a long time ago. She had buried that naive Cinderella-wanting-Prince-Charming part of herself in the closet along with her Barbie dolls and other childish fantasies and beliefs. "To be honest, I don't read those."

The woman looked offended. "Why not?"

"One man, one woman. Happily-ever-after. Forever and ever . . . bologna."

The woman shook her head at her. "My name's Esther," she said, extending her hand.

"Taryn," she said as she shook a hand that felt like warm velvet in her palm.

Esther gave her a probing stare. "Now, tell me about this man who stole that dream from you."

Taryn had never been the kind of person to confide in anyone much, least of all a perfect stranger, and yet before she knew it, her entire history with Rob Carpenter came pouring out of her right down to the grittiest of details.

"It was horrible!" she said, taking a tissue from Esther to

dab at her eyes as she continued to tell her the whole miserable event. "I believed in that snake and he lied to me."

Esther led her to a small table in the café area and made her a cup of coffee.

"So you see," Taryn said before she blew her nose, "he told me that I was the only woman for him. That he would love no one else. And then the next thing I knew, he was calling me by the wrong name when he answered the phone. Good giveaway, you know?" She sighed. "I should have known then, but I stupidly believed his lies and now . . ."

Again, she saw Rob and his secretary on the desk, their clothes scattered on the floor around them.

Taryn fisted her hand in her hair as pain, embarrassment, and grief assailed her anew. "How could I have been so stupid? How could he be so damned clichéd?"

Esther patted her hand. "It's all right, love, and I am so sorry, but you shouldn't base your opinion of all men on the actions of one thoughtless ass."

Taryn smiled at that, even though her heart was broken. "He *was* an ass."

"Of course he was. You're a beautiful young woman with your entire life before you. The last thing you need is to be so jaded. What you need is a good old-fashioned hero."

Taryn sighed dreamily at the thought as that buried part of her reared its ugly head. Whether she wanted to admit it or not, there was that tiny, infinitesimal part of her that still believed in fairy tales. At least, it wanted to. "Some knight in shining armor, come to sweep me off my feet. It does sound nice, doesn't it?"

"Yes, it does."

She watched while Esther got up and went to the shelves on her left. After a minute Esther came back with a book in her hand. "You need a champion, my dear, and I know just the man. Sparhawk the Brave, the fourth Earl of Ravensmoor."

Taryn studied the purple paperback where a handsome, bare-chested man with a sword grinned roguishly at her. The wind swept at his ebony hair, and his honest eyes were a deep, vibrant green. A wicked green that was tinged with a look of esoteric knowledge and intelligence, and they bore the glint of a man who knew his way around a woman's body. A man who would take his time and make sure he did the job right.

Oh, yeah, he was a major hottie.

His smile was devilish and there was something captivating about him. His arms bulged with strength and power, and he wore a gold, wolf-tipped torc that deepened the perfect tan of his skin.

He was striking and gorgeous, and the woman in her responded automatically to such overt masculinity. It might only be a drawing, but it was a damn good drawing. The kind that made a woman wish for one minute that she could find such perfection in the flesh.

At least for a night or two.

The title, *Knightly Dreams,* swept across the cover in gold foil, but the name of the author appeared to have been worn off.

Oddly enough there was no blurb on the back and she didn't recognize the publisher. *"Ma Souhait?"*

"They're an old publisher," Esther said. "Been around since before I was born."

"Really?"

"Oh, yes. You'll like it, trust me." Esther looked out the windows to where Taryn's Firebird was waiting. "Your tow truck is here. You'd better run."

Taryn pulled her wallet out.

Esther waved her hand at her. "Oh, pooh, dear, after the day you've had, consider it a gift."

"Are you sure?"

"Absolutely." Esther walked her to the door. "Good luck to you and Sparhawk. And remember, sometimes our dreams appear where and when we least expect it. Sometimes, just sometimes, you can even find them waiting in your own bed when you open your eyes."

Taryn arched a brow at the odd comment, but then Esther was quite a wonderfully eccentric character. "Thank you, Esther."

With Sparhawk in her hand, Taryn headed across the parking lot, then crossed the street and told the driver where to take her car.

o   o   o

Later that night, after she'd had a good cry over Rob, a pint of Phish Food, and a long geld-the-useless-bastard conversation with Janine, Taryn pulled out her book and decided to give Sparhawk a try.

And reading this book will help you how?

It was stupid, she knew that, and yet she couldn't seem to help herself from wanting to read the book and get Rob-the-Prickless-Bastard off her mind before she fell asleep.

She skimmed the first paragraph.

*The Earl of Ravensmoor was a hero like no other.
Tall, powerful, and magnetic, he had windswept jet
hair and a ruggedly handsome face that was neither
pretty nor feminine. He was all male.*

*Rumor said he'd killed over a thousand men in
battle, and as he walked through the crowded hall of
bejeweled nobles with one masterful hand on his
gilded sword hilt, his arrogant swagger bespoke a
man whose very presence had devastated over a
thousand women. . . .*

Taryn smiled at the image. Oh, yeah, he definitely sounded
like someone who could get Rob Dickhead off her mind.

She sighed as she read more about the wandering rogue
champion and his quest to claim his fair, if somewhat in-
sipid, maiden. It was a pity they didn't make guys like this
in modern-day America.

"Sparhawk," she whispered, smiling slightly, "I wish for
two seconds that you were real."

Closing the book, Taryn laid it on her nightstand, turned
out the light, and settled down to sleep. But as she lay there,
all she could see was the last image she'd read of the hero.

A knight in armor on the back of his huge white stallion,
riding into the forest to seek out the village enchantress . . .

o   o   o

Sparhawk dismounted halfway through the forest, his
heart pounding in expectation. The brush was so thick, he
knew from this point on he'd have to travel afoot.

Not that he minded. He would traverse the very fires of
hell to escape that which he was sworn to.

Life with Alinor.

A shiver of revulsion went down his spine. He had to find some way to escape his fate, and if the town gossips were to be believed, the old witch in the woods should have some miracle that could save him.

He picked his way through the dense underbrush. No one ever ventured this deeply into the forest. No one except the Hag. This was her home, and it kept her safe from any who would see her harmed.

As he walked, he felt an eerie presence. Almost as if the trees themselves were watching him.

But he feared not at all. Not this man who had stared down the heathens in Outremer. This man who had built his wealth on the strength of his sword arm and the sweat of his brow. There was no ghoul or demon inhabiting these woods that was more dangerous than he.

Indeed, it was said that the devil himself was terrified of Sparhawk.

He walked forward until at last he found the earthen hut draped with twisted vines. The only sign of life from within was the flicker of a large tallow candle.

More determined than before, Sparhawk knocked upon the vine-encrusted door. "Witch?" he called. "I mean you no harm. I come seeking your guidance and help."

After a brief pause the door slowly creaked open to reveal an old woman with long, silvery-gray hair. Her old brown eyes glowed with the vigor of a much younger soul, and her long gray hair fell loose about her frail shoulders.

"Milord," she greeted, opening the door to allow him entrance. "Come and be seated and tell me of this matter that has you venturing into my realm."

Sparhawk did as she bade him. He followed her into the small, cramped hut and took the seat she indicated by the window. He sat there for a few minutes to collect his thoughts. 'Twas the first time he'd told anyone of his problems with Alinor, and once he started to speak, all the sordid details came pouring out.

"So, you see," he said gently as the old woman handed him a strange black and bitter concoction she'd brewed by the fire. "'Tis not my duty I find offensive so much as milady's presence. I would give aught I own to have a lady who . . ." Sparhawk didn't finish the sentence. He couldn't.

What he wished for was something more fable than reality. No one married for love in this day and age.

No one.

Not that he knew anything of love anyway. He who had never known a kind touch. Never known what it felt like to be welcomed. He'd spent the whole of his life alone and aching.

His parents had died when he was scarce more than a babe, and he had been cast off first to his uncle, who despised his very presence, then squired to a man who thought nothing of him at all.

While other boys looked forward to trips home to their families, he had been left to muck out the stables and fetch for his lordly knight. He'd spent his holidays in a corner of the hall watching the families around him celebrating their gifts while he had nothing at all to call his own.

As a man, he'd carved out his destiny with the point of his sword and found plenty of women eager for his titles, wealth, and body, but none of them were ever eager for his heart. He'd found them all selfish and vain.

All he'd ever wanted was to see one face, either fair or foul, light up when he entered a room. To find a pair of open arms to greet him when he returned and a pair of eyes to weep for him when he was gone.

But it was a foolish wish and well he knew it.

"I want out of this story," he said at last. "I cannot marry Alinor and live here with her another moment. I have seen my ending and it is a pale one indeed. Please, I beg you, tell me how to change this."

The old woman touched him lightly on the arm. "I can help you, milord."

"Can you?" he asked, noting the lack of enthusiasm in his voice. He doubted if even the saints above could aid him through this plight. But he hoped. He always had hope.

She nodded. "I shall send you to a world of many miracles. A world where anything is possible . . . A place where your ending isn't yet set."

Sparhawk held his breath. Dare he even hope for such? "At what cost?"

She smiled gently. "There is no cost, milord. What I do, I do for love."

"For love?"

"Aye. I know I am not to meddle, but every so often—it's rare mind you—but every once in a while there are special cases that call for special measures. And you, good Sparhawk, are just such a case. Have no fear, I won't see you suffer through this anymore."

Sparhawk offered her a smile. The villagers were wrong about this woman. She wasn't a witch. She was an angel.

"Have you a name that I may know so that I can say a prayer of thanks for you?"

She smiled kindly at him. "Aye. They call me Esther."

"Then I owe you much more than I can every repay, good Esther."

"But," she said, a note of warning in her voice, "what I give you is only a chance. My powers, such as they are, are limited. I can give you no more than seven days to work your miracle. If you cannot find love within that time, then you must return here and marry Alinor."

His stomach turned with the thought of it. Still, the woman before him offered him a chance, and the good Lord knew he had been given far worse odds than that and returned victorious.

"Then I shall work this miracle," he breathed. "No matter what it takes."

"Then drink, milord," she said, lifting his hand that held the cup. "And remember, sometimes our dreams appear where and when we least expect it. Sometimes, just sometimes, you can even find them waiting in your bed when you open your eyes."

TWO

Sparhawk came awake with a start. His head pounded from a severe ache as if he'd drunk far too much mead the night before. By the light of the early morning sun, he would judge the day to be just starting. The faint butter rays spilled from the unshuttered window across the wooden floor and onto the bed wherein he lay.

'Twas a bed he knew not at all.

Immensely large, with a light yellow blanket, the bed easily accommodated his full six-foot-four height. As well as that of the woman lying beside him.

Arching his brow, he studied her beautiful brown hair that barely swept past her shoulders. It was thick with strands of russet and honey laced liberally through the darkness. She was not Alinor, but a new heroine for him to pursue.

His lips curling into a smile, he felt a stab of desire lance

131

through his middle. What treasure was this to be found in this bed?

And truly she was a treasure, all warm and soft as she slumbered. Her long lashes resting gently on her cheeks, her rosy lips parted.

He reached out to touch the silken curls of her hair. The soft strands wrapped about his fingers, firing his blood instantly.

Who was she? And how had he happened into her bed?

He frowned as he struggled to recall what had happened. The last thing he could remember was leaving the witch's hut and coming face-to-face with a most angry Alinor.

Alinor.

He flinched at her name. He was supposed to marry her in a handful of days, and yet the very sound of her voice grated on his ears. Even though she was without a doubt the most beautiful woman on earth, the image of her face and form turned his stomach.

Cease! She is to be your lady-wife and you will honor her.

Aye, he would. Even if it be the death of him.

And quite frankly, he might one day cast himself off the nearest mountainside to be rid of her. It was quite an intriguing possibility.

But not nearly as intriguing as this stranger at his side.

This stranger with the small pixie face and dark brows that arched above eyes closed in sweet slumber. He slid his thumb over her rosy cheek that was softer than the king's down and touched the gentle petals of her lips.

She lacked the great beauty of Alinor, and yet something about her drew his notice anyway, letting him know that even as he lay here, his story was changing. He thanked the Lord for that. Finally he'd found something new.

And she was a fetching morsel. Her looks were earthy and sweet, not perfect and sharp like Alinor's. Before he could stop himself, he pulled back the blanket to better study her. And as his gaze roamed her partially clothed body, heat surged through him, straight to his groin, which ached with want of her.

By her clothes he would guess her to be a tavern maid of some sort, though the color and style of her garment was unlike anything he had ever seen before.

The short gown barely trailed past her hips and betrayed a pair of stunningly smooth and shapely legs. Legs he desperately wanted to sample with his lips. Legs he ached to feel wrapped around his hips as he made love to her slowly and completely until they were both well spent and fully sated.

Sucking in his breath in appreciation, he ran his palm down her outer thigh. His body grew even harder in response as the woman sighed in her sleep and shifted dreamily.

His heart stopped as the gown rose higher, betraying a tiny, thin covering that concealed the moist, female part of her.

Just who was this temptress?

Was she the one the old witch had told him of?

She must be. Only that would account for his presence here in this very strange place.

And as he watched her respond to his touch, he knew he wanted nothing more of Alinor and her mewling ways. He wanted this woman by his side with a ferocity that was as stunning as it was demanding.

Her and her lush, full curves so unlike Alinor's thin, frail frame. This woman's body was made to comfort a man on a cold winter's night. Aye, her high breasts would spill freely over his palms, and her thighs were made for cradling a man's hips as he sank himself deep inside her body.

Hungry and aching, he slid his hand back up the curve of her thigh to the hem of the short, dark blue gown.

∘ ∘ ∘

Taryn sighed from her hot dream of a hero larger than life. Of a man who controlled the world around him and made no apologies.

All night long she'd been dreaming of the handsome, dark stranger who had flashing green eyes and strong arms to hold her. He had whispered to her in a deep, evocative voice. Tormented her with images of his life and with a need to make his life better.

Sparhawk the Brave.

What a stupid name and yet . . .

Somehow it suited the hero of the story.

Even now in her dreams she could see his handsome face from the book's cover, feel his warm hand sliding down her outer thigh, then up the front of her leg. Her body rolling into his caress, urging him on as a fire and fever consumed her.

She held her breath as that hand moved to her waist, then higher. Over the curve of her stomach and up to her . . .

Her eyes flew open as someone touched her breast.

Screaming, Taryn jumped out of bed to see a tall man dressed in medieval clothing staring at her with one arched, arrogant brow.

"Who the hell are you!" she demanded, realizing too late she had jumped to the wrong side of the bed.

He was between her and the door.

Dear God, help her!

But he didn't make a move toward her. He merely watched her from the bed with a look that could only be called patience. His silver chain-mail suit shimmered in the light, and he wore a white surcoat that held a red crescent moon and a stag.

He looked just like . . .

Her head swam at the implication. It couldn't be. *It just could not be.*

"I am the Earl of Ravensmoor. And you are?"

"Totally freaking out," she said.

"'Tis a most peculiar name, milady. Are you by chance Welsh?"

Taryn struggled to catch her breath as she stared at the gorgeous man on her bed who talked with a deep, evocative English accent. A man who looked entirely too much like the hero on the cover of her book.

He even wore the same gold torc around his neck. . . .

What the hell was going on here?

In that moment she half expected to hear the theme from *The Twilight Zone* start playing and for Rod Serling to begin his spiel about dimensions.

"How did you get into my house?" she asked.

It was only then he moved from the bed. Like some languid, graceful predator coming out of a crouch, he approached her. His muscles literally rippled with movement as his mail suit rasped slightly with his steps. A wickedly warm smile toyed at the edges of his handsome lips as he tilted her chin to where he could stare down into her eyes.

The power of him overwhelmed her. He was massive and tall, and so incredibly gorgeous that all she really wanted to do was take a bite out of him. The manly scent of sandalwood and leather invaded her head, making her breathless and warm.

His fingers stayed against her jaw, raising chills over her as she looked into eyes so incredibly green they barely seemed real. Eyes that hypnotized her with the danger and intelligence they revealed about the man who possessed them.

He was being gentle with her, but there was no doubt he could be lethal. No doubt he had the strength to do with her as he pleased.

And yet he made no other move to touch her. He merely stared at her with a leashed hunger that burned her from the inside out.

When he spoke, the deep possessiveness of his voice actually sent a shiver through her. "In truth, milady, I know not. I only know that I am here to win you."

Win me? She frowned at his strange choice of words. "Win me how?"

"With whatever it takes."

Oh, yeah, this was weird. Had she hit her head on something? Was she still dreaming? Maybe she had a fever that was causing delusions. Early dementia? Taryn bit her lip as she tried to sort through this to come up with a plausible explanation for why this gorgeous piece of anachronistic male flesh was in her house and not trying to rape her.

Maybe this was just some hallucination brought on by too much stress and too much caffeine.

But the hand on her face felt too real and the man before her too commanding to be imagined.

"Look, Mr. Freaky Man, I don't know how you got in here, but you need to leave or I'm calling the cops."

"Cops?"

"Police. Bobbies. You know, *the law.*"

He frowned at that. "I am the law, milady. I answer to no one save myself."

Oh, this was so *not* good.

He dipped his head down until his dark whiskers scraped her cheek, and he whispered in her ear. "Never fear me, little one," he breathed huskily. "You are my heroine and I have no intention of harming you. Ever."

"Then what do you intend to do?"

He pulled back and gave her a devilish grin. "I intend to woo you. To make you head over heels in love with me by week's end."

Nervous laughter bubbled up through her. This was just too bizarre for words.

"You don't believe me?" he asked with an arrogant look.

"Buddy, I don't know what to believe." She really didn't. "How did you get into my house anyway?"

He shrugged. "One moment I was in front of my . . ." His eyes turned sharp with anger as he hesitated. He cleared his throat. "I blinked and here I was."

"You blinked like Jeannie, right?"

"Jeannie?"

"Never mind."

He moved his fingers down her jaw, then laced them through her hair. And when he dipped his head toward hers, she quickly stepped out of his embrace and moved to the door. Halfway there, she stumbled to a standstill as her gaze caught the book on her nightstand.

Her dark knight with the sword was gone, and in his place was a blond guy holding a bouquet of flowers.

Nuh-uh!

Disbelief ran through her. It couldn't be. It just could not be. . . .

"Sparhawk?"

He cocked his head at her. "You know my name?"

"Okay," she said slowly. "I'm on drugs." It didn't really matter to her that she had never once taken any, but there seemed no other logical explanation. Esther must have slipped her a mickey in her coffee. Though why it had taken seventeen hours for it to work, she didn't know.

There just had to be some sane, logical reason why the stupidly named Sparhawk the Brave, Earl of Ravensmoor, was here in his armor and she was losing her mind.

But there really wasn't one.

I need to call Esther.

If anyone knew what was going on, it would surely be her. After picking up the phone and dialing for information, Taryn quickly learned there was no listing for the store.

And honestly, it wasn't really a surprise. Somewhere deep in the back of her mind, she had figured as much.

Still, she felt the need to find out whatever she could. "Tell you what, I'm going to get dressed real fast and you and I are going to take a trip."

"Where?"

"To a little bookstore."

He frowned at her. "What is a bookstore?"

She rubbed her temple. "I guess they didn't have those in the Middle Ages, did they?"

"Middle Ages? Lady, you use very strange words."

She gave another nervous laugh. "Yeah, okay, let me not tarry," she said, using words she hoped he'd understand better. "I shall dress forthwith and hasten myself back to thee or thou or whatever it is."

If anything his frown increased, and as she headed for the bathroom, she could have sworn she heard him say, "She's a strange demoiselle, but a highly amusing one."

Sparhawk ventured from the room as he waited for Lady Totally Freaking Out to return. The witch had not been jesting when she said this world would be filled with strange marvels. There were plants inside containers that held no water or soil. Strange furniture covered in dark green fabric. Nothing in this woman's dwelling appeared even remotely familiar to him.

What was this place the witch had sent him to? Was it another planet perhaps? A world of sorcerers?

Perhaps he should fear for his immortal soul, but then, given the thought of returning to Alinor, even something that threatened his eternity had to be better than her cloying smile and lackluster wit.

As he poked at the plant that had a strange, unnatural texture to it, he felt a presence behind him. Turning his head, he froze. His new lady wore a strange short-sleeved tunic and a pair of breeches that had been shorn off high on her thighs. The sight of those long legs made him think of how soft her skin had felt in his palm and of how much better it would taste under his tongue.

He trailed his gaze over her lush curves to her face, where her pink cheeks told him his stare made her uncomfortable. He smiled at the knowledge.

Taryn couldn't move as she watched Sparhawk watch her. The man was so incredibly hot. His green eyes filled with heat and carnal knowledge. She knew what he was thinking, and quite honestly, she was thinking it, too. Imagine having *that* naked and spread out on her bed . . . over her body.

Yeah, boy!

He filled out that armor in the way she was sure medieval smiths had meant for it to be worn. His broad shoulders were thrown back with pride, and he bore the presence of a man confident in himself.

The man in him devastated the woman in her.

And it was then she realized she couldn't really take him into public wearing medieval armor. Not unless they were going to a Ren Faire. People might begin to ask questions she couldn't even begin to answer, and the last thing she needed was for this to turn into some bad low-budget B movie with the two of them ending up in a lab somewhere.

Or worse, an asylum.

While she stared, he crossed the room to stand before her. "Tell me, milady, where is your guardian?"

She frowned. "You mean my parents?"

"I mean whoever is responsible for your future."

"That would be me."

A puzzled look crossed his handsome features until they

melted into one of amusement. "Truly? You answer only unto yourself?"

"Just like you."

He smiled at that, and before she realized what he intended, he captured her lips with his.

Taryn tensed for a moment and started to step back, but his arms quickly surrounded her, drawing her closer to his heat as he opened her mouth and ravished it. There was no other word for the complete possession he took.

She'd been kissed plenty of times in her life, but never like this. Never with such heated intensity. His tongue coaxed hers, his lips demanding.

And the smell of him . . .

So manly. So warm. So sexual.

Rising up on her tiptoes, she moaned from the feel of him, wanting to draw him in deeper. To taste more of this incredible male.

Sparhawk growled at the passion in her caress as she wrapped her arms about him. She clung to him and met his kiss with a hunger that surprised him. Aye, she was a wild one. One who would bed him well, and he in turn would never leave her wanting more. Never leave until she was completely spent and satisfied.

In that moment he knew she was the one he would take as his own. He would never go back to Alinor.

Never.

He cupped her face in his hands and reluctantly pulled back. She kept her eyes closed as if savoring the moment.

He smiled.

When she opened her large, doe-like eyes and stared up

at him, he felt a strange surge through him. It was raw and aching and it demanded her in a way that stunned him.

"That was nice," she said breathlessly.

He laughed. 'Twas the first time any woman had said that to him.

∘ ∘ ∘

Taryn tried to regain her equilibrium, but it wasn't easy. Not when all she really wanted to do was step back into his arms and have her most wicked way with him. Worse was the little tiny voice in the back of her mind that kept saying having sex with a character from a romance novel didn't count anyway. Right?

She could do anything she wanted to with him, and no one would ever know. . . .

Oh, yeah, that could be fun.

"Okay, Spar . . ." She paused on his name. *Sparhawk* just sounded too ludicrous for words when spoken out loud.

What had the writer been thinking?

Oh, do me, great big Sparhawk. You the man. Taryn laughed in spite of herself. Nope, that name did not work in reality.

"What would you like me to call you?" she asked.

He cocked an arrogant brow at her. "You may call me Earl."

Taryn bit back another laugh. Yeah, right. That was probably the only thing worse than Sparhawk. And for some unholy reason the Dixie Chicks song "Goodbye Earl" started going through her head.

Oh, good grief!

"Okay, look, your majesty or grace or whatever, Earl and Sparhawk aren't going to cut it for the moment, okay?"

Somehow Sparhawk managed to look ever more regal and arched. "I beg your pardon? This from a woman called Totally Freaking Out?"

This was rapidly disintegrating into even more chaos and bizarreness. "My name isn't Totally Freaking Out. It's Taryn. Taryn Edwards."

He seemed to relax a bit. "Lady Taryn?"

"No, just Taryn."

"Very well, Taryn. You may call me Sparhawk."

Taryn bit her lip as she winced. "You know, big guy, I just can't really do that."

"Then call me milord," he said, totally missing her point.

Taryn took a deep breath. "Let me explain my world to you. If I call you milord and you call me milady, people are going to lock both of us up."

"In the stocks?"

"Sure. Um, so I need a name I can call you that won't make anyone look at us strangely." *Or make me laugh out loud every time I use it.*

"Since this is your world, mi—" He broke off his words as she cocked a brow. "Taryn. Tell me, what name should I use?"

Taryn stared at him for several minutes as she ran over the possibilities. He was too incredible to be something simple like Tom or Ken or Robert. He needed a more studly name.

Finally she settled on just shortening it. "How about just Hawk?"

Still a little ridiculous, but better.

He nodded. "Very well, Taryn. For you, I shall be known as Hawk."

A strange flutter shot through her at his words. *For you.* No doubt he had meant nothing special by them; still they warmed her.

"Now we have to do something about those clothes."

"You would change my name and my clothing, milady. Is there nothing about me you find acceptable?"

A hurt look flashed across his eyes so fast that she thought she might have imagined it. And it was then she remembered what she had read about him in the book. . . .

Alinor's words made his old wounds bleed anew.

He had cut his teeth on criticism and had long ago ceased holding any tolerance for it. No one needed to point out his shortcomings to him, for he knew each fault he possessed quite intimately as it had been pointed out with crystal clarity in his youth, under the violent tutelage of his lord.

If this was really the Sparhawk character come to life, then he would have had the same past as the Sparhawk in the book.

Her heart lurched at the thought. The man in the book had borne solitude and suffering the whole of his life. It was his pain that had kept her up late reading about him, her need to see him happy that had her turning page after page as she hoped Alinor would get a clue and realize what a great guy she had.

Taryn paused at the thought.

No, it's not real. He's not real. Sparhawk is a book knight. He can't come to life.

And yet . . .

"What happened to your parents?" she asked.

His eyes turned dull. "My mother died birthing my still-born brother, and my father died of grief a few months later."

"Had you been worth anything, boy, your father wouldn't have damned himself to the devil by taking his own life to be rid of you. . . ."

Taryn flinched as she remembered the words Sparhawk's uncle had said when they delivered the frightened boy to his door. Barely eight, Sparhawk had dared to argue at his un-fair treatment, and his uncle had struck him so hard, the cut from the man's ring had left a scar.

A scar on his left cheek, right below his eye.

A scar that would probably look just like the faint one Hawk had on his left cheek.

Her heart stopped.

"You were sent to live with your uncle when you were eight?" she asked, hoping he would deny it.

"How did you know that?"

Taryn felt ill. Taking deep breaths, she sat on the arm of her dark blue sofa. "Oh, boy," she breathed.

Her head swam from the possibilities. How could this be real? How could he have gotten into her world? How?

Hawk moved toward her, taking her arm. "Are you all right, Taryn? You look faint."

In all honesty, she felt faint. "I'm fine," she said, staring at the long tapered fingers grasping her arm. Fingers that were as flesh and bone as the man at her side.

"We need to see Esther." Oh, yeah, they really did. She had to have some real answers.

"Esther? The witch?"

"Pardon?"

"The witch who sent me here. Her name was Esther. Do you know of her?"

Taryn's eyes widened. "Little gray-haired woman with brown eyes?"

"Aye."

"*She* sent you here?"

He nodded.

Oh, that figured. "Did she happen to say why you were sent here?"

"I asked for it. I wanted a way to escape my impending doom with Alinor, and she told me that I would find myself in a miraculous world, which I have. But I don't know the script here, only that you are my heroine and that I should make you fall in love with me."

Oh . . . good . . . grief. "Why would you ask such a thing? Your world didn't seem so bad."

By the look on his face, she could tell he disagreed. "I have my reasons, milady. There are many unpleasantries at home that I would soonest avoid."

She could understand that. She had her own unpleasantries she'd like to avoid. Taking a deep, fortifying breath, she forced herself up and returned to the issue that had started it all. His clothes.

She had some of Rob's sweats that she'd borrowed one night when she had accidentally spilled Coke all over herself at his house. Though Rob wasn't nearly as large as Hawk, the sweats should stretch enough to at least be decent.

Ten minutes later after she'd given them to Hawk, she recanted that idea as Hawk came out of the bedroom wearing navy sweats that hugged a rump so prime she was amazed the USDA hadn't stamped it. And her XXL T-shirt was pulled taut over a chest so well-toned she could hire him out for a muscle magazine ad.

Worse, those sweats rode low on his lean hips, showing his six-pack of abs off to perfection.

Oh, mama, she wanted a bite of that.

And in that moment she wanted to thank the unknown author of his book. The woman was a goddess! And her taste in men should be applauded until the cows came home and tap-danced on the front lawn.

Sparhawk paused as he caught the heated stare of Taryn's large brown eyes. She never so much as blinked as she sized him up. He smiled from the knowledge.

Lust he could work with. It was indifference that would spell the end to his plans.

"Are my clothes appropriate?" he asked.

She nodded, blinked, then met his gaze. "What was that?"

He laughed. "I asked if my clothing was now acceptable to you."

"Mmm-hmmm," she said, the noise carrying her approval. "All we need are tennis shoes and we're in business."

He didn't ask. In truth, he feared the answer. Tennis shoes sounded almost painful. "I have my boots."

She shook her head. "No offense, chain-mail footwear and sweats just don't go together well."

"I'll take your word for it."

Taryn decided he was dressed enough to take to the bookstore anyway. Grabbing her keys from the kitchen counter, she led the way out of the house and showed him to her car in the driveway.

He walked toward it with a frown on his face. A frown that deepened considerably as another car drove by and he watched it with fear and curiosity warring on his face. "How do these things move with no horses?"

"They have engines, which probably makes no sense whatsoever to you."

"'Tis one term I understand, milady. We had engines in my world as well."

"Really?"

"Aye, but nothing like this." He ran his hand over the top of her car as if marveling at it.

She smiled at the enthused look on his face, and something inside told her he was going to love riding in her rental car.

A wildly appreciative look came over his face as he took a seat on the passenger side and she started it.

Once they pulled out of the drive and started down the street, his eyes glowed like a child seeing the ocean for the very first time.

"'Tis like wings," he said, watching the scenery fly past. "This is incredible!"

"It's all right. Not as fast as my Firebird, though."

His eyes lit up even more. "You ride on a bird that flies faster than fire?"

"Not exactly. It's a car like this one, only cooler and faster." At least on the days when it ran. Laughing, she drove to the interstate and headed toward where she'd been yesterday.

A half hour later they stood outside the vacant store where Esther's bookstore had been the day before. The windows were covered, and it looked as if nothing had been there for at least a year. There was no sign, no books. Nothing.

"This can't be," she said under her breath.

"What is it?"

"Yesterday the store was here."

He gave her a puzzled stare. "Are you in error?"

She shook her head. "No, I swear. I sat in there just yesterday and drank coffee while I talked to Esther, who said her book would help me. . . ."

It was unbelievable.

"So what does this mean?" Hawk asked.

Taryn shook her head. "I guess it means I need to teach you to read modern English. 'Cause, buddy, it looks like you're stuck here."

Sparhawk saw the disbelief in her eyes, and it was on the tip of his tongue to correct her. But he didn't.

She seemed too eager for him to leave. As had most people of his acquaintance. Mayhap if he could convince her to spend time with him, she could come to care for him, at least somewhat.

But then why would she when even your own kind can't tolerate you?

He squelched that voice. Surely the witch wouldn't have sent him here unless she believed it were possible to make this strange woman crave him in this story.

Holding on to that thought, he took Taryn's hand from

the door and held it in his. "Tell me, milady, would being stuck with me be so terribly bad?"

Taryn wanted to say yes, but she couldn't. "I don't know, Hawk. I know nothing about you other than what I've read in my book."

"And I know nothing of you, my lady Taryn, other than you seem a decent and kind woman."

"Yeah." So decent and kind that her boyfriend tossed her over for a cheap thrill in his office. "C'mon, we need to get you some more clothes and some shoes."

She took him across the busy road to TJ Maxx so that they could start to outfit him. It was actually kind of fun since Hawk had no idea what was fashionable and what wasn't. He wore whatever she told him to, and hon, he looked damned good in jeans. When he came out of the dressing room, one woman actually walked into a rack of ties because she couldn't stop staring at him.

Not that Taryn blamed her. She was feeling rather giddy herself. Hawk didn't seem to notice the stir he was causing with other women. He only seemed to see her, which was really nice for a change.

"Do these fit correctly?" he asked.

Taryn bit her lip as she nodded impishly. "Oh, yeah, babe, those fit the way God and Calvin meant for jeans to fit a man."

"Calvin?"

"It's just an expression." She reached up to unbutton his collar so that the long-sleeved dark green shirt wouldn't choke him. The color of it made his eyes even more vibrant. Made his skin more tan, delectable.

It was all she could do not to shove him into the dressing

room and rip those clothes off him for her viewing and fondling pleasure.

Really, no guy should be this hot and tempting.

Taryn sent him back in to undress while she went to pick out underwear and socks. When he returned to her, he was again dressed in his sweats with the clothes held in his arms.

Once they had those bought, Taryn took him to a sports store for shoes.

"You have the biggest feet," she said as they measured them. He really was a fourteen. "Good grief, they're earth pads."

"Are you mocking me?"

"Nope," she said with a grin. "Trust me, in my world those are a vital asset."

"How so?"

"Well, women equate foot size to . . ." She dropped her gaze to an area of his body that she had been curious about for hours now.

His eyes widened as he caught her meaning. "Milady!"

"I know, I'm wicked, but I can't help myself. Have you seen yourself in a mirror?"

He smiled at her as he rose to pull her toward him. He dipped his head down so that he could whisper in her ear. "Anytime my Lady Wicked wishes to appease her curiosity, I am a most willing supplicant." Those words sent a shiver over her as did the sensation of his hot breath against her neck.

Taryn closed her eyes as she inhaled the scent of him. It really was all she could do not to pull him flush to her body and kiss the daylights out of him.

"Don't tempt me," she said quietly. "We need to find earth-pad covers."

But before she could escape, he did place a very quick, very powerful kiss to her lips. Taryn melted. "You are too good to be true."

But then he wasn't. Not really.

Was he?

She pulled back with a frown. "How did you get here, Hawk?"

He let his fingers linger in her hair as he smiled down at her. "I asked the old witch for a miracle that would keep me from Alinor's clutches, and the witch sent me to you."

"How, though?"

"I know not. One moment I was there with Alinor screaming at me, and the next I awoke in your bed."

"Can you get home again?"

Sparhawk hesitated. If he didn't make Lady Taryn fall in love with him, the witch had said he would be forced back into his own story. That was the last thing he wanted. He'd had enough of Alinor all these past years. Truly, he would rather be dead than forced to woo her one more time.

"Nay," he lied, unwilling to think of his life in his own book. "I was sent here for you, Taryn. You needed a hero and I am here to be him."

On her face he saw the joy and the pain his words wrought.

"Do you not want me with you? Is there another hero you would prefer?"

She sighed. "It's not that exactly. I just don't know what to do with a man from the Middle Ages. I mean, it's not like you can work a job or anything. There's not much opportunity for a knight in shining armor in twenty-first-century America."

"Then you do want me to return to my book?"

She looked confused. "No . . . Yes . . . I don't know. I'm just not sure what I should be doing with you."

"What is it you want to do with me?"

Taryn swallowed at his question. The images in her mind were hot and wicked and wholly inappropriate while she was standing in a public place. "I don't know, Hawk," she answered truthfully.

"Then pretend that I am only here for seven days. Pretend that at week's end you will never have to see me again. That I will just go back whence I came. What would you do with me then?"

She smiled wistfully at that. "I'm not sure."

"Give me seven days of your time, Lady Taryn. Just seven. Then I swear to you that if you no longer wish for me to be near you, I shall vanish from you forever and return to my book to marry Alinor."

Taryn bit her lip at the wonderful idea. A hot boyfriend for seven days who wouldn't break her heart. Esther had been right; it was just what the doctor ordered. "All right, then. Seven days."

Moving away from him, she went to buy his shoes, then led him out of the store, to her car, and then back to her house.

It was so odd to have him with her after what had just happened with Rob, and yet there was some part of her that really enjoyed his company. Hawk doted on her in a way no man ever had.

He stayed by her side the entire afternoon, and he was

actually helping her cook dinner even though he didn't really have a clue about how to do the simplest thing. In fact, the electric can opener had completely mystified him.

At first he had thought it was possessed and had tried to kill it with her serving spoon. Finally she had convinced him that it was a good thing and had showed him how to use it.

She frowned as she tried to get the lid off her jar of spaghetti sauce.

"Here, my lady, allow me."

She handed it to Hawk, who immediately whisked it open.

"Thanks," she said, taking it back. So there was something he was really good at.

Hawk inclined his head before he went to the stove to examine the burners. "There's no fire and yet 'tis hot."

"It's electricity."

He turned his frown to her. "Electricity?"

Taryn tried to explain the concept, then realized she didn't really understand it herself. "It's magic," she said at last. "Cool magic."

"Hot magic more like," he said, replacing the pot. "You have a most remarkable world here in your book, Lady Taryn."

"This isn't a book. This is reality."

He looked puzzled by that. "Nay, milady. I am a character and you are a character. Our world is a book that is being written by another even as we speak. Our every action and every word is being carefully scripted."

"No," she said, trying to explain it to him. She went

to her bookcase and pulled out a paperback. "These are books and this is reality. We're not in a book. We're in my house."

"Are you sure, Taryn? How do you know this isn't a book and that we're not just puppets being led about by someone else's whims?"

"Because I am a real, flesh-and-blood person. No one controls me. I control myself."

"And if you asked me that, I would say the same, so how do you know it is true?"

He had a very weird point that made her horribly uncomfortable. "Let's not do this, okay? I'm starting to feel like those people in *The Twilight Zone* who were trapped in the giant kid's toy town for his amusement." She shivered, then stopped. "If this is a book, then how is it everything here is crisp and clear? All the colors are vivid and the world is never ending."

"'Tis the same in my book."

That surprised her. She would have thought everything would be sketchy and vague. "Really?"

"Aye. There is nothing different in terms of tactile or sensory experience. Only the setting has changed."

Oh, that was just creepy.

He offered her a kind smile. "But I have to say that I much prefer your world to mine."

"Why is that?"

His green eyes burned her with their intensity. "Because you are in it."

She melted at those words. Damn, the man could be unreasonably charming at times. What was it about him that made her want him so? Was that magic, too?

155

She tried to imagine what it would be like to have a real-life modern-day Hawk. Would he be so enamored of her? Would she be so enamored of him? It was hard to know for sure.

Perhaps all of this was because he was a hero and not a real man. But then, what was *real*? Wasn't real something that could make her feel emotions? Wasn't it something she could see, taste, touch, smell, and hear? If that were true, then Hawk was every bit as real as Rob had been.

And that thought actually terrified her.

As soon as dinner was ready, she served him a plate of spaghetti, then took it to the dining room so that they could eat. Something that proved easier said than done. Hawk had no concept of how to eat with a fork.

He stared at it as if it were some alien creature.

"Don't you have forks?" she asked him.

"Nay, milady. I've never seen anything like this before."

"Oh." She took it from him and showed him how to wrap the angel hair pasta around the tines. He tried to lift it to his mouth, but it slid off the fork, into his lap.

Taryn forced herself not to laugh at him as she reached to pick it up, but the minute she touched him, she knew she'd made a mistake. As her hand brushed up against his body, she realized he was completely hard. His eyes flamed as he sucked his breath in sharply between his teeth.

Clearing his throat, he shot to his feet and moved away from her. The spaghetti landed with a splat on her floor. "Forgive me, milady," he said as he stooped to clean it up. "I didn't mean to offend you."

"Offend me how?"

"With my, um . . . my untoward condition. I realize that you are a lady of proper virtue, and I apologize if I caused you any discomfort."

The only thing that caused her discomfort was his embarrassment. "It's okay, really," she said, helping him clean the floor. "I'm not offended."

He paused to look at her. "Nay?"

She shook her head. "I'm actually flattered."

Those green eyes turned dark, probing. "Are you?"

"Aye," she said, using his own language. She moved closer to him until they were almost touching. She could see the longing on his face. See the need he had for her. She felt it, too. It was hot and wicked. Demanding. And all it wanted was to taste this man in front of her.

Sparhawk wasn't prepared for her kiss. He growled at the taste of her as his body hardened even more. All day long his groin had been aching for her. It was all he could do not to force himself upon her, but he would never do such a thing. She was his heroine and as such deserved nothing but his utmost respect and admiration.

His head spun at the sweetness of her mouth and the scent of her hair that invaded his head. She clutched him to her as she ran her hands over his back, making him ache even more.

And then she did the most unexpected thing of all. She dipped her hand down into the waistband of his breeches. Sparhawk hissed as he felt her hot hand against his bare flesh. Chills ran the length of his body as her hand moved slowly over his hip to his waist.

"Taryn." He breathed her name like a prayer.

She kissed him deeply, sweeping her tongue against his as her fingers brushed against his hard cock. He clenched his hands in her hair and groaned as she touched him for the first time. Every part of his body shivered in bittersweet need.

Taryn's head swam at the feel of him in her hand. Her knight was a large man, and she melted at the thought of having him inside her. She brushed her fingers lower to the base of his shaft so that she could cup him in her hand. He growled deep in his throat as she gave a light squeeze.

Laughing in excitement at pleasing him, she nipped at his prickly chin. She'd never been the kind of woman who slept with a guy she just met, and yet she felt as if she knew him intimately. And in a weird way, she did. She knew more about his life from what she'd read than she'd ever known about Rob. More to the point, she knew the truth about Hawk, whereas Rob had filled her with lies.

Sparhawk couldn't think straight with her hand on him. In all his life he'd never had a woman so eager to bed him. Could it be his newfound lady might actually have a tenderness in her heart where he was concerned?

Dare he even hope it?

It was all he'd ever dreamed of. All he'd ever wanted. In all the battles he'd fought and in all the women he'd met, it was the thought of finding the one true heart who could love him that kept him going through his life.

She pulled her hand away before she whisked his shirt off over his head. "I know we shouldn't do this, Hawk," she whispered. "But I want you too much to just throw myself in a cold shower."

"I am yours to do with as you please."

She smiled at that. "Then come, milord champion, and let me please us both."

She stood up first and started for her bedchamber. Sparhawk took two long strides before he scooped her up in his arms and carried her to the bed.

Taryn laughed at his enthusiasm. It felt so good to be this desired. She couldn't remember any man ever being this excited to be with her. And definitely not a man who looked as fine as this one.

He placed her carefully on the bed before he joined her there. He gathered her into his arms and kissed her soundly.

She moaned at the taste and feel of all that delectable weight pressing against her. His entire body was on top of hers, and she reveled at the exquisiteness of it. His every muscle rippled under her hands. Desire burned through her, pooling itself into a deep thrumming need at the center of her body.

He pulled back to stare down at her as he slowly, carefully unbuttoned her shirt. He spread the fabric open, then frowned at the sight of her bra.

"What is this?" he asked, tracing the cup of it with his fingers.

"A bra." She showed him how to unsnap it from the front.

His eyes glowed as soon as she was exposed to him. "You are beautiful," he moaned, cupping her breast in his hand.

Taryn's entire body sizzled as he dipped his head to

suckle her taut nipple. His mouth was hot and magical. His breath was scorching against her skin. Desire spread through her like liquid fire that wanted more and more of his touch.

She ran her hand down his hard back so that she could feel his muscles flex as he moved.

He was incredible.

Sparhawk took his time tasting the sweet morsel of her flesh. He nipped at her swollen peak before he pulled back to rub it gently with his whiskers. She shivered underneath him. He smiled in satisfaction, delighting in the way she reacted to his touch.

Taryn cradled him with her body. It was so good to have a man hold her again.

She trembled as he pulled her pants from her, then kissed his way up her body, all the way to her lips. She'd been right yesterday when she first saw his picture. He did know his way around a woman's body. This man had some serious skills.

Wanting to explore more of his talents, she peeled his jeans off his body so that she could feel every inch of that lush, masculine body against hers. His legs were dappled with dark hairs that tickled her skin.

Her heart pounded. She'd been hurt so badly in the past that a part of her couldn't help but wonder if Hawk would hurt her as well. But how could he?

Maybe all of this really was just some bizarre dream. Maybe a bus had hit her after all and she was lying in a coma and this was her mind's way of holding on to life.

Or maybe he was real and she could find some way to keep him.

It was that last thought that was most appealing to her.

Sparhawk gently placed his body between her thighs. Closing his eyes, he savored the feel of her body beneath his. Of her crisp hairs teasing at his stomach.

She smiled up at him as she reached down between their bodies to find him. He held his breath as she closed her hand around him, then guided his cock, inch by slow inch, deep inside her.

He moaned at the sleek, wet heat of her body. No woman had ever sheathed him better. Gathering her into his arms, he held her close to his chest as he started moving against her.

Taryn moaned as pleasure tore through her as he started thrusting against her hips. Every stroke echoed through her body, filling and teasing her. It was the most incredible sensation she had ever known.

If she didn't know better, she'd swear he loved her. He held her like some precious object. His every stroke soothed and thrilled her. It reached that deep-seated ache that wanted only to have him fill her and ease it.

Taryn arched her back as her body exploded into pleasure.

Sparhawk growled as she came beneath him. She cried out, clutching at him. The sound of her pleasure drove him over the edge as he, too, found his own paradise.

He collapsed on top of her, letting the softness of her body soothe his. 'Twas the most miraculous feeling he'd ever known. He felt connected to her. A part of her.

It didn't make sense.

She sighed contentedly as she ran her hands over his back. "That was incredible."

"Aye, it was."

She laughed and then kissed him. Sparhawk nuzzled her neck so that he could inhale the sweetness of her scent. It was enough to almost make him grow hard again. He licked her tender skin, marveling at the texture of it. "I don't ever want to leave this bed, my lady Taryn."

"Me either," she said before she gave a light laugh. "But if we don't, it could get ugly after a few days. We'd shrivel up from lack of water."

"I can think of no better way to go."

"That makes two of us."

Sparhawk rolled to his side, then pulled her against him. She lay herself over him like a blanket and traced circles on his chest.

"Thank you, Lady Taryn."

"For what?"

"For making me feel like this."

Taryn smiled at that. No man had ever given her thanks for making love to him, and she found that she liked it. A lot. "My pleasure, Hawk. Anytime you need to feel this way again, just give a whistle."

He grinned at that, then whistled low.

She laughed again. "You are evil."

"Nay, my lady. I am only in awe of you."

Taryn crawled even more on top of him so that she could feel the whole length of his body under hers. If she could have one wish, it would be to stay like this forever. But she knew in her heart that they couldn't.

Sooner or later they would have to leave this bed.

And sooner or later they would have to part company. No doubt forever. She winced at the thought, but in her heart she knew it was true. She didn't know what "magic" had brought him here; however, this couldn't last. He was a character from a book. He could never be hers to keep, and whatever had brought him here would most likely return him to his world.

Yet even the mere thought of it made her want to scream out in denial at the injustice. How weird. She barely knew him and already she wanted to keep him.

If only she could . . .

THREE

The next four days were the best of Taryn's life. Hawk stayed at her house during the day while she worked, and every night when she came home, he was there with something special for her. One night he'd raided her rosebushes out back and had the entire house covered in roses and candles lit for her. It looked like something out of a movie. Or better yet, a dream.

He'd even learned to work the stove, and though his cooking left much to be desired, it was so sweet of him to try that she didn't even mind eating burned bread. In fact, she was developing a taste for "blackened" chicken and steak.

But more than that, she was developing a taste for whipped-cream-basted Hawk as they spent their nights naked and in her bed. There was nothing she loved more than lying in his arms while she explored every inch of him.

He was funny and supportive, which for a man who had been a barbaric knight said something.

"Are all knights so gentle?" she'd asked him the night before.

"I know not, Taryn, since I don't make it my habit to lie abed with other knights."

She'd laughed at that while he stroked her hair.

"But to be honest, there is only so much battle a man can take. I think all of us crave a quieter life with a tender touch."

Taryn closed her eyes as he kissed her until her knees were weak from it. There was pure magic in his touch. Magic in his kiss. She pulled back to stare down at him while she straddled his hips. She had a sneaking suspicion that she was starting to fall in love with this man.

How could that be? How could she be in love with a character from a book? And yet all she could think of was him. The sound of his voice, the curve of his jaw, the masculine beauty of his face. He haunted her day and night. Called to her every time she left him. All she could think about at work was getting home to spend time with him alone.

It was spooky just how much of herself she had already given him, and they had just met. He cupped her face in his hands. Taryn turned her face into his palm so that she could taste the salty-sweet flesh as she slowly lowered herself onto him.

Hawk groaned as she took him in all the way to his hilt. Smiling up at her, he arched his back as she started to move against him.

"I love being inside you, Lady Taryn."

She had to admit she liked feeling him so deep inside her. There was something special about this connection to him. He lowered his hands to her breasts, where he gently cupped her as he lifted his hips to drive himself even deeper inside her.

Taryn rode him slow and easy, reveling in the sensation of his thick fullness.

Sparhawk closed his eyes as he let her take complete control of their pleasure. He didn't know what it was about this woman, but she touched him in ways no one ever had before. In her arms he felt loved. Cared for. He lived only for the sight of her face, the touch of her hand. The thought of living without her . . .

He would rather be dead than even contemplate it. How could such a thing be possible?

He ran his hand over her taut nipples, letting them caress his palm. She hissed in response to his touch. Wanting to please her even more, he trailed his hand slowly from her breast, down the curve of her stomach, down to the moist dark curls at the juncture of her thighs.

His gaze locked with hers, he sank his thumb deep into the folds of her body to find her sensitive nub. She cried out in pleasure as he gently stroked her. Even better, she quickened her strokes against him, pulling him in deeper and deeper.

Taryn couldn't think with his hand on her. All she could do was feel him, his strokes, the depth of him inside her. She wanted satisfaction, and when she got it, she screamed in pleasure.

Her heart pounding, she fell forward, over him.

Sparhawk rolled with her in his arms, their bodies still

joined until he was on top of her. Her body continued to spasm around his. He drove himself in deep and quickened his strokes so that he could elongate her orgasm. She kissed him fiercely, her tongue spiking against his as she clawed at his back.

Delighted with her reaction, he thrust himself into her over and over again until his own body found its release. He growled in pleasure. She wrapped her body around his and held him close as they lay in the sweaty aftermath of their play.

Taryn drew a ragged breath as she waited for her body to calm. This was her favorite part of the night. The time after they were both spent and all she could hear was the sound of his breathing. Skin to skin, heartbeat to heartbeat. There was nothing else like it in the world.

With the smell of her champion enchanting her, she let the sound of his heartbeat lull her into sleep.

She woke in the morning, late for work. Sparhawk was still asleep. Unwilling to wake him, she took a minute to ogle the gorgeous backside that was completely bare. His dark tawny skin was a perfect contrast to her cream sheets. She smiled at the sight of his black hair tousled and the whiskers that darkened his cheeks.

"Do me, Sparhawk," she said under her breath with a short laugh.

It took every ounce of her self-control not to fondle him awake and have a quickie before she left. But she was already late. Pouting, she forced herself into the bathroom to get ready.

But the memory of him in her bed and the feel of his body against hers kept her company all day at work. And it had her rushing home to find him dressed in a dark blue shirt and jeans, waiting for her.

Tonight, they were going out. She'd gotten the idea the day before from one of her coworkers whose daughter had just had a birthday. It was something she was sure Hawk would enjoy . . . dinner at Medieval Times.

She greeted him with a quick kiss, then herded him out to the car so that they would get there in plenty of time.

"I do not understand the rush," Hawk said as he paused outside the car.

By the disappointed look on his face, she could tell what he was thinking. "We can't spend every second in the bedroom, babe."

"Why not?"

She laughed at him. "Are you sure you weren't in an erotic novel?"

He frowned at that. "What is that?"

"A book where they do nothing but have sex all the way through it."

His green eyes sparkled at that. "There is such a thing? Methinks I should have had another conversation with Esther and made my demands more clear. I feel I may have chosen poorly with our story."

Taryn rolled her eyes at him. "I keep telling you, this is not a story. You're a real man now."

"But I was real before."

Oh, he was never going to get it. To him the real world was every bit as real as his fictional one. And every time he insisted his world was real, she heard her mother's voice in her head. *"Put down the book and join the real world.*

There's more to life than words on a page, and I'm sick of watching you waste your time on such asinine things."

As a girl, she'd been like Hawk and had believed that those places and people were as real as the ones around her. But her mother had finally worn her down, and over time Taryn had read less and less as she followed her mother's advice.

But the truth was, she enjoyed being with Hawk more than she had ever enjoyed anything else. If Hawk was right and this was a book, then she didn't want reality. She only wanted this man who was climbing into her Firebird.

Taryn got in and headed out of the driveway.

By the time they reached the "castle," she was practically giddy in expectation of Hawk's reaction to the restaurant. She'd always thought of the place as kind of cheesy, but after Rachel had talked about it and Taryn had seen the website, she knew she had to bring Hawk to it. She hoped he would feel at home here.

Once they were parked in the lot, Hawk looked suspiciously at the building that was fashioned to resemble a medieval castle, complete with banners hanging outside.

"What is this place?" he asked.

"It's a restaurant modeled on your time. I think you'll like it."

He didn't say much as she took his hand to lead him inside, but she could tell by his face that he was completely baffled by it. As they waited for the arena to be opened for seating, she took him to the gift shop, where he gravitated toward the wooden swords and shields.

"Bring back fond memories?" she asked. One of the

169

things she'd learned about him was that his "memories" from the book were as real to him as her own past was to her. There really was no difference between fantasy and reality to Hawk.

He nodded. "We practiced with such when I was a squire." But it was the toy trebuchets that held his interest most.

"Would you like one?"

He shook his head. "Nay. I have seen more than my share of them."

She could see by the sadness in his eyes that it brought back unhappy memories. "You've spent much of your time at war, haven't you?"

"Aye. Too much. When I was younger, I never thought there could be anything better than the glory of battle."

"And now?"

His gaze met hers and the heat in those beautiful green eyes set her on fire. "Now I would much rather coax a smile from your face."

She laid her hand against his cheek before she gave him a quick kiss to tide them both over until later.

Wrapping her arm around his, she led him toward the arena and made sure to get them a seat right up front so that he could see the show in all its glory.

"What is this?" he asked as he looked around the staged medieval tournament field.

"While we eat, they're going to reenact knights fighting and practicing."

When their server came up in wench's garb, Hawk did a double take.

"This is all very strange," he said to her once they were alone again. "Familiar and yet not."

Taryn smiled and waited until the knights appeared. Hawk sat forward, his eyes alight with bemused interest.

She was actually thrilled to watch him. It reminded her of a child experiencing his first trip to the circus. "So what do you think?"

He gave her a smug look. "They are most skilled, but I could defeat them."

She laughed at his arrogance, not doubting his abilities in the least.

Taryn was enjoying the show immensely until something went terribly wrong during one of their fight scenes. One of the special effects was a blast of fire that shot too close to one of the horses. The red knight's horse threw its rider and began to run wildly about, shrieking and spooking the other horses. As the red knight stood up, the horse charged him, then dodged before it made contact to run at the barrier wall. The crowd started screaming, which only added to the chaos as the horse reared too close to the wall. Its hooves came dangerously close to the metal barrier.

The red knight tried to catch his horse, only to have it rush at him and trample him.

Taryn cringed. "I think he's hurt. Bad."

Before she realized what was happening, Hawk vaulted over the side of the arena and ran toward the panicking horse. Taryn came to her feet, terrified of what he was about to do.

The horse pawed at him while the staff shouted for him to get back into the stands. Hawk didn't listen. He dodged the horse's flailing hooves and in a move that was poetic and beautiful, he whirled himself into the saddle.

Taryn watched in awe as he took the reins and then carefully brought the animal back under control while the other knights ran to the red knight to make sure he was okay.

Hawk slid from the back of the horse and patted it gently while talking to it in a slow and calm voice.

A man in a black T-shirt and jeans, who must have been the horse's trainer, came out to take the horse away. He said something to Hawk before Hawk inclined his head.

"Our champion!" the king said from his dais, indicating Hawk with a grand extension of his hand. "Truly, he is a marvel. We thank thee, gracious knight."

Hawk turned toward the king and placed his right fist to his left shoulder before he bowed regally. "'Tis an honor to be of service, Your Majesty," he said in a tone that sounded as if he enjoyed playing along with them. Then he ran at the wall and did a flip over it to land just before Taryn.

"Wow," she said, amazed by his ability. "Most impressive."

He shrugged. "Thank you, but it's more impressive in a full suit of armor." He winked at her.

Taryn laughed while the staff cleared the arena and then picked up the show where it had left off.

A few minutes later the man in black came up to them. "Hey," he said, taking the vacant seat next to Taryn. "I just wanted to say thanks for what you did. This was Goliath's first show, and I hate that he got spooked."

"I am just glad that I was able to help," Hawk said.

"You're English?"

"Aye."

The man smiled as he extended his hand to Hawk. "I'm Danny Fairfield."

He shook his hand. "Hawk."

Danny laughed. "So do you do reenactments?"

"All the time," Taryn said. "He can joust with the best of them."

"Really?" Danny looked extremely interested in that tidbit.

"I've trained many a man and squire for battle."

"Well, hey, anytime you want to audition for a position here, just give me a call. We're always on the lookout for new talent."

"Thank you," Hawk said.

Danny got up and paused between them. "By the way, dinner's on us tonight."

"Cool," Taryn said. "We appreciate it."

Danny inclined his head and left them alone. But as he walked away, Taryn's mind whirled.

Hawk could get a job. . . .

"Is something wrong, Taryn?"

She shook her head at Hawk. "No. I was just thinking that we might have found something you are more than qualified to do."

"Is this a good thing?"

"Oh, yeah," she said excitedly. "It means if you were to stay here that you would have a job."

"Do you want me to stay?" he asked with a note of hope in his tone.

Taryn stared at him for a full heartbeat. How could she not want this man to become a permanent part of her world? "Yeah, I think I do."

Sparhawk's heart pounded at that. It was the first time Taryn had said anything about him staying longer than his seven days. It was a good sign. A very good one.

173

But she still said nothing about love, and there were only three more days before he returned to Alinor. It was the last thing he wanted. These last few days with Taryn had been wonderful. Magical. What would he do without her?

In truth, he didn't want to know.

They didn't speak much during the rest of the meal, and once it was over, they returned to Taryn's house.

As they entered the living room, something odd started to happen. Hawk's skin turned grayish.

He looked as if he were completely ill. "What is happening?" he asked.

"I don't know." Taryn helped him toward her couch. He was writhing as if he were in pain. She put her hand on his brow to feel a severe fever. "Baby, are you okay?"

Holding his stomach as if something were rupturing, he grimaced and cursed.

Suddenly her hand passed right through him. "Hawk?"

He looked at her with panic in his eyes. It was as if he were fading out of existence.

"Hawk?"

The next thing she knew, he was gone. There wasn't even a scrap of fabric left behind.

"No!" Taryn screamed as she found herself completely alone in her living room. "You said we had seven days."

Come back to me.

The words whispered through her head as if Sparhawk had said them.

"How?" she asked out loud.

There was no answer. None. He was gone now. Taryn sat there in stunned disbelief as pain washed over her. How could he be gone like this?

o o o

Sparhawk jolted awake to find himself back in his own bed. It was early light by the looks of it. Rolling over on the large hand-carved mahogany bed, he found himself face-to-face with Alinor, who stared at him as if she wanted to run him through with his sword.

"Good," she said, narrowing her gaze on him. "You're back, milord."

"There is nothing good about this," he grumbled, getting up. He had to find the witch and return to Taryn. He hadn't had enough time with her.

Alinor blocked his way to the door. "Where is it you go?"

"'Tis none of your business. Now stand aside."

She lifted her chin defiantly as she held her arms out. "Nay! I most certainly will not. Nor will you leave this castle again. You are my hero, Sparhawk. Mine. You don't belong in that other story with that other woman. Taryn. What sort of name is that anyway? 'Tis a man's name and yet you would sooner be with her than me? I will not allow such."

Sparhawk went cold at her words. "How do you know about Taryn?"

She stamped her foot at him. "Because you cheated!" She threw a book at him.

"Ow!" Sparhawk said as he picked it up. It was the original book of his story, only now it had Alinor's name listed as the author. "What did you do?"

"Me?" She snorted at him. "You're the one who changed it first. I was minding my own business, doing what I was supposed to be doing when you decided to go off and change our lives. Well, I'm not having it. I was supposed to be the damsel you grew to love and you are supposed to be my champion, so now I have created a new master book."

He couldn't breathe as her words sank in. If she had created her own version of their lives, there was nothing he could do to alter it. God help him if she really were the author. "Where is the master book?"

She gave him an arrogant, taunting smile. "Someplace *you* can't find it. But don't worry, I'm writing the story now and we're going to be just fine, you and I. We're going to have lots of children and castles all over Christendom. We'll be the envy of everyone."

It was a nightmare even to contemplate. "I do not love you, Alinor. I love Taryn."

She shrieked at him. "You are going to love me, Sparhawk! You're *my* hero! I know you're resisting it right now because that's what heroes do. But you will settle into this role just as soon as I finish shopping for my wedding clothes. You just wait here and be thoughtful for a bit while I attend my role like a good character."

Sparhawk gaped as she spun about and left the room. Taking three steps, he opened the heavy wooden door. "I will not stay here, Alinor!" he shouted out the door after her.

She paused halfway down to the hall to look back at him with smug satisfaction beaming on her beautiful face. "Oh, yes, you will. I wrote the old witch out of the book entirely, so even if you go into the woods, all you'll find now is a creek that goes nowhere."

Sparhawk slammed the door, then opened it again immediately. He wasn't about to take her word for what was happening. He wasn't going to blithely submit to this storyline. He was Sparhawk the Brave. The king's champion. No one was going to take charge of his life without a fight.

Sprinting through the castle, he ran out to the stable to find his horse waiting for him. He saddled his stallion, then headed back toward the witch's hut.

Only this time, just as Alinor had predicted, there was nothing there but a creek, with large overgrown trees surrounding it. No sign of the hut or witch existed anywhere.

"Damn you, Alinor!" he shouted at the sky above. "I love Taryn."

But there was no one to hear him. Taryn was gone and now it was his fate to marry Alinor again. Heartsick and weary, he wheeled his horse about and headed back to the castle.

Tears gathered in his eyes, but he refused to let them fall. There had to be some way out of this. Some way to reach Taryn again. He couldn't give up, not on his lady.

By the time he reached the castle's gate, he'd decided on a new course of action. He had to find Alinor's master copy of the book. If he did, then there was a chance he could change it as Alinor had done, so that he could return to Taryn and her story.

If not, then he was doomed to stay here forever.

o   o   o

Taryn sat on her bed with voices speaking in her head. She swore she could hear Sparhawk's deep baritone and another woman she'd never met before. The voice was high pitched and whiny. Shrill. It went through her head like shattering glass.

Alinor?

It was eerie what was going on in her head. She could see Sparhawk searching the castle in her mind like a movie. She could feel his despair and his pain as he ached for her and sought his book. Every thought, every emotion he felt, was in her, too. It was as if she was experiencing it with him.

"I'm completely losing my mind."

"No, dear, you're not."

Taryn turned sharply at the old voice behind her. It was Esther. "What are you doing in my house?"

Esther sighed as she came farther into the room to sit beside her. "I'm breaking all kinds of rules . . . again. I'm not supposed to be here, but then I wasn't supposed to be there in the store either, when your car broke down, but I had no choice. I still don't. I have to make this right before it's too late."

"Make what right?"

Esther smiled at her. "Your happy ending."

Taryn rubbed her head as a severe pain started in her right temple. This was it. She had lost her mind. There was nothing more to be done about it. Maybe she should call the psycho ward now.

"You're not crazy," Esther said quietly. "Please don't even think it. We lose enough of you to that as it is."

"Enough of you who?"

"Writers," Esther said simply. "For some reason, a lot of you reject what you hear and see in your heads. If you go too long ignoring it, it builds up and then you do all sorts of weird things. Mumble to yourself. Nightmares. Day-dreams. Total anarchy and chaos. Before you know it, the writer is either sitting in a corner feverishly humming to his- or herself or on Prozac." She hesitated. "You're not on Prozac, are you?"

No, but she was beginning to think she ought to be.

Taryn frowned at her and completely disregarded every-thing she was saying. "How did you get into my house anyway?"

"The front door. You left it unlocked."

No, she hadn't. However, she wasn't about to argue. "How did you know where I lived?"

"I know where all good writers live."

The ache increased. "I'm not a writer," Taryn insisted. "I've never been one."

Esther patted her hand in an extremely patronizing manner. "That's what Hemingway said, too, when I sent him *A Farewell to Arms,* and then look at what he went on to do."

Okay, they were both nuts. But insanity aside, there was only one matter that was weighing heavily on her. "Can you get me back to Sparhawk?"

Esther sighed heavily. "No."

Tears welled in Taryn's eyes as she heard the last word she needed to. She didn't even want to think about not see-ing him again.

Esther leaned forward and spoke in a low tone. "But *you* can."

Taryn swallowed as hope began to swell inside her. "What do you mean I can? If I could, don't you think I'd be there?"

179

"Hon, you already are. Why do you think you can hear him in your head right now?"

"Because I've gone insane."

Esther laughed and shook her head. "No, sweetie. You hear him because *you're* a writer."

Here we go again.

"I don't have time—"

"Remember a few weeks ago, when you had that strange dream about a man lost in the woods?" Esther asked, interrupting her denial.

Taryn snapped her mouth shut. That dream had haunted her for days as she tried to figure out what it meant. She hadn't told a soul about it. Not even Janice.

"How do you know about that?" she asked the old woman.

Esther shrugged as if it were nothing unusual. "I'm the one who sent that dream to you. I'm the repository for romance novels."

"The what?"

"Repository," Esther said in a patient voice. "There are several dozen of us, and we are the keepers of books written and those yet to be written."

Taryn was about to reach for the phone to call the cops when her room suddenly changed from her bedroom to what appeared to be a giant library.

Her heart hammering, she looked about at the glistening shelves that were covered with thousands and thousands of leather-bound books as far as her eyes could see. It was the most incredible thing she'd ever heard of. "I have totally snapped a wheel."

"No, dear. I knew you wouldn't believe it unless you saw

180

it yourself." Esther, who was now dressed in a glowing red robe, walked down a row of shelves, dragging her finger lovingly along the edge of the carved wood. It was obvious the old woman cherished every volume in the room.

"Where is this place?" Taryn asked.

"Let's just say it's 'other.' There's no place like it on earth . . . exactly."

Esther walked over to the shelf on her right and swept her hand across the spines that held no author name whatsoever. "These are all the books that have yet to be written. Each one is a very special creation, and I am one of the overseers who is charged with making sure that the people who live inside the books get to the writer who can birth them properly." She pinned Taryn with a dark stare. "You were destined to be a writer, Taryn, but you have gone astray. Do you remember when you were a girl and you wrote all the time about all the people who talked to you whenever you closed your eyes?"

"Yeah," she said defensively, "and my mother told me to get my head out of the clouds and focus on what was important."

Esther sighed. "I hate it when that happens. We lose so many wonderful stories that way. 'Be practical. Stop listening to the characters who only want to live.' It's why we have people like Sparhawk, and it's why we end up losing them, too. Such a tragedy, really."

Taryn frowned at her words. "What do you mean, losing them, too?"

Esther indicated a steel vaulted door that was on the wall behind Taryn. "That is the Valley of Lost Souls. It's where we send the books whose characters have revolted."

"Revolted?"

She nodded. "You see the characters for the books that haven't yet been written are in a holding pattern while they wait for their stories to be finished. We, the repositories, send out an idea, usually the first chapter or a snippet from later in the book, to the writer. It plays over and over again in the writer's head until the writer is forced to sit down to write it. If the writer fails to follow the idea and commit it to paper, then the characters can get caught in a loop where they relive the same scenes over and over again, sometimes with only minor changes until they essentially go mad from the monotony. Then they can get a little cranky and revolt against the writer and us."

Esther shivered as if the very mention of it horrified her. "So whenever we sense that is happening, we pull the characters out of that writer's mind, then send them on to another writer where the process repeats until someone finally pens the story of their lives."

Taryn stared at all the volumes of "unwritten" books. "I don't understand. Where do all these ideas come from?"

Esther shrugged as she glanced over the infinity of books. "They are gifts from the universe to mankind. Honestly, we don't know where they come from. They just appear on the shelves, and we are charged with bringing them to life. It's kind of like a child being born. Where does his or her soul come from? Some call it God, others fate, whatever you believe or want to call it, it sends the books to us. Our personal theory is that a baby's soul and a character's soul are born from the same place. Some are destined to be living, breathing people in the flesh, and the others are living, breathing people on paper."

Esther picked up a book off the shelf closest to her and handed it to Taryn.

Just like the copy of *Knightly Dreams* Esther had given her in the store, there was no author listed. The cover showed a dark-haired Regency rake holding on to a scantily clad blond woman. "This book has been sent out over and over again these last few years. The first writer decided she didn't want to do romances and went on to write mysteries instead. The next one was all excited to write it until she got married. Another one got all the way to the middle of the book before she got rejected one time too many and decided she couldn't take the rejections anymore. She quit and burned what she'd written. The last writer we sent it to finished the first three chapters, but has since become distracted by a rumor that no one wants to read historical romances anymore. So she has set the book aside to write something she thinks is more marketable."

Esther sighed as if her heart were broken. "All we have now are the first three chapters and they repeat over and over again. The characters are in London, in the Regency period, where they attend the same party and speak the same lines ad nauseam. Miles is a rake, but he, like Sparhawk, is tired of listening to Henrietta rant about her season and her boorish uncle out to steal her inheritance. If the writer doesn't return soon, then I shall have to send this off to another to write before we lose the characters completely."

"Lose them how?"

Esther took the book back and held it lovingly in her arms. "They essentially start writing the story themselves and refuse to take orders from a writer. If we have a strong enough writer who loves them, then she can save them. If there is no writer, then they can no longer be corralled and the story falls apart. You have medieval knights abducting Regency governesses, dogs sleeping with chickens. Chaos. Total chaos. The story is then lost for all time, and we are forced to place the book in that room." She indicated the vault again. "It's truly tragic. The greatest book of all time is in there now because the author who was destined to write it thought he was losing his mind when he started hearing the characters talking to him. He's now on Prozac, living in an isolated cabin in Montana."

Taryn was still confused by all of this. "Are you telling me that Sparhawk isn't real?"

"Oh, no," she said sincerely. "They're *all* real. All of them. Just like you or I, only they live in their own world that is apart from ours. I allowed Sparhawk to cross over from his world into yours in a more tangible form so that he could win you. I knew that if you didn't fall absolutely head over heels in love with him, you wouldn't save him, and if he had to go back on the shelf one more time, he would rebel and take over his book so that no one would ever be able to finish it. Now it appears that Alinor has rebelled instead of him and threatens the whole thing."

Esther handed her a copy of *Knightly Dreams*. Sparhawk was again on the cover, just as he'd been originally. Only now the author's name read Alinor de Blakely.

Taryn ran her hand over the embossed letters. "How can she do this?"

"Alinor has found the original copy and has taken it over. She wanted Sparhawk back and so she has written his return." Esther opened the book to show her the parts that now held her name on the pages.

Taryn's heart stilled as she saw her life laid out in ink. It was horrifying. "This can't be."

"Yes, hon, it can and it is." Esther turned to the last page of the book, where it showed Alinor marrying Sparhawk.

Taryn's heart sank. The book was over and she wasn't mentioned at the end.

"Don't despair," Esther said quickly. "Notice there is room on the page and if you turn to the last page of the book, it's completely blank."

"Most books are like that."

"Yes, but not all. Those with no blank pages are the ones that are completely finished. There is nothing more to be done with them. But books like this one, where they have blank pages, can still be added to."

A glimmer of hope went through Taryn. "What exactly are you saying?"

Esther handed her a pen that appeared out of thin air. "I'm saying that you can alter Alinor's book and make it your own. We are all the authors of our own lives, Taryn. We make the rules of our world, and we are the ones who decide which road to take. It's all up to you and you alone. This story ends the way you want it to. But only if you have the courage and the imagination to see it through."

It sounded too good to be true. Too easy. "But it won't be a published book."

Esther held her hand out to indicate all the books around them. "Only a small percentage of all books written ever get published, dearest. Many more stay in the hearts, minds, and closets of their authors forever after they are committed to paper. They are there solely for the author's pleasure and benefit alone. But more importantly, they are there for the characters because until they are on paper, the characters aren't truly alive. Every author owes it to her people to birth them as best as he or she can."

Esther urged her toward a table that also appeared out of thin air. "Sparhawk the Brave is in desperate need of a champion of his own. Someone who can save him from certain death and torment. Otherwise he will spend eternity with Alinor lost in the vault."

Taryn knew from the short time they had been together just how much Sparhawk hated the thought of being stuck with Alinor. Esther was right. It would kill him.

If what she said could be believed, then Taryn was his only hope. . . .

Esther gave her a hopeful look. "So what's it to be, Taryn?"

FOUR

Taryn was still confused even after Esther had dropped her back into her home. Then again, who wouldn't be confused after being dropped in and out of places? She still wasn't completely sure she wasn't in the middle of some psychotic episode. Her entire concept of reality was completely altered now. Maybe she *was* in a book.

Maybe nothing was real.

No, she thought as she pinched herself for the eighth time. She was real. This was her house. Her life. And there for a time, Hawk had shared it all with her.

Now, as she lay on her bed with the paperback that had Sparhawk on the cover, her mind drifted through the last few days—something that was easy to do since everything they had shared was there in black-and-white. Everything. Every time they had made love, every meal, every line. It even had her in the library or whatever that place had been.

It was so odd to see her name on the pages, to read in the book what the two of them had done.

But even scarier than the passages with her in them were the ones where she was off in her own world and Hawk was in his. Alone. Those were horrible scenes with Hawk being wounded and tortured for no apparent reason. Perhaps it was Alinor's way of getting back at him for his having escaped in the first place.

Taryn didn't know. All she knew was that she didn't want him to suffer any more than she wanted to face the rest of her life without him. He'd been wonderful.

God help her, but he really had been her hero and she wanted him back.

"I have to save him," she whispered as she read one particularly painful page where he was gored by a wild boar in the woods while saving Alinor from pygmy bandits. . . . Pygmy bandits? Ay! If Alinor really was writing this, she had lost her mind completely.

Taryn sat up with the book. "Okay, let's pretend that I'm not hallucinating and that everything Esther has told me is the truth. . . ."

Then she could save him. She laughed in spite of herself. This had to be the most ludicrous thing she'd ever done. But what the heck? What did she really have to lose?

"Either I'll get him back or they'll lock me up," she said under her breath as she grabbed the pen. "Okay, Esther. Here goes nothing."

Closing her eyes, Taryn conjured up a picture of Sparhawk in her mind as he was on page 342 in the book, just after his return to his world.

He should be alone, sitting at the table with his head in

his hands. The chapter ended there, but there was blank space at the end of the paragraph. . . .

Taryn opened her heart and listened carefully until she could see and hear Hawk clearly. Her chest tight in fear of failing, she started writing. . . .

Sparhawk sat in his hall, completely bereft of hope. Alinor had hidden the master book so well that he had no idea where it might be. There was no way back to Taryn. No way to get out of this so long as Alinor had control of their story.

Damn her for this! How could she be so selfish? But then, that was what had caused him to want to escape her clutches to begin with.

"I miss you, Lady Taryn," he breathed.

"I missed you, too."

Sparhawk shot to his feet as he heard the tender voice behind him. It couldn't be, and yet as he turned, he saw his lady there, watching him with a guarded expression. Her smile was gentle as she looked up at him.

"Wow," she said, looking around his hall. "It really worked."

He couldn't believe what he was seeing. Was it possible? "How is it that you are here?"

Taryn held the book up in her hand, and this time the author's name on the cover was hers. "I'm making some changes in how the story goes."

He frowned. "What?"

She drew near him. "Esther said that I was supposed to be the writer of your book, so here I am . . . writing for the first time since I was a kid. It's actually kind of fun. Did you know Alinor is off shopping?"

"'Tis what she told me."

"Yeah, but she has tacky taste in jewelry," Taryn said as she made a note in the book. "But that's okay. The jeweler is about to look a lot like my ex-boyfriend. In fact, I'm thinking Rob really should end up with Alinor. She's demanding and beastly. They should be quite happy together, especially after I give Rob some very choice moles in awkward locations." She wagged her brows at him.

Hawk shook his head at her. "And what about me?"

Taryn sat down at the table where he'd been and started writing. One minute they were in his castle, and in the next they were back at her house, naked in her bed.

Hawk frowned at her. "I don't understand this."

"Neither do I. At least not exactly. But that's okay. Esther said that I was the author of my own life, so I am going to make sure that . . ." Taryn paused as a bad thought struck her. "Wait. I'm being extremely selfish here. I didn't even ask you what you wanted."

Fear gripped her as she realized that for all she knew, Hawk wanted to return to the Middle Ages and be with someone else.

His gaze hooded, he looked rather hesitant. "Do you want the truth?"

Be careful what you ask for; you just might get it. . . .

Her mother's favorite phrase went through her as panic swelled in her heart. *C'mon, Taryn, you're a big girl. You can handle whatever he says.*

As a character, Hawk had never had any say in his life. The least she could do was give him a choice in this. "Yeah," she said quietly. "I want the truth."

He reached out to brush the hair back from her face. "What I want . . ."

She waited for him to speak as he continued to play with her hair. "Is . . . ?" she prompted.

"You," he said before he pulled her into a sizzling kiss.

Taryn groaned at the taste of her medieval knight. Hawk was everything she had ever dreamed of. Everything she'd ever wanted. She nipped at his lips before she pulled back. "Okay, then, we shall have a big wedding. . . ."

Sparhawk watched as she started writing lines in her book. Every time she got to the bottom of the page, she turned it over and a new blank page appeared magically at the end of the book so that she could continue onward with her writing.

He tried to read what she was writing, but couldn't understand it. "What are you putting there, Taryn?"

"I am making you independently wealthy, 'cause we know that all good heroes are, and I'm making sure that Alinor's copy of the book is spontaneously combusting into flames."

"Can you do that?"

She smiled at him. "Baby, I'm the writer. According to Esther, I can do anything I want to."

"And so what do you wish to do now?"

Taryn bit her lip as she raked a hungry gaze over his naked body. "Right now I wish to spend the rest of my day making love to you."

She kissed him on his cheek, then scribbled a few more words.

"What are you saying now?" he asked.

She smiled at him. "I'm writing that we go on to live happily ever after."

And then Taryn made sure to do the one thing that Alinor had forgotten to do. It was the one thing to make sure that no one added any more pages to her future or altered her life with Sparhawk.

She wrote the three most powerful words on the planet. "I love you."

"Do you?" Hawk asked her.

Taryn paused as she realized that she had spoken those words out loud. "Yes, Sparhawk the Brave. I do."

"Good," he whispered, nuzzling her neck as his whiskers gently scraped her skin. "Because I love you, too."

Her heart melted at his words. And then she quickly added the other two most powerful words on earth . . . The End.

DRAGONSWAN

ONE

"**Be** kind to dragons, for thou art crunchy when roasted and taste good with ketchup."

Dr. Channon MacRae paused in her note-taking and arched a brow at the peculiar comment. She'd been staring at the famous Dragon Tapestry for hours, trying to decipher the Old English symbolism, and in all this time no one had disturbed her.

Not until now.

With her most irritated look, she pulled her pen away from her notepad and turned.

Then she gaped.

No annoying, irreverent little man here. He was a tall, mind-blowingly sexy god who dominated the small museum room with a presence so powerful that she wondered how on earth he had entered the building without shaking it to its foundations.

Never in her life had she beheld anything like him or the seductive smile he flashed at her.

Good grief, she couldn't take her eyes off him.

Standing at least six feet five, he towered over her average height. His long black hair was pulled back into a sleek ponytail, and he wore an expensively tailored black suit and overcoat that seemed at odds with his unorthodox hair yet perfectly fitting with his regal aura.

But the most peculiar thing of all was the tattoo covering the left half of his face. A faded dark green, it spiraled and curled from his hairline to his chin like some ancient symbol.

On anyone else such a mark would be freakish or strange, but this man wore it with dignity and presence—like a proud birthright.

Yet it was his eyes that captivated her most. A rich, deep, greenish-gold, they were filled with such warm intelligence and vitality that it left her completely breathless.

His grin was both boyish and roguish and framed by inviting dimples that enchanted her. "Rendered you speechless, eh?"

She loved the sound of his voice, which was laced with an accent she couldn't quite place. It seemed a unique blending of the British and Greek. Not to mention, deep and provocative.

"Not quite speechless," she said, resisting the urge to smile back at him. "I'm just wondering why you would say such a thing."

He shrugged his broad shoulders nonchalantly as his golden gaze dropped to her lips, making her want to lick them. Worse, his prolonged stare sent a rush of desire coiling though her.

Suddenly, it was so extremely warm in this little glass room that she half expected the gallery windows to fog up.

He folded his hands casually behind his back, yet he seemed coiled for action, as if he were ready and alert to take on anyone who threatened him.

What a strange image to have . . .

When he spoke again, his deep voice was even more seductive and enticing than it had been before, almost as if it were weaving some kind of magical spell around her. "You had such a serious frown while you were staring at the tapestry that it made me wonder what you would look like with a smile in its place."

Oh, the man was beguiling. And just a little too cocksure of his appeal, judging by his arrogant stance. No doubt he could get any woman who caught his eye.

Channon swallowed at the thought as she glanced down at her tan corduroy jumper and her hips, which were not the fashionable, narrow kind. She'd never been the type of woman who drew the notice of a man like this. She'd been lucky if her average looks ever garnered her a second glance at all.

Mr. Do-Me-Right-Now must have lost a bet or something. Why else would he be speaking to her?

Still, there was an air of danger, intrigue, and power about him. But none of deceit. He appeared honest and, strangely enough, interested in her.

How could that be?

"Yes, well," she said, taking a step to her left as she

closed her pad and slid her pen down the spiral coil, "I don't make it my habit to converse with strangers, so if you'll excuse me . . ."

"Sebastian."

Startled by his response, she paused and looked up. "What?"

"My name is Sebastian." He held his hand out to her. "Sebastian Kattalakis. And you are?"

Completely stunned and amazed that you're talking to me.

She blinked the thought away. "Channon," she said before she could stop herself. "Shannon with a C."

His gaze burned her while a small smile hovered at the edges of those well-shaped lips and he flashed the tiniest bit of his dimples. There was an indescribable masculine aura about him that seemed to say he would be far more at home on some ancient battlefield than locked inside this museum.

He took her cold hand into his large, warm one. "So very pleased to meet you, Shannon with a C."

He kissed her knuckles like some gallant knight of long ago. Her heart pounded at the feel of his hot breath against her skin, of his warm lips on her flesh. It was all she could do not to moan from the sheer pleasure of it.

No man had ever treated her this way—like some treasured lady to be quested for.

She felt oddly beautiful around him. Desirable.

"Tell me, Channon," he said, releasing her hand and glancing from her to the tapestry. "What has you so interested in this?"

Channon looked back at it and the intricate embroidery

that covered the yellowed linen. Honestly, she didn't know. Since she'd first seen it as a little girl, she'd been in love with this ancient masterpiece. She'd spent years studying the detailed dragon fable that started with the birth of a male infant and a dragon and moved forward through ten feet of fabric.

Scholars had written countless papers on their theories of its origin. She, herself, had done her dissertation on it, trying to link it to the tales of King Arthur or to Celtic tradition.

No one knew where the tapestry had come from or even what story it related to. For that matter, no one knew who had won the fight between the dragon and the warrior.

That was what intrigued her most of all.

"I wish I knew how it ended."

He flexed his jaw. "The story has no ending. The battle between the dragon and the man lives on unto today."

She frowned at him. He appeared serious. "You think so?"

"What?" he asked good-naturedly. "You don't believe me?"

"Let's just say I have a hefty dose of doubt."

He took a step forward, and again his fierce, manly presence overwhelmed her and sent a jolt of desire through her. "Hmmm, a hefty dose of doubt," he said, his voice barely more than a low, deep growl. "I wonder what I could do to make you believe?"

She should step back, she knew it. Yet she couldn't make her feet cooperate. His clean, spicy scent invaded her head and weakened her knees.

What was it about this man that made her want to stand here talking to him?

Oh, to heck with that. What she really wanted to do was jump his delectable bones. To cup that handsome face of his in her hands and kiss his lips until she was drunk from his taste.

There was something seriously wrong here.

Mayday. Mayday.

"Why are you here?" she asked, trying to keep her lecherous thoughts at bay. "You hardly look like the type to study medieval relics."

A wicked gleam came into his eyes. "I'm here to steal it."

She scoffed at the idea, even though something inside her said it wouldn't be too much of a stretch to buy that explanation. "Are you really?"

"Of course. Why else would I be here?"

"Why else, indeed?"

Sebastian didn't know what it was about this woman that drew him so powerfully. He was involved in grave matters that required his full attention, yet for the life of him, he couldn't take his gaze from her.

She wore her honey-brown hair swept up so that it cascaded in riotous waves from a silver clip of old Welsh design. Several strands of it had come free of the clip to dangle haphazardly around her face as if the strands had a life of their own.

How he longed to set free that hair and feel it sliding through his fingers and brushing against his naked chest.

He dropped his gaze down over her lush, full body and stifled his smile. Her dark blue shirt wasn't buttoned properly and her socks didn't match.

Still, she drove him crazy with desire.

She wasn't the kind of woman who normally drew his interest, and yet . . .

He was beguiled by her and her crystal blue gaze that glowed with warm curiosity and intelligence. He longed to sample her full, moist lips, to bury his face in the hollow of her throat where he could drink in her scent.

Gods, how he yearned for her. It was a need borne of such desperation that he wondered what kept him from taking her into his arms right now and satisfying his curiosity.

He'd never been the kind of man to deny himself carnal pleasures—especially not when the beast inside him was stirred. And this woman stirred that deadly part of him to a dangerous level.

Sebastian had only come into the museum to get the lay of it for tonight and to find out where they housed the tapestry. He hadn't been looking for a woman to pass the lonely night with until he could return home where he would be . . . well, lonely again.

However, he still had hours before he could leave. Hours that he would much rather spend gazing into her eyes than waiting in his hotel room.

"Would you care to join me for a drink?" he asked.

She looked startled by his question. But then he seemed to have that effect on her. She was nervous around him, a bit jumpy, and he longed to set her at ease.

"I don't go out with men I don't know."

"How can you get to know me unless you . . ."

"Really, Mr. Kat—"

"Sebastian."

She shook her head at him. "You are persistent, aren't you?"

She had no idea.

Suppressing the predator inside him, Sebastian put his hands in his pockets to keep from reaching out to her and scaring her off. "I'm afraid it's ingrained in me. When I see something I want, I go after it."

She arched a brow at that and gave him a suspicious look. "Why on earth would you want to talk to me?"

He was aghast at her question. "My lady, do you not own a mirror?"

"Yes, but it's not an enchanted one." She turned away from him and started away.

Moving with the incredible speed of his kind, Sebastian pulled her to a stop.

"Look, Channon," he said gently. "I fear I have bungled this. I just . . ." He stopped and tried to think of the best way to keep her with him for a while longer.

She looked to his hand, which still gripped her elbow. He reluctantly let go, even though every part of his soul screamed for him to hold her by his side, regardless of the consequences. She was a woman with her own mind. And the first law of his people ran through his head: Nothing a woman gives is worth having unless she gives it of her own free will.

It was the one law not even he would break.

"You what?" she asked softly.

Sebastian drew a deep breath as he fought down the animal part of himself that wanted her regardless of right or laws, the part of him that snarled with a need so fierce that it scared him.

He forced a charming smile to his lips. "You seem like a

very nice person, and there are so few of you in this world that I would like to spend a few minutes with you. Maybe some of it might rub off."

Channon laughed in spite of herself.

"Ah," he teased, "so you *can* smile."

"I can smile."

"Will you join me?" he asked. "There's a restaurant on the corner. We can walk there, in plain sight of the world. I promise, I won't bite unless you ask me to."

Channon frowned lightly at him and his quirky humor. What was it about him that made him so irresistible? It was unnatural. "I don't know about this."

"Look, I promise I'm not psychotic. Eccentric and idio-syncratic, but not psychotic."

She still wasn't completely sure about that. "I'll bet the prisons are full of men who have told women that."

"I would *never* hurt a woman, least of all you."

There was such sincerity in his voice that she believed him. Even more convincing, she didn't feel any inner warnings, no little voice in her head telling her to run.

Instead, she was drawn to him and felt a most peculiar kind of serenity in his presence, almost as if she were supposed to be with him. "Down the street?"

"Yes." He offered her his arm. "C'mon. I promise I'll keep my fangs hidden and my mind control to myself."

Channon had never done anything like this in her life. She was a woman who had to know a guy for a long time before she'd even consider a date.

Yet she found herself pulling on her coat and placing her hand in the crook of his arm, where she felt a muscle so taut and well formed that it sent a jolt through her.

By the feel of that arm, she could tell his fashionable black suit and overcoat hid one incredible body.

"You seem so different," she said as he walked her out of the room. "Something about you is very Old World."

He opened the glass door that led to the museum's foyer. "*Old* being the operative word."

"And yet you're very modern."

"A Renaissance man trapped between cultures."

"Is that what you are?"

He cast a playful sideways look to her. "Honestly?"

"Yes."

"I'm a dragon slayer."

She laughed out loud.

He scoffed. "Again you don't believe me."

"Let's just say it's no wonder you said you wanted to steal the tapestry. I suppose there's not much call for slaying a mythological beast, especially in this day and age."

Those greenish-gold eyes teased her unmercifully. "You don't believe in dragons?"

"No, of course not."

He *tsk*ed at her. "You are so skeptical."

"I'm practical."

Sebastian ran his tongue over his teeth as a sly half-smile curved his lips. A practical woman who didn't believe in dragons yet studied dragon tapestries and wore a misbuttoned shirt. Surely there wasn't another soul like her in any time or place. And she had the strangest effect on his body.

He was already hard for her, and they were barely touching. Her grip on his arm was light and delicate, as if she was ready to flee him at any moment.

That was the last thing he wanted, and that surprised him most of all.

A reclusive person, he only interacted with others when his physical needs overrode his desire for solitude. Even then, those encounters were brief and limited. He took his lovers for one night, making sure they were as well sated as he, then he quickly returned to his solitary world.

He'd never dawdled with idle conversation. Never really cared to get to know more about a woman than her name and the way she liked to be touched.

But Channon was different. He liked the cadence of her voice and the way her eyes sparkled when she talked. Most of all, he liked the way her smile lit up her entire face when she looked at him.

And the sound of her laughter . . . He doubted if the angels in heaven could make a more precious melody.

Sebastian opened the door to the dark restaurant and held it for her while she entered. As she swept past him, he let his gaze travel down the back of her body. He hardened even more.

What he wouldn't give to have her warm and naked in his arms so that he could run his hands down her full curves, nibble the flesh of her neck, and hold her to him as he slowly slid himself deep inside her while she writhed to his touch.

Sebastian forced himself to look away from Channon and to speak to the hostess. He sent a mental command to the unknown woman to sit them in a secluded corner. He wanted privacy with Channon.

How he wished he'd met her sooner. He'd been in this cursed city for well over a week, waiting for the opportunity to go home, where if not the comfort of warmth, he at least had the comfort of familiarity. He'd spent his nights in this city alone, prowling the streets restlessly as he bided his time.

At dawn, he would have to leave. But until then, he intended to spend as much time with Channon as he could, letting her company ease the loneliness inside him, ease the pain in his heart that had burned him for most of his life.

Channon followed the hostess through the restaurant, but all the while she was aware of Sebastian behind her—aware of his hot, predatorial gaze on her body and the way he seemed to want to devour her.

But even more unbelievable was the fact that she wanted to devour *him*. No man had ever made her feel so much like a woman or made her want to spend hours exploring his body with her hands and mouth.

"You're nervous again," he said after they were seated in a dark corner in the back of the pub.

She glanced up from the menu to catch sight of those greenish-gold eyes that reminded her of some feral beast. "You are incredibly perceptive."

He inclined his head toward her. "I've been accused of worse."

"I'll bet you have," she teased back. Indeed, he had the presence of an outlaw. Dangerous, dark, seductive. "Are you really a thief?"

"Define the term *thief*."

She laughed even though she wasn't quite sure if he was joking or serious.

"So tell me," he said as the waitress brought their drinks, "what do you do for a living, Shannon with a C?"

She thanked the waitress for her Coke, then looked to Sebastian to see how he would deal with her occupation. Most men were a bit intimidated by her job, though she'd never been able to figure out why. "I'm a history professor at the University of Virginia."

"Impressive," he said, his face genuinely interested. "What cultures and times do you specialize in?"

She was amazed he knew anything about her job. "Mostly pre-Norman Britain."

"Ah. Hwæt wē Gār-Dena in geār-dagum Þēod-cyninga Þrym gefrūnon, hū ðā æÞhelingas ellen fremedon."

Channon was floored by his Old English. He spoke it as if he'd been born to it. Imagine a man so handsome knowing a subject so dear to her heart.

She offered him the translation. "So. The Spear-Danes in days gone by and the kings who ruled them had courage and greatness. We have heard of those princes' heroic campaigns."

His inclined his head to her. "You know your *Beowulf* well."

"I've studied Old English extensively, which, given my job, makes sense. But you don't strike me as a historian."

"I'm not. Rather, I'm a sort of reenactor."

That explained the way he looked. Now his presence in the museum and knightly air of authority made sense to her.

"Is your study of the Middle Ages what had you in the museum today?" he asked.

She nodded. "I've studied the tapestry for years. I want to be the person who finally unravels the mystery behind it."

"What would you like to know?"

"Who made it and why? Where the story of it comes from. For that matter, I would love to know how the museum got it. They have no record of when they acquired it or from whom it was purchased."

His automatic answers surprised her. "They bought it in 1926 from an anonymous collector for fifty thousand dollars. As for the rest, it was made by a woman named Antiphone back in seventh-century Britain. It's the story of her grandfather and his brother and their eternal struggle between good and evil."

His gaze was so sincere that she could almost believe him. In a strange way, it made sense, since the tapestry had no ending.

But she knew better. "Antiphone, huh?"

He shook his head. "You just don't believe anything I tell you, do you?"

"Why, kind sir," she said impishly with a mock English accent. "'Tis not that I don't believe you, but as a historian I must align myself with fact. Have you any proof of this Antiphone or transaction?"

"I do, but I somehow doubt you would appreciate my showing it to you."

"And why is that?"

"It would scare the life out of you."

Channon sat back at that, unsure of how to take it. She didn't really know what to make of the man sitting across from her. He kept her on edge all the while he lured her toward his danger. Lured her against all her reason.

They remained quiet as their food was placed on the table.

While they ate, Channon studied him. The candlelight in

the pub danced in his eyes, making them glow like a cat's. His hands were strong and callused—the hands of a man who was used to hard work—yet he had the air of wealth and privilege, the air of a powerful man who made his own rules.

He was a total enigma, a walking dichotomy who made her feel both safe and threatened.

"Tell me, Channon," he said suddenly, "do you like teaching?"

"Some days. But it's the research I like best. I love digging through old manuscripts and trying to piece together the past."

He gave a short half laugh. "No offense, but that sounds incredibly boring."

"I imagine dragon slaying is much more action-oriented."

"Yes, it is. Every moment is completely unpredictable."

She wiped her mouth as she watched him eat with perfect European table manners. He was definitely cultured, yet he seemed oddly barbaric. "So, how do you kill a dragon?"

"With a very sharp sword."

She shook her head at him. "Yes, but do you call him out? Do you go to him . . . ?"

"The easiest way is to sneak up on him."

"And pray he doesn't wake up?"

"Well, it makes it more challenging if he does."

Channon smiled. She was so drawn to that infectious wit of his. Especially since he didn't seem to notice the women around them who were ogling him while they ate. It was as if he could only see her.

As a rule, she stunk at this whole male-female thing. Her

last boyfriend, a D.C. correspondent, had educated her well on every personal and physical flaw she possessed. The last thing she was looking for was another relationship in which she wasn't on equal terms with the man.

For her next love interest, she wanted someone just like her—a historian of average looks whose life revolved around research. Two comfortable peas in a pod.

She wasn't looking for some hot, mysterious stranger who made her blood burn with desire.

Channon, would you listen to yourself and what you're saying! You are insane not to want this man!

Perhaps. But things like this never happened to her.

"You know," she said to him, "I keep having this really weird feeling that you're going to take me someplace later and tie me up naked so that your friends can come laugh at me."

He arched a brow at her. "Does that happen to you often?"

"No, never, but this night has the makings for a *Twilight Zone* episode."

"I promise no Rod Serling voice-overs. You're safe with me."

And for some reason that made absolutely no sense whatsoever, she believed him.

Channon spent the next few hours having the dinner and conversation of her life. Sebastian was incredibly easy to talk to. Worse, he set her hormones on fire.

The longer they were together and the more laughs they shared, the more incredible he seemed.

She glanced at her watch and gasped. "Did you know it's almost midnight?"

He checked his watch.

"I hate to cut this short," she said, placing her napkin on the table and sliding her chair back, "but I have to go or I'll never get a taxi out of here."

He placed his hand lightly on her arm to keep her at the table. "Why don't you let me drive you home?"

Channon started to protest, but something inside her refused. After the evening they had spent together, she felt oddly at ease with him. There was an aura about him that was so comforting, so open and welcoming.

He was like a long lost friend.

"Okay," she said, relaxing.

He paid for their food. Then he helped her up and into her coat and led her from the restaurant.

Channon didn't speak as they made their way toward his car down the street, but she felt his magnetic, masculine presence with every single cell of her body.

Though not a social butterfly by any account, she'd had plenty of dates in her life. She'd had a number of boyfriends and even a fiancé, but none of them had ever made her feel the way this stranger did.

Like he fit some missing part of her soul.

Girl, you are crazy.

She must be.

Channon paused as they neared his sporty gray Lexus. "Someone travels in style."

Winking devilishly at her, Sebastian opened the car door. "Well, I would turn into a dragon and fly you home, but something tells me you would protest."

"No doubt. I imagine the scales would also chafe my skin."

"True. Not to mention, I once learned the hard way that they really do call the military out on you. You know, fighter jets are hard to dodge when you have a forty-foot wing-span." He closed her door and walked to his side of the car.

She laughed yet again, but then she'd been doing that most of the night. Goodness, she *really* liked this man.

Sebastian got into the car and felt his body jerk the instant they were locked inside together. Her feminine scent permeated his head. She was so close to him now that he could almost taste her.

All night long he had listened to the dulcet sound of her smooth Southern drawl, watched her tongue and lips move as he imagined what they would feel like on his body, imagined her in his arms while he made love to her until she cried out from pleasure.

His attraction to her stunned him. Why did he have to feel this now, when he couldn't afford to stay in her time and explore more of her?

Cursed Fates. How they loved to tamper in mortal lives.

Pushing the thought out of his mind, he drove her to the hotel where she was staying.

"You don't live here?" he asked as he parked in the lot.

"Just here for the weekend to study the tapestry." She unbuckled her seat belt.

Sebastian got out and opened her door, then walked her to her room.

Channon hesitated at the door as she looked up at him and the searing heat in his captivating eyes. The man was so hot and sexy in the most dangerous of ways.

212

She wondered if she would ever see him again. He hadn't asked for her number. Not even her email.

Damn.

"Thank you," she said. "I had a really good time tonight."

"I did, too. Thanks for joining me."

Kiss me. The words rushed across her mind unexpectedly. She really wanted to know what this man felt like against her.

To her amazement, she found out as he pulled her into his arms and covered her lips with his.

Sebastian growled at the feel of her as he fisted his hands against her back. He clutched her to him as every fiber of his body burned and ached to possess her. Her tongue swept against his, teasing him, tormenting him.

She brushed her hand against the nape of his neck, sending chills all over his body, making him so hard for her that he throbbed painfully. He closed his eyes while he let all of his senses experience her. Her mouth tasted of honey, and her hands were soft and warm against his skin. She smelled of woman and flowers, and he thrilled at the sound of her ragged breathing as she answered his passion with her own.

Take her. The animal inside him stirred with a fierce snarl. It snapped and clawed at the human part of him, demanding he cede his humanity to it. It wanted her.

He was almost powerless against the onslaught, and his hands trembled from the force of holding himself back. He growled from the effort of it.

Channon moaned at the fierce feel of his powerful arms locked around her. She was pressed so tight against his

213

chest that she could feel his heart pounding against her breasts.

His intensity surrounded her, filled her, made her burn with volcanic need. All she could think of was stripping his clothes off him and seeing if his body really was as spectacular as it felt.

He pressed her back against her door, pinning her to it as he deepened his kiss. His warm, masculine scent filled her senses, overwhelming her.

He kissed his way from her lips and down across her cheek, then he buried his lips against her neck. "Let me make love to you, Channon," he breathed in her ear. "I want to feel your warm, soft body against mine. Feel your breath on my naked skin."

She should be offended by his suggestion. They barely knew each other. Yet no matter how hard she tried to talk herself out of this, she couldn't.

Deep inside, she wanted the same thing.

Against all reason—all sanity—she ached for him.

Never in her life had she done anything like this. Not once. Yet she found herself opening the door to her room and letting him in.

Sebastian breathed deeply in relief as he struggled for control. He'd never come so close to using his powers on a woman. It was forbidden for his kind to interfere with human freewill unless it was in defense of their lives or someone else's. He'd bent that rule a time or two to serve his purposes.

Tonight, had she refused him, he held no doubt he would have broken it.

But she hadn't refused him. Thank the gods for small favors.

He watched her as she set her key card on the dresser. She hesitated and he felt her nervousness.

"I won't hurt you, Channon."

She offered him a tentative smile. "I know."

He cupped her face in his hands and stared into those celestial blue eyes. "You are so beautiful."

Channon held her breath as he pulled her to him and recaptured her lips. None of this night made sense to her. None of her feelings. She clung to Sebastian as she sought for an explanation for why she had let him into her room.

Why she was going to make love to him. A stranger. A man she knew nothing about. A man she would like as not never see again.

Yet none of that mattered. All that mattered was this moment in time—holding him close to her and keeping him here in her room for as long as she could.

She felt his hands free her hair to cascade down her back. He slid her coat from her shoulders, and she let it fall to the floor. Running his hands up her arms, he pulled back to stare down at her with hungry eyes. No man had ever given her such a look. One of fierce longing, of total possession.

Scared and excited, she helped him from his overcoat. His eyes dark with unsated passion, he removed his jacket and tossed it aside without care that it would be wrinkled later. So much for his impeccable suit. It thrilled her that she meant more to him than that.

He loosened his tie and pulled it over his head.

His eyes softened as she moved to unbutton his shirt. He caught her right hand in his and nibbled her fingertips, sending ribbons of pleasure through her, then he led her hand to his buttons and watched her intently.

Hot and aching for him, Channon worked the buttons through the buttonholes of his shirt. She trailed her gaze after her hands, watching as she bared his skin inch by slow, studied inch. Oh, good heavens, the man had a body that had been ripped from her dreams. His muscles were tight and perfect and covered by the most luscious tawny skin she'd ever seen. Dark hairs dusted his skin, making him seem even more like a predator, even more dangerous and manly.

Channon paused at the hard abs that held several scars. She traced her hand over them, feeling his sharp intake of breath as her fingers brushed the raised, lighter skin. "What happened?"

"Dragons have sharp talons," he whispered. "Sometimes I don't get out of the way quickly enough."

She placed her hand over one really nasty-looking scar by his hipbone. "Maybe you should fight smaller dragons."

"That wouldn't be very sporting of me."

She swallowed as he removed his shirt and she saw his unadorned chest for the first time. He was scrumptious. She ran her palm over his taut, hard pecs, delighting in the way they felt under her hands. She ran her fingers up his chest and across his lean, hard shoulder, which was tattooed with a dragon. "You do like dragons, don't you?"

He laughed. "Yes, I do."

Sebastian was doing his best to be patient, to let her get used to him. But it was hard when all he really wanted to do was lay her down on the bed and relieve the fierce ache in his loins.

He nibbled at her neck as he unfastened the buttons on her jumper and let it fall to the floor. She stood before him wearing nothing but her shoes and her misbuttoned shirt. It was the sexiest thing he'd ever seen in his four hundred years of living. "Do you always button your shirts like this?"

She looked down and gasped. "Oh, good grief. I was in a hurry this morning and—"

He stopped her words with a kiss. "Don't apologize," he whispered against her lips. "I like it."

"You're a very strange man."

"And you are a goddess."

Channon shook her head at him as he picked her up in his arms and moved with her toward the bed. She placed her hands over his muscles, which were taut from his strain. The feel of them made her mouth water. He laid her gently on the mattress, then ran his hands down her legs to her feet so he could remove her shoes and socks and toss them over his shoulder.

Her heart pounding, Channon watched as he nibbled his way over her hip to her stomach. He moved his hands to her shirt and slowly unbuttoned it, kissing and licking every piece of her skin that he bared.

She moaned at the sight and feel of his mouth on her, at the way he seemed to savor her body. Spikes of pleasure pierced her stomach as her body throbbed and ached for him to fill her.

She wanted him inside her so much that she feared she

might burst into flames from the fire tearing through her body.

Sebastian felt her wetness on his skin as he slid himself against her. His body screamed for hers, but he wasn't through with her yet. He wanted to savor her, to commit every inch of her lush body to his memory.

What he felt for her amazed him. It was unlike anything he'd ever experienced. On some strange level she gave him peace, sanctuary. She filled the loneliness in his battered heart.

He buried his face in her neck while her hardened nipples teased the flesh of his chest and her hands roamed over his back. "You feel so good under me," he whispered as he soaked her essence into him.

Channon took a deep, ragged breath. His words delighted her.

He nuzzled her neck, his whiskers softly teasing her flesh while his hand skimmed over her body to touch the burning ache between her legs. She hissed at the pleasure of his fingers toying with her and arched her back against him as he slowly dragged his mouth from her neck to her breast. His tongue swept against the hardened tip, making her tingle and throb.

She bit her lip as a wave of fear went through her. "I want you to know that I don't normally do this sort of thing."

He lifted himself up on his arms to look down at her. He pressed his hips between her legs so that she could feel the large bulge of him while his expensive wool pants slightly chafed her inner thighs. The hot feel of him there was enough to drive her wild with need.

"If I thought you did, my lady, I wouldn't be here with you now." His gaze intensified, holding her enthralled. "I see you, Channon. You and the barriers you have around you that keep everyone at a distance."

"And yet you're here."

"I'm here because I know the sadness inside you. I know what it feels like to wake in the morning, lost and lonely and aching for someone to be there with me."

Her heart clenched as he spoke the very things that really were a part of her. "Why are *you* alone? I can't imagine a man so handsome without a line of willing women fighting behind him."

"Looks aren't all there is in this world, my lady. They are certainly no protection against being alone. Hearts never see through the eyes."

Channon swallowed at his words. Did he mean them? Or was this all some lie he was telling her to make her feel better about what she was doing with him? She didn't know.

But she wanted to believe him. She wanted to comfort the torment she saw in his hungry eyes.

He pulled away from her and removed his shoes and pants. Channon trembled as she finally saw him completely naked. Like a dangerous, dark beast moving sinuously in the moonlight, he was incredible. Absolutely stunning.

Every inch of him was muscled and toned and covered by the most scrumptious tanned skin she'd ever beheld. The only flaws on his perfect body were the scars marking his back, hips, and legs. They really did look like claw and bite marks from some ferocious beast.

When he rejoined her on the bed, she pulled the tie from

his hair, letting it fall forward to surround his sinfully hand-some face.

"You look like some barbaric chieftain," she said, running her hand through the silkiness of his unbound hair. She traced the intricate lines of the tattoo on his face.

"Mmm," he breathed, taking her breast in his mouth.

Channon held his head to her as his tongue teased her. Ripples of pleasure tore through her.

She ran her hands down his muscled ribs, then along his arms and shoulders as she drifted through a strange hazy fog of pleasure. Something strange was happening to her. With every breath he expelled, it was like his touch intensified. Multiplied. Instead of one tongue stroking her, she swore she could feel a hundred of them. It was as if her skin was alive and being massaged all over at once.

Sebastian hissed as his powers ran through him. Sex always heightened the senses of his breed. The intensity of physical pleasure was highly sought by his people for the elevation it gave them and their magic. The beauty of it was that the surge of power usually lasted a full day, and in the case of truly great sex, two days.

Channon was definitely a two-day high.

He looked into her eyes to see her gaze unfocused and wild. His powers were affecting her, too. The physical stimulation to a human was even greater than it was to his breed.

He knew the moment she lost herself to the ecstasy of his sorcerer's touch. Her barriers and inhibitions gone, she threw her head back and cried out as an orgasm tore through her. "That's it," he whispered in her ear. "Don't fight it."

She didn't. Instead, she turned toward him and grabbed

feverishly at his body. Sebastian groaned as he obliged her eagerness.

She sought out every inch of his flesh with her hands and mouth. He rolled over and pulled her on top of him, where she straddled his waist, letting him feel her wetness on the hollow of his stomach. He knew she was past the ability to speak now and a part of him regretted that. She was all need. All hot, demanding sex.

Her eyes wild and hungry, she took his hands in hers and led them to her breasts as she slid herself against his swollen shaft. She leaned forward to drag her tongue along the edge of his jaw as she nibbled her way to his lips.

She kissed him passionately, then pulled back. "What have you done to me?" she asked hoarsely, her words surprising him.

"It's not exactly me," he said honestly. "It's something I can't help."

She moaned and writhed against him, making his body burn even more. "I need you inside me, Sebastian. Please."

He wasted no time obliging her. Rolling her over, he curled his body around hers as they lay with her back to his front. He draped her leg over his waist.

He tucked her head beneath his chin and held her close as he drove himself deep inside her sleek wetness. He growled at the warm, wet feel of her while she leaned her head back into his shoulder and cried out.

Channon had never felt anything like this. No man had ever made love to her in such a manner. Her right hip was braced against his inner thigh while he used his left knee to hold her left leg up so that he had access to her body from behind her. She didn't know how he managed it, but his strokes were deep and even, and they tore through her with the most intense pleasure she had ever known. He was so hard inside her, so thick and warm.

And she wanted more of his touch. More of his power.

He slid his hand down over her stomach, then lower until he touched her between her legs. She hissed and writhed as pleasure tore through her while his fingers rubbed her in time to his strokes. And still it felt as if a thousand hands caressed her, as if she were being bathed all over by his touch, his scent.

Out of her mind with ecstasy, she met him lush stroke for lush stroke. Her body felt as if it held a life of its own, as if the pleasure of her was its own entity. She needed even more of him.

Sebastian was awed by her response to him. No human woman had ever been like this. If he didn't know better, he'd swear she was part Drakos. She dug her nails into the flesh of the arms he had wrapped around her, and when she came again she screamed out so loudly, he had to quickly put a dampening spell around them to keep others from hearing her.

His powers surging, he smiled wickedly at that. He loved satisfying his partner, and with Channon he took even more delight than normal.

She rolled slightly in his arms, capturing his lips in a frenzied kiss.

Sebastian cupped her face as he quickened his strokes and buried himself even deeper in her body. She felt so incredibly good to him. So warm and welcoming. So perfect.

He held her close against him as his heart pounded and his groin tightened even more. The feel of her, the taste of her, cascaded through his senses, making him reel, making him ache, yet at the same time soothing him.

The beast in him roared and snapped in satisfaction while the man buried himself deep in her and shook from the force of his orgasm. With the two parts of him sated and united, it was the most incredible moment of his entire life.

Channon groaned as she felt his release inside her. Still wrapped around her, he pulled her even closer to his chest. She heard his ragged breathing and felt his heart pounding against her shoulder blade. The manly scent of him filled her head and her heart, making her want to stay cocooned by his body forever.

Slowly, the throbbing pleasure faded from her and left her weak and drained from the intensity of their love-making.

When he withdrew from her, she felt a tremendous sense of loss.

"What did you do to me?" she asked, turning onto her back to look at him.

He kissed his way across her collarbone to her lips. "I did nothing, *ma petite*. It was all you."

"Trust me, I've never done that before."

He laughed softly in her ear.

She smiled at him and dropped her gaze to the small gold medallion he wore around his neck. Odd, she hadn't noticed it before.

She traced the chain with her fingers, then took it into her hand. It was obviously quite old. Ancient Greek if she didn't miss her guess. The gold held a relief of a dragon coiled around a shield. "This is beautiful," she breathed.

Sebastian looked down at her hand and covered her fingers with his. "It belonged to my mother," he said, wondering why he spoke of it. It was something he'd never shared with anyone else. "I don't really remember her, but my brother said she told him to give it to me so that I would know how much she loved me."

"She died?"

He nodded. "I was barely six when . . ." His voice trailed off as his memories of that night scorched him. Inside his head he could still hear the screams of the dying and smell the fires. He remembered the terror and the arms of his brother, Theren, pulling him to safety.

He'd always lived with the horrors of that night close to his heart. Tonight, with Channon, it didn't seem to hurt quite so much.

She ran her hand over the markings on his face. "I'm sorry," she whispered, and inside his heart, he could feel her sincerity. "I was nine when my mother died of cancer. And there's always this little piece of me that wishes I could hear the sound of her voice just one more time."

"You're without family?"

She nodded. "I grew up with my aunt, who died two years ago."

He felt her ache inside his own heart and it surprised him. He hated that she was alone in the world. Like him. It was a hard way to be.

Tightening his arms, he let his body comfort her.

Channon closed her eyes as he ran his tongue around and into her ear, sending chills over her. She leaned into his arms and pulled him close for another scorching kiss. A tiny part of her wanted to beg him not to leave her in the morning. But she refused to embarrass herself.

She'd known going into this that tonight would be all they would ever have. Yet the thought of not seeing him again hurt her more than she could fathom. She literally felt that losing him would be like losing a vital part of herself.

Sebastian knew he should leave now, but something inside him rebelled.

It wasn't much longer until dawn. He still had to retrieve the tapestry and return home.

But right now, all he wanted was to spend a little more time holding this woman, keeping her in the warm shelter of his arms.

"Sleep, Channon," he whispered as he sent a small sleeping spell to her. If she were awake and looking at him, he would never be able to let her go.

Immediately, she went limp in his arms.

Sebastian ran his fingers over the delicate curve of her cheek as he watched her. She was so beautiful by his side.

He clenched his hand against her silken curls and took a deep breath in her hair. Her floral scent reminded him of warm summer days of shared laughter and friendship. Her bare hips were nestled perfectly against his groin, her lower back against his stomach. Her smooth legs were entwined with his masculine ones. Gods, how he ached to keep her here like this.

He felt himself stirring again. He felt the need within him to take her one more time before he upheld his obligation.

You must go.

As much as he hated to, he knew he had no choice.

Sighing in regret, he withdrew from the warmth of her and crept from the bed, still amazed by the night they had shared. He would never forget her. And for the first time in his life, he actually considered coming back here for a while.

But that was impossible.

His kind didn't do well in the modern world, where they were easily hunted and found. He needed wide-open spaces and a simpler world where he could have the freedom and solitude he needed.

Clenching his teeth against the pain of necessity, he dressed silently in the dark.

Sebastian stepped away from the bed, then paused.

He couldn't leave like this, as if the night had meant nothing to him.

Pulling his mother's medallion from his neck, he placed it around Channon's and kissed her parted lips.

"Sleep, little one," he whispered. "May the Fates be kind to you. Always."

Then, he shimmered from her room and out into the dark night. Alone. He was always alone.

He'd long ago accepted that fact. It was what had to be.

But tonight he felt that loneliness more profoundly than he had ever felt it before.

As he rounded the hotel's building and headed toward his car, he collided with a middle-aged woman who was walking, huddled from the cold, in a worn jacket. She wore the faded uniform of a waitress and the old shoes of a woman who had no choice but to be practical.

"Hey," he said as she started past him. "Do you have a car?"

She shook her head no.

"You do now." He handed her the keys to his Lexus and pointed it out to her. "You'll find the registration in the glove box. Just fill it out and it's yours."

She blinked at him. "Yeah, right."

Sebastian offered her a genuine smile. He'd only bought the car to use while he'd been trapped in this time period. Where he was going, there was no need for it.

"I'm serious," he said, nudging her toward it. "No strings attached. I took a vow of poverty about fifteen minutes ago, and it's all yours."

She laughed incredulously. "I have no idea who you are, but thank you."

Sebastian inclined his head and waited until the woman had driven off.

Cautiously, he stepped into the alley and looked around to make sure there were no witnesses. He called forth the powers of Night to shield him from anyone who might happen by, then he shifted into his alternate form. The power of the Drakos rushed through him like fire as the ions in the air around him were charged with electrical energy—electrical energy that allowed him to shed one form and shift into another.

In his case, his alternate form was that of a dragon.

Spreading his bloodred wings out to their full forty-foot span, he launched himself from his hind legs and flew into the sky, careful to stay below radar level this time.

Sebastian had one last thing to do before he could return

to his time. Yet even as he headed back to the museum, he couldn't shake the image of Channon from his mind.

He could still see her asleep in the bed, her hair spread out around her shoulders. He could still feel the texture of the honey-laced strands in his palm.

His dragon form burned with need, and he yearned to return to her.

Not that he could. One-night stands with humans were all he dared. The risk of exposure was too great.

Sebastian crossed town in a matter of minutes and landed on the roof of the museum. He summoned the electrical field that allowed the molecules of his body to transform from animal to human and flashed back into his man form.

With a flick of his hand, he dressed himself all in black, then shimmered from the roof into the room that held the tapestry.

"There you are," he said as he saw Antiphone's work again. Sadness, guilt, and grief tore through him as he recalled his baby sister's gentle face.

After he'd sold this tapestry, he had never wanted to see it again.

But now he had to have it. It was the only way to save his brother's life. Not that he should care. Damos had never given a damn about him.

After all the things Damos had done to break him, Sebastian still couldn't turn his back on his brother and let the man die. Not when he could help it.

"I'm a bloody fool," he said disgustedly.

He willed the tapestry from the museum case into his hand. Then he folded and tucked it carefully into a black leather bag to protect it.

As he began to shimmer from the room back to the roof, an odd burning started in the palm of his left hand.

"What the . . . ?"

Hissing from the pain, he dropped the case and pulled off his glove. Sebastian blew cool air across his hot skin and frowned as a round geometric design appeared in his palm.

"No," he breathed in disbelief as he stared at it.

This wasn't possible, yet there was no denying what he saw and felt. Worse, there was a presence inside him, a tickling in the depth of his heart that made him curse even louder.

Against his will, he was mated.

TWO

This was a nightmare. The absolute worst kind of nightmare.

It was wrong. It had to be.

Sebastian left the museum immediately, all the while debating his next step. On the building's roof, he paused. He needed to take the tapestry back to Britain of a thousand years earlier. He was sworn to it. He'd destroyed Antiphone's future, and now the fate of his brother was in his hands.

But the mark . . .

He couldn't leave his mate here while he went home. Nor could he stay in this time period where the danger of being inadvertently struck by an electrical charge was so strong—that was his one Achilles' heel.

Because he relied on electrical impulses to change forms, any kind of outside electrical jolt could involuntarily transform him. It was why his kind avoided any time period after Benjamin Franklin, the so-called Satan of his people.

But Arcadian law demanded he protect his mate.

At any cost.

Centuries of war had left the Drakos branch of the Arcadians virtually extinct. And since Sebastian hunted down and executed the evil animal Drakos, their kind would make it a point to track and kill his mate should they ever learn of Channon's existence.

She would be dead and it would be all his fault.

Should she die, he would never mate again.

"Mate, my bloody hell," he muttered. He looked up at the clear, full moon above. "Damn you, Fates. What were you thinking?"

To mate a human to an Arcadian was cruel. It happened only rarely, so rarely that he'd never even considered the possibility of it. So why did it have to happen now?

Leave her.

He should. Yet if he did, he would leave behind his only chance for a family. Unlike a human male, he was only given one shot at this. If he failed to claim Channon, he would spend the rest of his exceptionally long life alone.

Completely alone.

No other woman would ever again appeal to him.

He would be doomed to celibacy.

Oh, bloody, damned hell with that.

There was no choice. At the end of three weeks, the mark on her human hand would fade and she would forget he'd ever existed. The mark on his Arcadian hand was eternal, and he would mourn her for the rest of his life. Even if he went back for her later, it would be too late. After the mark faded, his chance was over.

It was now or never.

Not to mention the small fact that during the three weeks she was marked by his sign, Channon would be a magnet to the Katagaria Draki who wanted him dead.

For centuries, he and the animal Katagaria had played a deadly game of cat and mouse. The Katagaria routinely sent out mental feelers for him, just as he did for them. Their psychic sonar would easily pick up his mark on Channon's body, allowing them to hone in on her.

And if one of them were to find his mate alone without a protector . . .

He flinched at the image in his mind.

No, he had to protect her. That was all there was to it.

Closing his eyes, Sebastian transformed himself into the dragon and went back to Channon's hotel, where he shifted forms again and entered her room as a man.

He was about to break nine kinds of laws.

Sebastian laughed bitterly. So what else was new? And why should he care? His people had banished him long ago. He was dead to them. Why should he abide by their laws?

He didn't care about them. He cared for nothing. For no one.

Yet as he stared at Channon lying asleep in the moonlight, something peculiar happened to him. A feeling of possessive need tore through him. She was his mate. His only salvation.

For whatever twisted reason, the Fates had joined them. To leave Channon here unprotected would be wrong. She had no idea about the kind of enemies who would do anything to have him, enemies who wouldn't hesitate to hurt her because she was his.

Sebastian lay down by her side and gathered her into his arms. She murmured in her sleep, then snuggled into him. His heart pounded at the sensation of her breath against his neck.

He looked down and saw her right palm, which bore the same mark as his left hand, laying upright by her cheek. He'd waited an eternity for her.

After all these centuries of empty loneliness, dare he even dream of having a home again? A family?

Then again, dare he not?

"Channon?" he whispered softly, trying to wake her. "I need to ask you something."

"Hmm?" she murmured in her sleep.

"I can't remove you from your time period unless you agree to it. I need you to come with me. Will you?"

She blinked open her eyes and looked up at him with a sleepy frown. "Where are you taking me?"

"I want to take you home with me."

She smiled up at him like an angel, then sighed. "Sure."

Sebastian tightened his arms around her as she fell back to sleep. She'd said yes. Joy ripped through him. Maybe he had done his penance after all.

Maybe, for once, he could have his one moment of respite from the past.

Holding her close, Sebastian stared out the window and waited for the first rays of dawn so that he could pulse them out of her world and into one beyond her wildest imagination.

o o o

Channon felt a strange tugging in her stomach that settled into a terrible queasiness. What on earth?

She opened her eyes to see Sebastian staring down at her. He wore an intriguing mask of black and red feathers that made the gold of his eyes stand out even more prominently. It reminded her of a *Phantom of the Opera* mask as it only covered his forehead and the left side of his face where his tattoo was.

She'd never considered masks sexy before, but on him, mmm, baby.

Even more inviting than that, he wore black leather armor over a chain-mail shirt—black leather armor covered in silver rings and studs that was laced down the front. The laces had come untied, leaving an enticing gap where she could see his tanned skin peeping through.

Ummm, hmmm.

Smiling, she started to speak until she realized she was on the back of a horse. A really, really *big* horse.

Even more peculiar, she was dressed in a dark green gown with wide sleeves that flowed around her like some fairy-tale princess garment.

"Okay," she breathed, running her hand along the intricate gold embroidery on her sleeve. "It's a dream. I can cope with a dream where I'm Sleeping Beauty or something."

"It's not a dream," he said quietly.

Channon laughed nervously as she sat up in his lap and glanced around. The sun was high above as if it were well into the afternoon, and they were traveling on an old dirt road that ran perpendicular to a thick, prehistoric-looking forest.

Something was wrong. She could feel it in her bones, and she could tell by the stiffness of his body and his guarded look. He was hiding something. "Where are we?"

"The where of it," he said slowly, refusing to meet her gaze, "isn't nearly as interesting as the *when* part."

"Excuse me?"

She watched the emotions flicker in his eyes, but the most peculiar one was a fleeting look of panic, as if he were nervous about answering her question. "Do you remember last night when I asked if I could take you home with me and you said sure?"

Channon frowned. "Vaguely, yes."

"Well, honey, I'm home."

An ache started in her head. What was he talking about? "Home? Where?"

He cleared his throat and still refused to meet her gaze. The man was definitely hedging. But why?

"You said you like research, right?" he asked.

Her stomach knotted even more. "Yes."

"Consider this a unique research venture then."

"Meaning what?"

His jaw flexed. "Haven't you ever wished you could go back to Saxon England and find out what it was really like before the Normans invaded?"

"Of course."

"Well, your wish is granted." He looked at her and flashed an insincere smile.

Okay, the guy was not Robin Williams, and unless she was missing something really important from last night, she didn't conjure him from a bottle. If he wasn't a genie . . .

She laughed nervously. "What are you saying?"

"We're in England. Or rather we're in what will one day soon become England. Right now, this kingdom is called Lindsey."

Channon went completely still. She knew all about the medieval Saxon kingdom, and this . . . this was not possible. No, there was no way she could be here. "You're joking with me again, aren't you?"

He shook his head.

Channon rubbed her forehead as she tried to make sense of all this. "Okay, you have slipped me a mickey. Great. When I sober up from this, you do realize I will call the cops."

"Well, it'll be about nine hundred years before there are cops to call, about a hundred more years after that before you have a phone. But I'm willing to wait if you are."

Channon clenched her eyes shut as she tried to think past the throbbing ache in her skull. "So you're telling me that I'm not dreaming and I'm not drugged."

"Correct on both accounts."

"But I'm in Saxon England?"

He nodded.

"And you're a dragon slayer?"

"Ah, so you remember that part."

"Yes," she said reasonably, but with every word she spoke after that, her voice crescendoed into mild hysteria. "What I don't remember is how the hell I got *here!*" she shouted, sending several birds into flight.

Sebastian winced.

She glared at him. "You told me there wouldn't be any Rod Serling voice-overs, yet here I am in the middle of a

Twilight Zone episode. Oh, and let me guess the title of it, *Night of the Terminally Stupid!*"

"It's not as bad as all that," Sebastian said, trying to decide the best way to explain this to her. He didn't blame her for being angry. In fact, she was taking all this a lot better than he had dared hope. "I know this is hard for you."

"Hard for me? I don't even know where to begin. I did something I've never done in my life and then I wake up and you tell me you have supposedly time-warped me into the past, and I'm not sure if I'm insane or delusional or what. Why am I here?"

"I . . ." Sebastian wasn't sure what to answer. The truth was pretty much out of the question. *Channon, I practically kidnapped you because you are my mate and I don't want to be alone for the next three to four hundred years of my life.*

No, definitely not something a man told a woman on their first date. He would have to woo her. Quickly. And win her over to wanting to stay here with him.

Preferably before a dragon ate one of them.

"Look, why don't you just think of this as a great adventure. Instead of reading about the history you teach, you can live it for a couple weeks."

"What are you? Disney World?" she asked. "And I can't stay here for a couple weeks. I have a life in the twenty-first century. I will be fired from my job. I will lose my car and my apartment. Good grief, who will pick up my laundry?"

"If you stayed here with me, it wouldn't be a problem. You'd never have to worry about any of that again."

Channon was aghast at him. *Oh, God, please let this be*

some bizarre nightmare. She had to wake up. This could not possibly be real.

"No," she said to him, "you're right. I wouldn't have to worry about *any* of that in Saxon England. I'd only have to worry about the lack of hygiene, lack of plumbing, Viking invasions, being burned at the stake, lack of modern conveniences, and nasty diseases with no antibiotics. Good grief, I can't even get a Midol. Not to mention, I'll never find out what happens next week on *Buffy!*"

Sebastian let out an elongated, patient breath and gave her an apologetic look that somehow succeeded in quelling a good deal of her anger.

"Look," he said quietly, "I'll make a deal with you. Spend a few weeks with me here, and if you really can't stand it, I'll take you home as close to the departure time as I can manage. Okay?"

Channon still had a hard time grasping all this. "Do you swear you're not playing some weird mind game with me? I really am *here*, in Saxon England?"

"I swear it on my mother's soul. You are in Saxon England, and I can take you back home. And no, I'm not playing mind games with you."

Channon accepted that, even though she couldn't imagine why. It was just a feeling she had that he would never swear on his mother's soul unless he meant it.

"Can you really take me back to the precise moment I left?"

"Probably not the precise moment, but I can try."

"What do you mean, *try?*"

He flashed his dimples, then turned serious. "Time-walking isn't an exact science. You can only move through the time fields when the dawn meets the night, and only under the power of a full moon. The problem is on the arrival end. You can try to get someplace specific, but you have only about a ninety-five percent chance of success. I might get you back that day, but it could also be a week or two after."

"And that's the best you can do?"

"Hey, just be grateful I'm old. When an Arcadian first starts time-walking, we only have about a three percent chance of success. I once ended up on Pluto."

She laughed in spite of herself. "Are you serious?"

He nodded. "They're not kidding about it being the coldest planet."

Channon took a deep breath as she digested everything he'd told her. Was any of this real? She didn't know, any more than she knew whether or not he was being honest about returning her. He was still very guarded. "Okay, so I'm stuck here until the next full moon?"

"Yes."

Oh, good grief, no. Had she been the kind of woman to whine, she'd probably be whining. But Channon was always practical. "All right. I can handle this," she said, more for her benefit than his. "I'll just pretend I'm a Saxon chick and you . . ." Her voice trailed off as she recalled what he'd said about time-traveling. "Just how old are you?"

"My people don't age quite the same way humans do. Since we can time-walk, we have a much slower biological clock."

Oh, she really didn't like the way he said *humans*, and if he turned fangy on her, she was going to stake him right through the heart. But she would get back to that in a minute. First, she wanted to understand the age thing. "So you age like dog years?"

Sebastian laughed. "Something like that. By human age, I would be four hundred sixty-three years old."

Channon sat flabbergasted as she looked over his lean, hard body. He appeared to be in his early thirties, not his late four hundreds. "You're not joking with me at all, are you?"

"Not even a little. Everything I have told you since the moment I met you has been the honest truth."

"Oh, God," she said, breathing in slowly and carefully to calm the panic that was again trying to surface. She knew it was real, yet she had a hard time believing it. It boggled her mind that people could walk through time and that she could really be in the Dark Ages.

Surely, it couldn't be this easy.

"I know there has to be more of a downside to all this. And I'm pretty sure here's where I find out you're some kind of vampire or something."

"No," he said quickly. "I'm not a vampire. I don't suck blood, and I don't do anything weird to sustain my life. I was born from my mother, just as you were. I feel the same emotions. I bleed red blood. And just like you, I will die at some unknown date in the future. I just come equipped with a few extra powers."

"I see. I'm a Toyota. You're a Lamborghini, and you can have really awesome sex."

He chuckled. "That's a good summation."

Summation, hell. This was unbelievable. Inconceivable. How had she gotten mixed up with something like this?

But as she looked up at him, she knew. He was compelling. That deadly air and animal magnetism—how could she have even hoped to resist him?

And she wondered if there were more men out there like him. Men of power and magic. Men who were so incredibly sexy that to look at them was to burn for them. "Are there more of you?"

"Yes."

She smiled evilly at the thought. "A *lot* more?"

He frowned before he answered. "There used to be a lot more of us, but times change."

Channon saw the sadness in his eyes, the pain that he kept inside. It made her hurt for him.

He looked down at her. "That tapestry you love so much is the story of our beginning."

"The birth of the dragon and the man?"

He nodded. "About five thousand years before you were born, my grandfather, Lycaon, fell in love with a woman he thought was a human. She wasn't. She was born to a race that had been cursed by the Greek gods. She never told him who and what she really was, and in time she bore him two sons."

Channon remembered seeing that birth scene embroidered on the upper left edge of the tapestry.

"On her twenty-seventh birthday," he continued, "she died horribly just as all the members of her race die. And when my grandfather saw it, he knew his children were destined for the same fate. Angry and grief-stricken, he sought unnatural means to keep his children alive."

Sebastian was tense as he spoke. "Crazed from his grief and fear, he started capturing as many of my grandmother's people as he could and began experimenting with them—

241

combining their life forces with those of animals. He wanted to make a hybrid creature that wasn't cursed."

"It worked?" she asked.

"Better than he had hoped. Not only did his sorcery give them the animal's strength and powers, it gave them a life span ten times longer than that of a human."

She arched a brow at that. "So you're telling me that you're a werewolf who lives seven or eight hundred years?"

"Yes on the age, but I'm not a Lykos. I'm a Drakos."

"You say that as if I have a clue about what you mean."

"Lycaon used his magic to 'half' his children. Instead of two sons, he made four."

"What are you saying?" she asked. "He sliced them down the middle?"

"Yes and no. There was a byproduct of the magic I don't think my grandfather was prepared for. When he combined a human and an animal, he expected his magic would create only one being. Instead, it made two of them. One person who held the heart of a human, and a separate creature whose heart was that of the animal.

"Those who have human hearts are called Arcadians. We are able to suppress the animal side of our nature. To control it. Because we have human hearts, we have compassion and higher reasoning."

"And the ones with animal hearts?"

"They are called Katagaria, meaning miscreant or rogue. Because of their animal hearts, they lack human compassion and are ruled by their baser instincts. Like their human brethren, they hold the same psychic abilities and shape-shifting, time-bending powers, but not the self-control."

That didn't sound good to her. "And the other people

who were experimented on? Were there two of them, too?"

"Yes. And we formed the basis of two societies: the Arcadians and the Katagaria. As with nature, like went with like, and we created groups or patrias based on our animals. Wolf lives with wolf, hawk with hawk, dragon with dragon. We use Greek terms to differentiate between them. Therefore, dragon is drakos, wolf is lykos, et cetera."

That made sense to her. "And all the while the Arcadians stayed with the Arcadians and Katagaria with Katagaria?"

"For the most part, yes."

"But I take it from the sound of your voice that no one lived happily-ever-after."

"No. The Fates were furious that Lycaon dared thwart them. To punish him, they ordered him to kill the creature-based children. He refused. So, the gods cursed us all."

"Cursed you how?"

A tic started in his jaw, and she saw the deep-seated agony in his eyes. "For one thing, we don't hit puberty until our mid-twenties. Because it is delayed, when it hits, it hits us hard. Many of us are driven to madness, and if we don't find a way to control and channel our powers we can become Slayers."

"I take it you don't mean the good vampire-slayer kind of slayer that kills evil things."

"No. These are creatures that are bent on absolute destruction. They kill without remorse and with total barbarism."

"How awful," she breathed.

He agreed. "Until puberty, our children are either human or animal, depending on the parents' base-forms."

"Base-forms? What are those?"

"Arcadians are human so their base-forms are human. The Katagaria have a base-form of whatever animal part they are related to. An Ursulan would be a bear, a Gerakian would be a hawk."

"A Drakos would be a dragon."

He nodded. "A child has no powers at all, but with the onset of puberty, all the powers come in. We try to contain those who are going through it and teach them how to harness their powers. Most of the time we succeed as Arcadians, but with the Katagaria this isn't true. They encourage their children to destroy both humans and Arcadians."

"Because we have vowed to stop them and their Slayers, they hate us and have sworn to kill us and our families. In short, we are at war with one another."

Channon sat quietly as she absorbed that last bit. So that was the eternal struggle he'd mentioned yesterday. "Is that why you are here?"

This time the anguish in his eyes was so severe that she winced from it. "No. I'm here because I made a promise."

"About what?"

He didn't answer, but she felt the rigidness return to his body. He was a man in pain, and she wondered why.

But then she figured it out. "The Katagaria destroyed your family, didn't they?"

"They took everything from me." The agony in his voice was so raw, so savage.

Never in her life had she heard anything like it.

Channon wanted to soothe him in a way she'd never wanted to soothe anyone else. She wished she could erase the past and return his family to him.

Seeking to distract him, she went back to the prior topic. "If you're at war with each other, do you have armies?"

He shook his head. "Not really. We have Sentinels, who are stronger and faster than the rest of our species. They are the designated protectors of both man- and were-kind."

Reaching up, she touched his mask that covered the tattoo on his face. "Do all Arcadians have your markings?"

Sebastian looked away. "No. Only Sentinels have them."

She smiled at the knowledge. "You're a Sentinel."

"I *was* a Sentinel."

The stress on the past tense told her much. "What happened?"

"It was a long time ago, and I'd rather not talk about it."

She could respect that, especially since he'd already answered so much. But her curiosity about it was almost more than she could bear. Still, she wouldn't pry. "Okay, but can I ask one more thing?"

"Sure."

"When you say long ago, I have a feeling that takes on a whole new meaning. Was it a decade or two, or—"

"Two hundred fifty-four years ago."

Her jaw dropped. "Have you been alone all this time?"

He nodded.

Her chest drew tight at that. Two hundred years alone. She couldn't imagine it. "And you have no one?"

Sebastian fell silent as old memories surged. He did his best not to remember his role of Sentinel. His family.

He'd been raised to hold honor next to his heart, and with one fatal mistake, he had lost everything he'd ever cared for. Everything he'd once been.

"I was . . . banished," he said, the word sticking in his throat. He'd never once in all this time uttered the word aloud. "No Arcadian is allowed to associate with me."

"Why would they banish you?"

He didn't answer.

Instead, he pointed in front of them. "Look up, Channon. I think there's something over there you'll find far more interesting than me."

Seriously doubting that, Channon turned her head, then gaped. On the hill far above was a large wooden hall surrounded by a group of buildings. Even from this distance, she could make out people and animals moving about.

She blinked, unable to believe her eyes. "Oh my God," she breathed. "It's a real Saxon village!"

"Complete with bad hygiene and no plumbing."

Her heart hammered as they approached the hill at a slow and steady speed. "Can't you make this thing move any faster?" she asked, eager to get a closer view.

"I can, but they will view it as a sign of aggression and might decide to shoot a few arrows into us."

"Oh. Then I can wait. I don't want to be a pincushion."

Sebastian remained silent and watched her as she strained to see more of the town. He smiled at her exuberance as she twisted in the saddle, her hips brushing painfully against his swollen groin.

After the night they had shared, it amazed him just how much he longed to possess her again, how much his body craved hers.

He still couldn't believe he'd told her as much as he had about his past and people, yet as his mate, she had a right to know all about him.

If she would be his mate.

He still hadn't really made up his mind about that.

The kindest thing would be to return her and let her go. But he didn't want to. He missed having someone to care for and someone who cared for him.

How many times had he lain awake at night aching for a family again? Wishing for the comfort of a soothing touch? Missing the sound of laughter and the warmth of friendship?

For centuries, his solitude had been his hell.

And this woman sitting in his lap would be his only salvation.

If he dared . . .

Channon bit her lip as they entered the bailey and she saw real, live Saxon people at work in the village. There were men laying stone, rebuilding a portion of the gate. Women with laundry and foodstuffs walking around, talking amongst themselves. And children! Lots of Saxon children were running around, laughing and playing games with each other.

Better still, there were merchants and music, acrobats, and jongleurs. "Is there a festival going on?"

He nodded. "The harvest is in and there's a celebration all week long to mark it."

She struggled to understand what the crowd around them said.

It was incredible! They were speaking Old English!

"Oh, Sebastian," she cried, throwing her arms around him and holding him close. "Thank you for this! Thank you!"

Sebastian clenched his teeth at the sensation of her breasts flattened against him. Of her breath tickling his neck.

His groin tightened even more, and it took all his human powers to leash the beast within. He felt the ripping inside as he set the two halves of him against each other.

It was a dangerous thing he did, but for both their sakes, it was a necessary action. Especially since both halves of him wanted the same thing—they wanted the Claiming where Channon would entrust herself to him, the ceremony that would bind them together for eternity. It wasn't something to be taken lightly. She would have to give up everything to be with him. Everything. And he wasn't sure if he could ask that of her.

It would be unfair to her, and he definitely wasn't worth such a sacrifice.

He saw the happiness in Channon's eyes and smiled at her.

But his smile faded as he looked around the town and saw all the innocent lives that would end if something went wrong.

Bracis had shown a rare streak of intelligence when he had set up this exchange. Sebastian was forbidden by his Sentinel oath to transform into his dragon form or to use his powers in any way that could betray his heritage to the humans. To the innocent, he must always appear human.

Bracis had sworn that the Katagaria would come in as humans to make the exchange and then leave peacefully. Unfortunately, Sebastian had no choice except to trust them.

Of course, Bracis knew the extent of Sebastian's powers, and the Katagari male would be an absolute idiot to cross him. And though the beast could be stupid, Bracis wasn't *that* stupid.

As soon as they reached the stable, Sebastian helped Channon down, then dismounted behind her. He pulled his hauberk lower so that no one could see just how much he craved the woman before him.

Channon watched as Sebastian removed his huge broadsword from his horse and fastened it to the baldric at his waist. She had to admit the man looked delectable like that, so manly and virile.

The chain-mail sleeves fell from the shoulders of the leather armor, clinking ever so slightly with his movements. The laces of the hauberk were open, showing a hint of the hairs on his chest, and all too well she remembered her hours of running her fingers and mouth over that lush skin.

And as she stared at the small scar on his neck, she ached to trace it with her tongue. This man had a body and aura that should be cloned and made standard equipment for all men. Prideful and dangerous, it made every female part of her sit up and pant.

Stop that! she snapped at herself. They were in the middle of town and . . .

And she had other people to study.

Yeah right. Like they were really more interesting than Sebastian.

He adjusted his sword so that the hilt came forward and the blade trailed down his leg, then pulled a leather bag from the saddle. A youth ran up to take his mount.

"What day is today?" he asked the boy in Old English.

"It be Tuesday, sir."

Sebastian thanked him and gave him two coins before relinquishing his horse to the boy's care.

He turned toward her. "You ready?"

"Absolutely. I've dreamed of this my whole life."

Channon held her breath as he led her through the bustling village.

Sebastian looked behind him to see Channon as she tried to watch everything at once. She was so happy to be here.

Maybe there was hope for them after all. Maybe bringing her here hadn't been a mistake.

"Tell me, Channon, have you ever eaten Saxon bread?"

"Is it good?"

"The best." Taking her hand, he pulled her into a shop across the dirt road.

Channon breathed in the sweet smell of baking bread as they entered the bakery. Bread was lined up on the wooden counter and in baskets on tables all over the room. An older, heavyset woman, stood to the side, trying to move a large sack across the floor.

"Here," Sebastian said, rushing to her side. "Let me get that."

Straightening up, she smiled in gratitude. "Thank you. I need it over there by my workbench."

Sebastian hefted the heavy sack onto his shoulder.

Channon watched, her mouth watering as his hauberk lifted and gave her a flash of his hard, tanned abs. His broad shoulders and toned biceps flexed from the strain. And when he placed the sack on the floor by the bench, she was gifted with a nice view of his rear covered by his black leather pants.

Oh, yeah, she'd love a bite of that.

"Now what can I do for you gentle folks?" the woman asked.

"What looks good to you, Channon?"

Was that a trick question or what?

Forcing herself to look at something other than Sebastian, she attempted to find a substitute to sink her teeth into. "What do you recommend?" she asked, trying out her Old English. She'd never used it before in conversation.

To her amazement, the woman understood her. "If you're in the mind for something sweet, I just pulled a honey loaf from the oven."

"That would be wonderful," Channon said.

The woman left them alone. Sebastian stood back while Channon examined the different kinds of bread in the shop.

"So what's in the bag?" she asked, indicating the black one Sebastian had removed from his horse.

"It's just something I need to take care of. Later."

Again with the hedging. "Is that why you came back here?"

He nodded, but there was something very guarded in his look, one that warned her this topic was quite closed.

The woman returned with the bread and sliced it for them. While Channon ate the warm, delicious slice, the woman asked Sebastian if he would help her move some boxes from a cart outside into the back of her shop.

He left his bag with Channon, then went to help.

Channon listened to them in the other room while she ate the bread and drank the cider the woman had also given her. Her gaze fell to the black bag and curiosity got the better of her. Leaning over, she opened it to see what it contained. Her breath left her body as she saw the tapestry inside.

He really had stolen it. But why?

The old woman came in, brushing her hands on her apron. "That's a good man you got there, my lady."

Blushing at being caught in her snooping, Channon straightened up. At the moment, she wasn't so sure about that. "Is he still unloading the cart?"

The woman motioned her to the back, then took her to look out the door. In the alley behind the shops, she saw Sebastian playing a game with two boys who were wielding wooden swords and shields against him while pretending to be warriors fighting a dragon. The irony of their game wasn't lost on her.

She took a minute to watch him laughing and teasing them. The sight warmed her heart.

The Sebastian she had come to know was a man of many facets. Caring, compassionate, and tender in a way she'd never known before. Yet there was a savage undercurrent to him, one that let her know he wasn't a man to be taken lightly.

And as she watched him playing with the children, something strange happened to her. She wondered what he would look like playing with his own children.

With their children . . .

She could see the image so plainly that it scared her.

"Why do you wear a mask?" one of the boys asked him.

"Because I'm not as pretty as you," Sebastian teased.

"I'm not pretty," the little boy said indignantly. "I'm a handsome boy."

"Handsome you are, Aubrey," a middle-aged man said as he moved a keg through the back door of the building across the way. The man looked to Sebastian.

He gaped widely, then wiped his hand on his shirt and moved to shake Sebastian's arm. "It's been a long time since I seen one of you. It's an honor to shake your arm, sir."

The boys paused in their play. "Who is he, grandfather?"

"He's a dragon slayer, Aubrey, like the ones I tell you about at night when you go to sleep." The man indicated Sebastian's mask and sword. "I was just your age when they came to Lindsey and slew the Megalos."

She wondered if Sebastian was one of the ones who had come that day.

As if sensing her, Sebastian turned his head to see her in the doorway. "If you'll excuse me," he said to the man and boys, then made his way toward her.

Sebastian could tell by Channon's face that something was troubling her. "Is something wrong?"

"Were you one of the ones who fought the Megalos?"

He shook his head as pain sliced through him. If not for his banishment, he would have been here that day. Unlike the other Sentinels, he had to fight the Katagaria alone. "No."

"Oh."

"Is something else wrong? You still don't look happy."

She met his gaze levelly. "You stole the tapestry from the museum," she said in modern English so no one else would understand her. "I want to know why."

"I had to get it back here."

"Why?"

"Because it's the ransom for another Sentinel. If I don't give them the tapestry on Friday, they will kill him."

Channon scowled at that. "Why do they want the tapestry?"

"I have no idea. But since a man's life was at stake, I didn't bother to ask."

Suddenly, she remembered what he'd said last night about the tapestry. *"It was made by a woman named Antiphone back in seventh-century Britain. It's the story of her grandfather and his brother and their eternal struggle between good and evil."*

On their way into town, he'd said it was the story of *his* grandfather.

"Antiphone is your sister?"

"Was my sister. She died a long time ago."

By the look on his face she could tell the loss was still with him.

"Why was her tapestry in the museum?"

"Because . . ." He took a deep breath to stave off the agony inside him, agony so severe that it made his entire being hurt.

He felt the tic working in his jaw as he forced himself to answer her question. "The tapestry was with her when she died. I tried to return it to my family, but they wanted nothing to do with me. I couldn't stand having it around me, so I took it into the future where I knew someone would preserve it and make sure it was honored and protected as she should have been."

"You plan on taking it back after all this is over with, don't you?"

He frowned at her astuteness. "How did you know?"

"I would say I'm psychic, but I'm not. I just figured a man with a heart as big as yours wouldn't just steal something without making amends."

"You don't know me that well."

"I think I do."

Sebastian clenched his teeth. No, she didn't know. He wasn't a good man. He was fool.

If not for him, Antiphone would have lived. Her death had been all his fault. It was a guilt that he lived with constantly. One that would never cease, never heal.

And in that moment he realized something. He had to let Channon go. There was no way he could keep her. There was no way he could share his life with her.

If anything should ever happen to her . . .

It would be his fault, too. As his mate, she would be prime Katagari bait. Even though he was banished, he was still a Sentinel, and his job was to seek and destroy every Slayer he could find.

Alone he could fight them. But without his patria to guard Channon while he fulfilled his ancient oath, there was always a chance she would end up as Antiphone had.

He would sooner spend the rest of his life celibate than let that happen.

Celibate! No!

He squelched the rebellious scream of the inner Drakos. For the next three weeks, he would guard her life with his own, and once his mark was gone from her, he would take her home.

It was what *had* to be done.

. . .

After they left the bakery, they spent the afternoon browsing the stalls and sampling the food and drink.

Channon couldn't believe this day. It was the best one of her entire life. And it wasn't just because she was in Saxon

Britain, it was because she had Sebastian by her side. His light teasing and easygoing manner wrapped around her heart and made her ache to keep him.

"Beg pardon, my lord?"

They turned to find a man standing behind them while they were watching an acrobat.

"Aye?" Sebastian asked.

"I was told by His Majesty, King Henfrith, to come and ask for the honor of your company tonight. He wishes to extend his full and most cordial hospitality to you and to your lady."

Channon felt giddy. "I get to meet a king?"

Sebastian nodded. "Tell His Majesty that it would be my honor to meet with him. We shall be along shortly."

The messenger left.

Channon breathed nervously. "I don't know about this. Am I dressed appropriately?"

"Yes, you are. I assure you, you will be the most beautiful woman there." Then, her gallant champion offered her his arm. Taking it, she let him lead her through town to the large hall.

As they drew near the hall's door, she could hear the music and laughter from inside as the people ate their supper. Sebastian opened the door and allowed her to enter first.

Channon hesitated in the doorway as she looked around in awe. It was more splendid than anything she'd ever imagined.

A lord's table was set apart from the others, and there were three women and four men seated there. The man with the crown she assumed was the king, the lady at his right, his queen, and the others must be daughters and sons or some other dignitaries perhaps.

Servants bustled around with food while dogs milled about, catching scraps from the diners. The music was sublime.

"Nervous?" Sebastian asked her in modern English.

"A little. I have no idea what Saxon etiquette is."

He lifted her hand to his lips and kissed her fingers, causing a warm chill to sweep through her. "Follow my lead, and I will show you everything you need to know to live in my world."

She cocked her brow at his words. There was something hidden in that. She was sure of it. "You are going to take me home at the next full moon, right?"

"I gave you my word, my lady. That is the one thing I have never broken, and I most assuredly would not break my oath to you."

"Just checking."

A hush fell over the crowd as they crossed the room and neared the lord's table.

Channon swallowed nervously. But she was there with the most handsome man in the kingdom. Dressed in his black armor and mask, Sebastian was a spectacularly masculine sight. The man had a regal presence that promised strength, speed, and deadly precision.

He stopped before the table and gave a low, courtly bow. Channon gave what she hoped was an acceptable curtsy.

"Greetings, Your Majesty," Sebastian said, straightening. "I am Sebastian Kattalakis, a Prince of Arcadia."

Channon's jaw went slack with that declaration. A prince? Was he for real or was it another joke?

He turned to her, his features guarded. "My lady, Channon."

The king rose to his feet and bowed to them. "Your Highness, it has been a long time since I've had the privilege of a dragon slayer's company. I owe your house more than I can ever repay. Please, come and be seated in honor. You and your lady-wife are welcomed here for as long as you wish to stay."

Sebastian led Channon to the table and sat her to his right, beside a man who introduced himself as the king's son-in-law.

"Are you really a prince?" she whispered to Sebastian.

"A most disinherited one, but yes. My grandfather, Lycaon, was the King of Arcadia."

"Oh my God," Channon said as pieces of history came together in her mind. "The king cursed by Zeus?"

"And the Fates."

Lycanthrope, the Greek word for werewolves, was taken from Lycaon, the King of Arcadia. Stunned, she wondered what other so-called myths and legends were actually real.

"You know, you are better than the Rosetta stone to a historian."

Sebastian laughed. "Glad to know I have some use to you."

More than he knew—and it wasn't just the knowledge he held. Today was the only day she could recall in an exceptionally long time when she hadn't been lonely. Not once. She'd enjoyed every minute of this day and didn't really want it to end.

She looked forward to spending the next few weeks with

Sebastian in his world. And deep inside where she best not investigate was a part of her that wondered if, when the time came, she'd be able to leave him.

How could a woman give up a man who made her feel the way Sebastian did every time he looked at her?

She wasn't sure it was possible.

Sebastian cut and served her from the roast of something she couldn't quite identify. Thinking it best not to ask, she took a bite and discovered it was quite good.

They ate in silence while others finished their meals and started dancing.

After a time, Channon glanced to Sebastian and noticed his eyes seemed troubled. "Are you all right?" she asked.

Sebastian ran his hand over the uncovered portion of his face. He felt ill inside. The harmony between his two halves had been disrupted by his inner fighting over Channon, and the pain of it was almost more than he could stand.

The Drakos wanted her regardless, but the man in him refused to see her endangered. The struggle between the two sides was so severe that he wondered how he was going to make it for the next three weeks without doing permanent damage to one or the other of his halves.

It was this kind of internal struggle that caused the madness in their youth. And if he didn't restore the balance soon, his powers would be permanently scarred.

"Jet lag from the time-jump," he said.

Forcing the dragon back into submission, he didn't speak to Channon while she ate. He allowed her the time to experience the life and beauty of this time without intruding on her.

Gods, how he ached to make her stay here. He could

take her right now and bind her to him for the rest of his life. It was fully within his power.

But he couldn't do that to her. The man in him refused to claim her against her will. It had to be her choice. He would never accept anything less than that.

Channon frowned as she noted the seriousness in Sebastian's eyes. "Are you sure you're all right?" she asked.

"I'm fine. Really."

She still didn't buy that. The musicians paused and the crowd clapped for them. As she applauded the musicians and dancers, Channon became aware of something on her hand. Frowning, she studied her palm. "What in the world?"

Sebastian swallowed. Up until now he'd used his powers to shield her from the marking. But his powers were weakening . . .

She tried to rub it off. "What is this?"

He started to tell her the truth, but it wedged in his throat. She didn't need to know that. Not right now. He didn't want to destroy the fun she was having by interjecting such a serious topic. "It's from the time-jump," he lied. "It's nothing major."

"Oh," Channon said, dropping her hand. "Okay."

The musicians started up again. Sebastian excused himself from her.

Channon frowned. Something in his demeanor concerned her.

He walked too deliberately with his spine rigid and his shoulders back.

Following after him, she watched as he left the hall and went outside. He rounded the side of the hall and headed toward a small well.

Channon stayed back while he pulled water from the well, then removed his mask and splashed the water over his face.

"Sebastian?" she asked softly, moving to his side. "Tell me what's wrong with you."

Sebastian raked his gloved hands through his hair, dampening it. "I'm okay, really."

"You keep saying that, but . . ."

She placed her hand on his arm. The sensation of her touch rocked him so fiercely that he wanted to growl from it. His body reacted viciously as desire tore through him.

The dragon snarled and circled, demanding her. *Take her. Take her. Take her.*

No! He would not cost her her life. He would not endanger her.

"I shouldn't have brought you here, Channon," he said as he turned his powers inward to harness the Drakos. "I'm sorry."

She smiled at him. "Don't be. It's not turning out so badly. It's actually kind of nice here."

He shut his eyes and turned away. He had to. The beast inside was snarling again. Salivating.

Claim her.

It wanted total possession.

And so did the man.

His groin tightened even more, and he wondered how much longer he could keep that part of him leashed.

Channon saw the feral look in his eyes as he raked a ravenous look over her. Her body reacted to it with a desire so powerful that it stunned and scared her. She wanted him to look at her like that. Forever.

261

His breathing ragged, he cupped her face in his hands and pulled her close for a fierce kiss. Channon moaned at the raw passion she tasted as she surrendered her weight to him.

She wrapped her arms around his neck and felt his muscles bunch and flex. Images of last night tore through her. Again she could see his naked body moving in the moonlight and feel him deep and hard inside her.

Sebastian growled at the taste of her, at the feel of her tongue sweeping against his. Out of his mind with passion, he pinned her against the wall of the gate.

He wanted her no matter the consequences, no matter the time or place.

Channon felt his erection as he held her between him and the wall. As if magnetized, her hips brushed against him. She wanted to feel him inside her again. She wanted nothing between them except bare skin.

"What is it you do to me?" she breathed.

Sebastian pulled back as her words penetrated the haziness of his mind. Still, all he could smell was Channon. Her scent spun around his head, making him even dizzier. He dipped his head for her lips, then barely caught himself.

Hissing, he forced himself to release her. If he kissed her again, he would take her here in the yard like an animal, without regard to her humanity, without regard for her choice.

Claiming was a special moment, and he refused to sully it like the Katagari. No, he wouldn't take her like this. Not out here where anyone could see them. He would not let the Drakos win.

"Channon," he whispered. "Please, go back inside."

Channon started to refuse, but the steeliness in his body kept her from it. "Okay," she said.

She paused at the corner of the hall and looked back at him. He was now leaning over the well with his head hung low. She didn't know what was wrong, but she was sure it wasn't good.

"Ha, take that!"

Channon turned at the sound of a child laughing. She saw the two boys with wooden swords who had been fighting Sebastian earlier. They ran across the yard.

"I will kill you, nasty dragon," one boy cried as they ran into a forge where the blacksmith cursed and chased them out, telling the tallest that he should be home eating.

She shook her head. Some things never changed, no matter the time period. Curious about what else reminded her of home, she crossed the yard.

∘ ∘ ∘

Sebastian breathed deeply, trying to summon his powers back to him. This was not good. If he stayed around Channon, by the time Friday arrived, he wouldn't be able to face the Katagaria trio.

He had to have his powers back, intact and strong, which meant that he would either have to claim her or find some place safe for her to stay so that he could get distance from her.

Because if he didn't, they would both die.

"Bas?"

Sebastian looked around the yard, trying to find the

source of that whispered call. It was a nickname no one had used in centuries.

Gold flashed to his right. To his shock, Damos appeared, then collapsed on the ground. Like a wounded animal, his brother held himself on all fours with his head hung low.

Unable to believe his eyes, Sebastian went to him. "Damos?"

Damos lifted his head to look at him. Instead of the hatred and disgust he expected to see, Sebastian saw only pain and guilt. "Did you get the tapestry?"

Sebastian couldn't answer as he saw his brother's face again. The two of them were almost identical in build and looks. The only real difference was in their hair color. Sebastian's hair was black while Damos's was a dark reddish-brown.

And as Sebastian looked into those eyes that were the same color as his own, the past flashed through his mind.

"You're nothing but a cowardly traitor. You've never been worth anything. I wish it had been you they tore apart. If there were any justice, it would be you lying in the grave and not Antiphone." The cruel words echoed in his head, and even now he could feel the bite of the whip as they delivered the two hundred lashes to his back.

Battered and bloody, Sebastian had been dumped in a cesspit and left there to die or survive as he saw fit.

He'd crawled from the pit and somehow found his way into the woods, where he'd lain for days floating in and out of consciousness. To this day, he wasn't sure how he'd survived it.

"Bas!" Damos snapped, wincing from the effort as he pushed himself slowly to his feet. He staggered, and against his will, Sebastian found himself helping his brother to the well where he propped him.

Damos's long reddish-brown hair was lank and clotted with blood and snarls. His face was battered and his clothes torn. "You look like hell."

"Yeah, well, it's hard to look good when you're being tortured."

Sebastian knew that firsthand. "You escaped?"

He nodded. "Where's the tapestry?"

"It's safe."

Damos locked gazes with him. "Were you really going to trade it for me?"

"I brought it here, didn't I?"

Tears gathered in Damos's eyes as he looked at him. "I am so sorry for what I did to you."

Sebastian was stunned. So, Damos did know what an apology was.

"The Katagaria told me what happened that day, how they tricked you." Damos placed his hand against the scar on Sebastian's neck that Sebastian had received while trying to save Antiphone's life. "I can't believe you survived them. And I can't believe you did this for me."

"Not like I had anything better to do."

Damos hissed and placed his hand to his eyes. "Those damned feelers. They're trying to find me."

Sebastian went cold. Without his powers, he couldn't sense the feelers, but if they were sending them out for Damos, then they would find . . .

Channon!

His heart pounding, he ran for the hall.

o o o

Channon wished she had her notepad to take notes on everything she saw. This was just incredible!

Enchanted, she walked idly past the stalls and huts, looking inside to see families eating and spending the evening together.

"You look lost."

She turned at the voice behind her. There were three men there, handsome all and quite tall. "Not lost," she offered. "Just out for a bit of fresh air."

The blond man appeared to be the leader of the small group. "You know, that can be quite dangerous for a woman alone."

Channon frowned as a wave of panic washed over her. "I beg your pardon?"

"Tell me, Acmenes." The blond spoke to the tall brunet beside him. "Why do you think an Arcadian would bring a human woman through time?"

Panic gone, sheer terror set in, especially since the man was speaking in modern English.

She tried to head back to Sebastian, but the third man caught her. He grabbed her right hand and showed it to his friends. "Because she's his mate."

The one called Acmenes laughed. "How precious is this? An Arcadian with a human dragonswan."

"No," the brunet said, "it's better. A lone Sentinel with a human mate."

They laughed cruelly.

Channon glared. She might look harmless, but she'd been on her own for quite some time, and as a woman alone, she'd learned a few things.

Tae Kwon Do was one of them. She caught the man holding her with her elbow and twisted out of his grasp. Before the others could reach her, she ran for the hall.

Unfortunately, the Katagaria moved a lot faster than she did and they grabbed her before she could reach it.

"Let her go." Sebastian's voice rolled across the yard like dangerous thunder as he unsheathed his sword.

"Oh no," Acmenes said sarcastically. "This is the best of all. A Sentinel who has *lost* his powers."

Channon's heart clenched at their words.

Sebastian's smile was taunting, wicked. "I don't need my powers to defeat you."

Before she could blink, the Katagaria attacked Sebastian.

"Run, Channon," Sebastian said as he delivered a staggering blow to the first one who reached him.

Channon didn't go far. She couldn't leave him to fight the men alone. Not that he appeared to need any help. She watched as they attacked him at once and he deftly knocked them back.

"Um, Acmenes," the youngest Katagari said as he picked himself up from the ground and panted. "He's kicking our butts."

Acmenes laughed. "Only in human form."

In a brilliant flash, Acmenes transformed into a dragon. The crowd that had gathered at the start of the fight shrieked and ran chaotically for shelter.

Channon stumbled back.

Standing at least twenty feet high, Acmenes was a

terrifying sight. His green and orange scales shimmered in the fading daylight while his blue wings flapped. He slung his spiked tail around, but Sebastian flipped out of the way.

The other two flashed into dragon form.

Sebastian held his sword tightly in his hands as he faced them. Even if he still held his powers unsevered, he wouldn't have been able to transform. Not while in the middle of a human village. It was forbidden.

Damn you, Fates.

"What's the matter, Kattalakis?" Acmenes asked. "Won't you breech your oath to protect your humans?"

Bracis laughed. "He can't, brother, his powers are too fragmented. He's powerless to stop us."

Acmenes shook his large, scaled head and sighed. "This is so anticlimactic. All these years you've chased us, and now . . ." He *tsk*ed. "To comfort you as you die, Sebastian, know that your dragonswan will be as well used by all of us as your sister was."

Raw agony ripped through Sebastian.

Over and over, he saw his sister's face and felt her blood on his skin as he held her lifeless body in his arms and wept.

"Kill him," Acmenes said. Then he turned toward Channon.

The dragon beast inside Sebastian roared with needful vengeance. He'd been unable to save Antiphone, but he would never let Channon die. Not like that.

Ceding his humanity, he let loose his shields. His change came so swiftly that he didn't even feel it. All he felt was the love in his heart for his mate, the animal desperation to keep her safe regardless of law or sense.

Channon froze at the sight of Sebastian's dragon form. The same height as Acmenes, his scales were bloodred and black. He looked like some fierce, terrifying menace, and she searched for something to remind her of the man he'd been two seconds ago.

She found none of him.

What she did see terrified her.

Acmenes swung about to face Sebastian as he savagely attacked the other two dragons. Fire shot through the village as they fought like the primeval beasts they were.

Then, to her horror, she saw Sebastian kill the dragon on his left with one sharp bite. The one on his right stumbled away from him in wounded pain, then took to the skies.

Acmenes reached for her, but Sebastian tackled him. The force of them hitting the ground shook it. They fought like men, slugging at each other, and yet like dragons, as their tails coiled and moved trying to sting one another.

She cringed as both dragons were wounded countless times by their fighting, but neither would pull back. She'd never seen anything like it. They were locked in the throes of a blood feud.

Acmenes hefted his body and threw Sebastian over his head, then rolled to his monstrous feet. He stumbled as he tried to reach the sky, but before he could leap, Sebastian caught him through the heart with his tail.

"Dragon!"

Now armed and prepared, the men of the village came

running back to do damage to the creatures who had invaded them.

At first Channon thought they came to help Sebastian, until she realized that they intended to attack him.

Without thought, she went to him. "Run, Sebastian," she said.

He didn't. He turned on her with frightening eyes, and in that moment she realized the man she knew was not in that body.

The dragon snarled at her as the crowd attacked him. Throwing his head back, he shrieked.

To her shock, he didn't attack the people.

Instead, he grabbed her in his massive claw and took flight.

Channon screamed as she watched the ground drift far away from her. She had no idea where he was taking her, but she didn't like this. Not even a little bit.

"Sebastian?"

Sebastian heard Channon's voice. But it came from a distance. He could only vaguely remember her.

Vaguely recall . . .

He shrieked as something flew past his head. Looking behind him, he saw Bracis coming for them.

And with the sight, his human memories came flooding back.

"Sebastian, help us. We're trapped by the Slayers."

"I can't, Percy. I can't leave Antiphone."

"She's safe in the hills. We are in the open, unprotected. Please, Sebastian. I'm too young to die. Please don't let them kill me. I know you can beat them. Please, please help me."

And so he had heeded the mental distress call and gone to protect his young cousin and brother, never knowing Percy's cry for help had been a trick, never knowing that Percy had deliberately summoned him from the cave.

He'd found his cousin barely alive and learned too late they had forced Percy to call for him.

By the time he'd returned to the cave where he'd left his sister hiding, the Slayers were gone.

And so was his sister's life.

Devastated on a level he'd never known existed, he'd refused to speak up in his own defense when his people had banished him.

He'd offered no argument at all against Damos's insults.

He should never have left Antiphone unprotected.

Now he looked at the woman he held cradled in his palm.

Channon.

The Fates had entrusted this woman to him, just as his brother had entrusted Antiphone to him.

He would not let Bracis have her. This time, he would see her safe. No matter what it cost him, she would live.

Sebastian headed for the forest.

Channon held her breath as they landed on the ground in a small clearing.

"Hide." The word seemed to sizzle out of Sebastian's dragon mouth.

She went without question, running into the trees and underbrush, looking for someplace safe. The forest was so thick that she quickly lost sight of the dragons. But she could hear them as they fought. She could feel the ground under her shake.

Grateful for the green dress, she found a clump of bushes and crawled into them to wait and to pray.

∘   ∘   ∘

Sebastian circled around Bracis, enjoying the moment, enjoying the feel of the dragon blood coursing through his veins. For two hundred and fifty years he had dreamed of this moment. He had dreamed of drinking from the fount of vengeance.

Now the moment was upon him.

Bracis was the last of the Slayers left from that day. One by one, Sebastian had hunted them all down. He had hunted them through time and even space itself.

"Are you ready to die?" Sebastian asked his opponent.

Bracis attacked. Sebastian caught him with his teeth and clamped down on the Katagari's shoulder. He tasted the blood of the beast as Bracis shredded at his back with his claws.

Sebastian barely felt it. But what he did feel was the fear inside Bracis. It swelled up with a pungent odor so foul that it made Sebastian laugh.

"You may kill me," Bracis rasped. "But I'm taking you with me."

Something stung Sebastian's shoulder. Snarling, he jerked his head around to see the dagger protruding from his back. But it wasn't the steel that stung; it was the poison that coated the blade. Dragon's Bane.

Roaring from the pain of it, he turned back and finished Bracis off quickly by breaking his long, scaled neck.

Sebastian stood over the body of his enemy, staring at it

blankly. After all this time, he'd wanted more out of the kill. He'd expected it to release the agony in his heart, to relieve his guilt.

It didn't.

He felt nothing except disappointed by it. Cheated.

No. In two hundred and fifty years only one thing had ever given him a moment's worth of peace.

Suddenly, a scream tore through the woods.

Channon.

Sebastian reared up to his full twenty foot height, searching for her through the trees with his dragon sight and senses.

He heard nothing more. His heart pounding, he ran for the woods where she'd vanished. With every step that closed the distance between them, all his feelings rushed through him. He relived every moment of Antiphone's death.

The guilt, the fear, the raw agony.

Under the onslaught of his human feelings, the dragon inside him receded again, leaving only the man. The man who had been crushed that day. The man who had sworn over his sister's grave to never let another person into his heart.

The same man who had looked into a pair of crystal blue eyes over dinner one night and had seen a future inside them that he wanted to live. A future with laughter and love. One spent in quiet serenity with a woman standing beside him to keep him strong and grounded.

Leaves and brambles tore at his flesh, but he paid no attention to them.

Like Antiphone, he'd left Channon alone to face an untold nightmare.

Left her to face . . .

He came to a stop as he caught sight of her.

Frowning, Sebastian struggled to breathe. His vision was so blurry from the poison that he wasn't sure he could trust it.

He blinked and blinked again. And still it stayed before his eyes. Channon stood with a sword in her hand, and it was angled at Damos's throat.

"Bas, would you please tell her I'm not a Katagari."

Channon glanced over her shoulder to see Sebastian standing naked in the woods. Human once more, he was pale and covered in sweat.

"Let him go."

By the sound of Sebastian's voice, she knew the man she held hadn't been lying to her. He was one of the good guys.

The instant she saw Sebastian stumble, she dropped the sword she'd taken from this stranger.

Channon ran to his side. "Sebastian?"

He was shaking in her arms. Together, they sank to the ground and she held his head in her lap.

"I thought you were dead," he whispered, running his hand over her forearms. "I heard you scream."

The man she'd cornered knelt beside them. "I startled her. I was trying to help you with Bracis. I sent out a feeler for your essence and it led me to her. You didn't tell me you were mated."

Channon ignored the man as Sebastian's body temperature dropped alarmingly.

Why was Sebastian trembling so? His wounds didn't look that severe. "Sebastian, what's wrong with you?"

"Dragon's Bane."

Channon frowned as the man cursed. What was Dragon's Bane?

"Sebastian," he said forcefully, taking Sebastian's face in his hands and forcing him to look up at him. "Don't you dare die on me. Damn you, fight this."

"I'm already dead to you, Damos," he said, his voice ragged as he turned away from him. "You told me to die painfully."

Sebastian closed his eyes.

Channon saw the grief in Damos's eyes as her own tore through her. This couldn't be happening. She wanted to wake up.

But it wasn't a nightmare; it was real.

Damos looked at her, his greenish-gold eyes searing her with power and emotion. "He's going to die unless you help him."

"What can I do?"

"Give him a reason to live."

Her hand started to tingle where the mark was. Channon scowled as it began to fade. "What the . . . ?"

"We're losing him. When he dies, your mark will be gone, too."

The reality of the moment hit her ferociously. Sebastian was going to die?

No, it couldn't be.

"Sebastian?" she said, shaking him. "Can you hear me?"

He shifted ever so slightly in her arms.

She wouldn't let him go like this. She couldn't. Though they had only known each other one day, it felt as if they'd been together an eternity. The thought of losing him crippled her.

"Sebastian, do you remember what you said to me in the hotel room? You said, 'I'm here because I know the sadness inside you. I know what it feels like to wake in the morning, lost and lonely and aching for someone to be there with me.'"

She pressed her lips against his cheek and wept. "I don't want to be alone anymore, Sebastian. I want to wake up with you like I did this morning. I want to feel your arms around me, your hand in my hair."

He went limp in her arms.

"No!" Channon cried, holding him close to her heart. "Don't you do this to me, Sebastian Kattalakis. Don't you dare make me believe in knights in shining armor, in men who are good and decent, and then leave me alone again. Damn it, Sebastian. You promised to take me home. You promised not to leave me."

The mark faded from her palm.

Channon wept as her heart splintered. Until that moment, she hadn't realized that against all known odds, against all known reason, she loved this man.

And she didn't want to lose him.

She pressed her wet cheek to his lips. "I love you, Sebastian. I just wished you'd lived long enough for us to see what could become of us."

Suddenly, she felt another tingle in her palm. It grew to a burning itch. It was followed by a slow, tiny stirring of air against her cheek.

Damos expelled a deep breath. "That's it, little brother. Fight for your mate. Fight for your dragonswan."

Channon looked up as Damos doffed his cloak, then wrapped it around Sebastian's body.

"Is he going to live?"

"I don't know, but he's trying to. The Fates willing, he will."

THREE

Channon bathed Sebastian's fevered brow while she prayed for his survival and whispered for him to come back to her.

After they had stabilized Sebastian, Damos had taken them to a small village in Sussex where humans and Arcadians lived and worked together. She learned that though Arcadians could only time-jump during a full moon, they could use their magic to make lateral jumps from one place to another in the same time frame any time they wanted to.

It didn't really make sense to her, but she didn't care. At the moment, all that mattered to her was the fact that Sebastian was still fighting his way back from death.

It was long after midnight now. They were alone in a large room where the only light came from three candles set in an iron fixture against the wall. Sebastian lay draped in a sheet on an ornate bed that bore the images of dragons and wheat and was shielded from drafts by shimmery white drapes.

The sounds of the night drifted in from the open window while she waited for some sign that he would wake up.

None came.

At some point before dawn, exhaustion overtook her and she curled up by his side and went to sleep.

"Channon?"

Channon felt as if she were floating, as if she had no real form at all.

Suddenly, she stood in a summer field with wildflowers all around her. She was dressed in a sheer white gown that left her all but bare. There was a medieval castle in the distance, highlighted against the horizon. It reminded her of one of the manuscript pages she studied.

None of it seemed real until she felt strong arms wrap around her.

Glancing over her shoulder, she looked up to find Sebastian behind her. Like her, he was practically naked, dressed only in a pair of thin white pants. The breeze stirred his dark hair around his handsome face, and he flashed those killer dimples. Her heart soaring, she turned in his arms, reached up, and placed her marked palm over his Sentinel tattoo. "Am I dreaming?"

"Yes. This was the only way I could reach you."

She frowned. "I don't understand."

"I'm dying."

"No," she said emphatically, "you're still alive. You came back to me."

The tenderness on his face as he looked at her made her

heart pound. "In part, but I still lack the strength I need to wake."

He sat down on the ground and pulled her down with him. "I missed you today."

So had she, in a way that made no sense whatsoever to her, but then feelings seldom did. The entire time he'd been unconscious, she had felt as if a vital part of her was gone.

Now, in the circle of his arms, leaning back against him, she felt right again. She felt whole and warm.

Sebastian took her hand into his and used his thumb to toy gently with her fingers.

"I can't lose you," she whispered. "I've spent hours thinking of my life at home. It was lonely and empty. I had no one to laugh with."

He placed his lips against her temple and kissed her tenderly. Then he cupped her head in his hands and leaned his forehead against her. "I know, love. I've spent my life alone in caves, my only company the sound of the wind outside. But the only way I can fight my way back to you is to regain my powers."

"Regain them how? How did you lose them?"

She felt his lips moving against her skin as he whispered the words while he nuzzled her. It was wonderful to have him holding her again. "I was using them against myself. I set the dragon and the human inside me at odds."

His touch burned through her. She didn't want to live another day without feeling him by her side, without seeing that devilish smile and those deep dimples.

In short, she needed this man.

"Why did you do that?" she asked.

He pulled back and kissed her fingertips. "To protect you."

"From what?"

"Me," he said simply.

Channon stared up at him, baffled by his words. He would never hurt her. She knew that. Even in his true dragon form he had done nothing but protect her. "I don't understand."

He ran his thumb over her palm, tracing the lines of her mark. Chills swept up her arm, tightening her breasts as she watched him.

When he met her gaze, she saw his sorrow. "I lied to you when you asked me about the mark on your hand. Part of the curse of my people is that we are only designated one mate for our entire existence, a mate we don't choose."

Channon frowned. Damos had refused to speak to her when she asked him what he meant when he had called her Sebastian's mate. He'd told her it was for Sebastian to do.

Sebastian kissed her marked palm. "The moment we Arcadians and Katagaria are born, the Fates choose a mate for us. We spend the rest of our lives trying to find our other half. Unlike humans, we can't have a family or children with anyone other than our mate. If we fail to find our other half, we are doomed to live out our lives alone.

"As a human, you have the freewill to love anyone. You can love more than once. But I can't. You, Channon, are the only woman in any time or place who I can love. The only woman I can ever have a family with. The only woman I will ever desire."

She remembered Plato's theory about the human race

281

being two halves of the same person—the male and female who were separated by the gods. Now she realized Plato's theory was based on the reality of Sebastian's people, not hers.

"So what do you need to regain your powers?"

He fingered her lips and stared at her with desperate need. She knew he was still holding himself back, still keeping himself from kissing her.

"You have to claim me as your mate," he said quietly. "Sex regenerates our powers. It heightens them. I was trying so hard to keep from forcing you into the Claiming that I buried them too deeply. There is a delicate balance in all Arcadians and Katagaria between the human and animal half. I was fighting myself so hard to protect you that I ruptured the balance."

"It can only be repaired by Claiming me?"

He nodded.

"And this Claiming, what is it exactly?"

He traced the line of her jaw, making her burn from the inside out. "When you claim me, you acknowledge me as your soulmate. The ceremony is really quite simple. You place your marked palm over mine and then you take me into your body. You hold me there and say, 'I accept you as you are, and I will always hold you close to my heart. I will walk beside you forever.'"

"And then?"

"I repeat the words back to you."

That seemed just a little too easy to her. If that was all there was to it, why had he fought it so hard? "That's it?"

He hesitated.

Inwardly, she groaned. "I know that look," she said, pulling back slightly from him. "Any time you're not telling me the whole truth you get that look."

He smiled at her and planted a chaste kiss on her cheek. "All right, there is something more. When we join, my natural instinct will be to bond you to me."

That still didn't sound so bad. "Bond me how?"

"With blood."

"Okay, I don't like this part. What do you mean *with blood?*"

He dropped his hands and leaned back on them to watch her. "You know how humans will bind themselves together as blood brothers?"

"Yes."

"It's basically the same thing—but with one major difference. If you take my blood into you, our mortal lives are completely conjoined."

"Meaning we will become one person?" she asked.

"No, nothing like that. Do you remember your Greek myths at all?"

"Some of them."

"Do you remember who Atropos is?"

She shook her head. "Nope, not a clue."

"She is one of the Moirae, the Fates. She's the one who assigns our mates to us at birth, and if we choose to bond with that mate, her sister Clotho, who is the spinner of our lives, combines our life-threads together. At the end of a normal life Atropos will cut the thread and cause a death. But if we are bonded together and our threads are one, then she can't cut one without the other."

"We die together."

"Exactly."

Wow, that was a big commitment. Especially for him. "So you will have a human life span."

"No. My thread is stronger. You will have an Arcadian life span."

She blinked at that. "Are you saying I could live several hundred years?"

He nodded. "Or we could both die tomorrow."

"Whoa. Is there anything else?" she asked, curiously. "Will I also get some of your powers? Mind control? Time-walking?"

He laughed at her. "No. Sorry. My powers are tied to my birth and my destiny. Bonding only extends to our life-threads."

Channon smiled as she rose up on her knees, between his legs. She crouched over him, forcing him to lean back farther on his arms as she hovered over him. She bit her lip as she stared at his handsome face, at those lips she was dying to taste.

"So, what you're offering me is a gorgeous, incredibly sexy man who is completely devoted to me for the next few centuries?"

"Yes."

She smiled even wider. "One who can never stray?"

"Never."

She forced him to lie back on the ground as she straddled his waist and leaned forward on her arms so that her face was just a few inches above his. She felt his hard erection through his pants, pressing against her core. How she wanted him. But first she wanted to make sure she under-stood all the consequences.

"You know," she said, "it's real hard to say no to this. What downside could there possibly be?"

He shifted his hips under hers, making her burn for him as he tucked a stray piece of her hair back behind her ear. Still, he didn't touch her, and she knew he was leaving it all up to her now.

"The Katagaria who want me dead," he said seriously. "They will never cease coming for us, and because I am banished, it will only be the two of us to fight them off. Our children will be Arcadian and not human, and they, too, will have to battle the Katagaria. But most important, you will have to remain here in the Middle Ages."

"Why?"

"Because of the electricity in your time period. Arcadians who are natural animals such as hawks, panthers, wolves, bears, and such can live in your world. If they are accidentally changed, their animal forms are small or normal enough to hide from humans."

"But if you become a dragon, then we have a Godzilla movie."

"Exactly. And in your time period, there are plenty of tasers and electrical devices that can completely incapacitate me. No offense, but I don't relish being someone's science experiment. Been there, done that, and sold the T-shirt for profit."

She sat up straight, still straddling him, as she digested all of this.

The man offered her the deal of a lifetime.

Sebastian watched her carefully. It was taking all his restraint to keep his hands off her when all he wanted to do was make love to her. He'd told her everything. Now it was up to her, and he trembled with the fear that she would leave him.

She took his hands in hers and held them to her waist. "Our babies will be normal, right?"

"Perfectly normal. They will age like human children with the only exception being that they won't be teenagers until their twenties."

"And that's a drawback?"

He laughed.

"Oh, by the way, you're no longer banished."

Sebastian scowled. "What?"

"While they were torturing Damos, the Katagaria admitted that they had tricked you so they could get the tapestry from Antiphone. But she refused to let them have it."

"Why? What was so important about it?"

"Unfortunately nothing, but they believed that it contained the secret for immortality. It seems Katagaria legend had it that the granddaughter of their creator had placed his secrets into the work she'd created to honor him. They captured Damos, thinking he had it, and when they found out you alone knew where it was, they arranged the bargain with you."

"My sister died for no reason?"

"Sh," she said, placing her hand over his lips. "Just be glad the truth is out and the tapestry is safe. Damos wants to make the past up to you."

Sebastian couldn't believe it. After all this time, his banishment was lifted?

That meant a real home for Channon where she would be safe. A home where their children would be safe.

Channon laid her body down over his and breathed him in. "Which means you're no longer alone, Sebastian. You don't really need me."

"That's not true. I need you more than I've ever needed anything else. My heart was dead until I looked into your eyes."

He cupped her face in his hands. "I want you to claim me, Channon," he said fiercely. "I want to spend the rest of my life waking up with you in my arms and feeling your hair in my palm."

She choked as he used her words. He'd heard her. "I want you, too."

Laughing, he rolled over with her, pinning her to the ground and letting her feel every hard, wonderful inch of his body.

They kissed each other in a frenzied hurry as they helped one another out of their clothes.

Channon pulled back as their naked bodies slid against each other. "Does it count if we do this in a dream?"

"This isn't really a dream. It's an alternate place."

"You know, you scare me when you talk like that."

He smiled at her. "I have much to teach you about my world."

"And I am willing to learn it all." Channon kissed those delectable lips as she wrapped her bare legs around his. She felt his erection against her hip, and it made her burn with need.

"Are you sure about this?" he asked, nibbling his way along her jaw. "You'll be giving up all your future *Buffy* episodes."

She drew her breath in sharply between her teeth as she

thought it over. "I have to tell you, it's a hard decision to make. Watching Spike prance around and be all Spikey, versus a couple hundred years of making love to a Greek god." She clucked her tongue. "What is a woman to do?"

She moaned as he ran his tongue around her ear and whispered, "What can I do to sway your verdict?"

"That's a real good start right there." She sighed as her body erupted into chills and he dipped his head to torment her breast with his hot mouth. "I guess I'll just have to find another pastime besides television watching."

"I think I can help you with that." He rolled over again to place her on top of him.

The intensity of his stare scalded her.

"Tradition demands you be in charge of this, my lady. The whole idea behind the Claiming is that the woman places her life and her trust into the hands of her mate. Once you accept me, the animal inside me will do whatever it takes to keep you safe."

"Like when you turned into a dragon in front of all those people?"

He nodded.

She smiled. "You know it's a pity I didn't know you in third grade. There was this bully—"

He cut her words off with a kiss.

"Mmm," she breathed. "I like that. Now, where were we?"

She nibbled her way down his chin to his chest.

Sebastian growled as she found his nipple and teased it with her tongue and lips. He felt his powers surging again, felt the air around them charging with the force of it.

Channon felt it, too. She moaned as the energy moved around her body, caressing her.

Sebastian held his left hand up. The mark in his palm glowed and shimmered. Looking into his eyes, Channon covered his mark with hers and laced her fingers with his.

Heat engulfed her entire body as she felt something hot and demanding rush through her. She saw the beast in his eyes and the man as he breathed raggedly.

It was the sexiest thing she'd ever beheld.

Arching her back, she lifted her hips and took him deep into her body.

They moaned in unison.

She watched Sebastian's face as she slowly ground herself against him. "Um, I forgot the words."

He laughed as he lifted his hips, driving himself so deep into her that she groaned. "I accept you as you are."

"Oh," she breathed, then remembering what she was doing, she repeated his words. "I accept you as you are."

"And I will always hold you close to my heart."

"Umm, hmmm. I will most definitely hold you close to my heart."

"I will walk beside you forever."

She placed her hand on his chest, over his heart. "I will walk beside you forever."

His eyes turned eerily dark. He reached up with his free hand and cupped her cheek. His voice was a deep, low growl, a cross between the voice of the dragon and the voice of the man. "I accept you as you are, and I will always hold you close to my heart. I will walk beside you forever."

He'd barely finished the words before his teeth grew long and sharp and his eyes darkened to the color of obsidian.

"Sebastian?"

"Don't be afraid," he said as he bared his fangs. "It's the dragon wanting to bond with you, but I have control of it."

"And if I want to bond with you?"

He hesitated. "Do you understand what you're doing?"

Channon paused with him inside her and locked gazes with him. "I've lived alone all my life, Sebastian. I don't want to do it another day."

He sat up, keeping them joined.

Channon hissed at how good he felt as she wrapped her free arm around his waist and he pulled her against him with his.

She lifted her hips, then dropped herself down on him.

"That's it, love, claim me as yours." Sebastian let her ride him slowly as he waited for more of his powers to return. He needed to be in total control for this.

Their marked hands still joined, he held her close to him so that he could feel her heart beating in rapid time to his.

When he was certain his powers were perfectly aligned, he leaned his head forward and sank his teeth gently into her neck.

Channon shivered at the feeling of his hot breath and teeth on her, but oddly enough, there was no pain at all. Instead, it was an erotic pleasure so intense that her entire body exploded into a sensation of colors and sound. Her head fell back as she felt the strength of him moving through her, the smell of him engulfing her. It was electrifying and terrifying.

Her sight grew sharper and clearer, and she felt her teeth elongate.

Growling, she knew instinctively what she was supposed to do. She clutched feverishly at his shoulders, pulling herself up in his arms. Then she leaned forward and sank her teeth into his shoulder.

For an instant, time stood still with them locked together. Channon couldn't breathe as her body and mind joined his in a place she'd never known existed. It was just the two of them. Just their hearts beating, their bodies joining.

Sebastian hissed as he felt their bonding. The air around them sizzled and spun as they came together in an orgasm so intense, so powerful, that they cried out in unison.

Panting and weak from it, he kissed her lips, holding her to him as he felt her teeth recede.

"That was incredible," she said, still clutching him to her.

He smiled. "Too bad it's a one-time thing."

"Really?"

He nodded. "You're fully human again. Except you have a long life ahead of you."

She bit her lip and gave him a hot, promising look. "And my own pet dragon."

"Aye, my lady. And you can pet him any time you want."

She laughed at him. "You know, since the moment I saw you, I keep having this strange feeling that all of this is just some weird dream."

"Well, if it is, I don't want to wake up."

"Neither do I, my love. Neither do I."

EPILOGUE

Two years later

Channon left the podium, her heart pounding in triumph. Every historian in the room had been left completely speechless by the paper and research she had just delivered to them. She'd done the one thing she'd always wanted to do.

She'd solved the mystery of the tapestry, which now hung back in the museum.

"Brilliant research, Dr. Kattalakis," Dr. Lazarus said, shaking her hand as she left the podium. "Completely groundbreaking. This takes us into a whole new area."

"Thank you."

She tried to step past him, but he cut her off.

"How ever did you find those answers? I mean that *Book of Dragons*, you said it was from the Library of Alexandria. How did you ever find it?"

She looked past his shoulder to see Sebastian leaning against the wall with his arms folded across his chest, waiting patiently for her. Dressed all in black, he cut a fearsome pose.

Still, she missed seeing him in his armor. Something about the mail over those luscious muscles . . .

She needed to get back home. Real soon.

She returned her attention to Dr. Lazarus and his questions.

The *Book of Dragons* had been her birthday present from Sebastian last year. He said he'd swiped it the day before the fire that burned the ancient library. With that book and Antiphone's tapestry, she had been able to concoct an entire mythology based on his people that was guaranteed to keep any "experts" from ever discovering the truth of the Draki people.

The Arcadian Draki were safe from human curiosity.

"The book was found in an estate sale. I've handed it over to the Richmond Museum." She patted his arm. "Now, if you'll please excuse me?"

She sidestepped him.

But before she could reach Sebastian, Dr. Herter stopped her. "Have you reconsidered coming back to work?"

She shook her head. "No, sir. I told you, I'm retired."

"But after that paper you just delivered—"

"I'm going home." She handed him the pages in her hand. "Publish it and be happy."

Dr. Herter shook his gray head at her. "'The Myth of the Dragon.' It's a brilliant piece of fiction."

She smiled. "Yes, it is."

As soon as she reached her soulmate, Sebastian wrapped his arms around her and drew her close. "I don't know if you helped us or hurt us with that."

"We can't let the humans know of you. This way, no one

will question the tapestry anymore. It's preserved as you originally wanted, and the academic community can stop nosing around for the truth."

She looked up and saw him staring at the tapestry on the museum's wall. Anytime he thought of his sister, he always looked so incredibly sad. "It's a pity the Fates won't let you guys change the past."

He sighed. "I know. But if we try, they make us pay for it tenfold."

She hugged him tightly, then pulled back so they could leave.

"Well," he said, draping his arm over her shoulders as he walked her out of the museum, "tonight's the full moon. Are you ready to go home?"

"Absolutely, Sir Dragon-Knight. But first . . ."

"I know," he said with a long-suffering sigh, "it's the *Buffy* marathon torture that you always put me through whenever we visit here."

She laughed. He'd been very patient with her on their infrequent visits to her time period, where she caught up on all her favorite shows. "Actually, I was thinking there is one thing I do miss most when we're in Sussex."

"And that is?"

"Whipped cream loincloths."

He arched a brow at that, then smiled a wicked smile that flashed his dimples. "Mmm, my lady, I definitely like the way your mind works."

"Glad to hear it, because you know what they say?"

"What's that?" he asked as he opened the door for her.

"Be kind to dragonswans, for thou art gorgeous when naked and taste good with Cool Whip."